Death
by Water

Books by Kerry Greenwood

The Phryne Fisher Series
Cocaine Blues
Flying Too High
Murder on the Ballarat Train
Death at Victoria Dock
The Green Mill Murder
Blood and Circuses
Ruddy Gore
Urn Burial
Raisins and Almonds
Death Before Wicket
Away With the Fairies
Murder in Montparnasse
The Castlemaine Murders
Queen of the Flowers
Death by Water
Murder in the Dark

The Corinna Chapman Series
Earthly Delights
Heavenly Pleasures
Devil's Food
Trick or Treat

Short Story Anthology
A Question of Death: An Illuminated Phryne Fisher Treasury

Death by Water

A Phryne Fisher Mystery

Kerry Greenwood

Poisoned Pen Press

Poisoned Pen
PRESS

Copyright © 2005, 2010, 2018 by Kerry Greenwood

First U.S. Trade Paperback Edition 2010

10 9 8 7 6 5 4 3

Library of Congress Control Number: 2018940949

ISBN: 9781464207808   Trade Paperback
ISBN: 9781464207815   Ebook

Poisoned Pen Press
4014 N. Goldwater Blvd., #201
Scottsdale, AZ 85251
www.poisonedpenpress.com
info@poisonedpenpress.com

Printed in the United States of America

This book is dedicated to my very dear and much admired Mr Witherspoon, my fourth grade teacher at Geelong Road State School, who not only believed I could read but gave me the key to the book cabinet, beginning my lifelong affair with literature. I have never had a better present. And at last I get a chance to say thank you.

With thanks to Catherine Howat's kind expertise on ships, Jean Greenwood's recall of music, Maggie Walsh's Maori wisdom, David Greagg's navigation, Dennis, Mark and Ben Pryor.

And in very loving memory of my cousin Muriel Wright, who died before she could read this. I hope she would have liked it. Missed much more than she would have believed.

Revenge is a kind of wild justice;
which the more man's nature runs to,
the more ought law to weed it out.

Francis Bacon, 1st Baron Verulam
'On Revenge'

Chapter One

Then pricketh him nature in hir corages
Thanne longen folke to go on pilgrimages.
Prologue to the *Canterbury Tales*
G Chaucer

Wednesday

Phryne Fisher was trying to read Chaucer. She liked Middle English for a certain mood. It had a cryptic crossword difficulty which usually absorbed the attention. Today, however, late in the year 1928, the list of distractions and inconveniences was simply too exasperating.

1. Her adopted daughters, Jane and Ruth, were playing a loud game of snakes and ladders.

2. Her admirable cook, Mrs. Butler, was expressing to the butcher's boy her opinion of last night's lamb, which had been tough even when later minced.

3. Her attentive houseman, Mr. Butler, had just reminded her that he and Mrs. Butler were embarking on the morrow on their yearly visit to Rosebud to stay with their married daughter for a fortnight.

4. Her sister Eliza, exiled from her own house by the discovery of an unexpected cesspit, had arrived to stay, bringing with her her partner in Good Works Lady Alice, seven trunks, a hatbox and a madly barking Pekingese mop dog called Ching.

5. The dog Molly and the cat Ember, had still not recovered from their resentment of this interloper in their own particular ways—Molly by giving the Pekingese a really good barking and Ember by fleeing up the curtains.

And even though the sun had not run his half-course in the Ram, the month was not April of the sweet showers and the local St Kilda birds always slept with opened eye anyway, Phryne Fisher thereupon decided to accept the free passage on the SS *Hinemoa* which the nice man from P&O had offered her the day before.

This being decided, she shut the book, made a telephone call to alert P&O to their good fortune and went upstairs to tell Dot, her maid and companion, to start packing.

'But you can't just go away and leave them all!' objected Dot, a plain young woman of stern moral principles.

'Why not? Eliza and Lady Alice will look after the girls and the house. My darling Lin is away in Castlemaine and won't be back for two weeks—a funeral, apparently, of a very old Chinese lady. The substitute staff will be here today to be briefed by Mr. Butler. And if I have to listen to any more noise, I am going to commit a mortal sin of some kind. Probably murder.'

Dot looked at Phryne. She wasn't smiling. Promptly, Dot stepped onto a chair, brought down the big suitcase, and listened to her instructions.

'Sports clothes, evening clothes, ordinary underwear, Dot—I do not expect dalliance. We'll only be away fourteen days. And the paste jewellery, if you please. Nothing real.'

'Why not?' asked Dot, grasping at events as they raced past her.

'Because I don't want to lose it,' said Phryne. 'The man from P&O wants me to find out who is pinching the passengers' gems.'

Dot started packing. Phryne sat down on her bed and explained.

'There have been four thefts in four voyages,' she said. 'Each time it was the most valuable piece on the ship. It vanished so completely that even the last search, where they practically disassembled the vessel, didn't find it.'

'I see,' said Dot, who didn't, but was folding chemises.

'Who cannot possibly be searched down to the bone when leaving a luxury cruise liner?' asked Phryne.

'Oh,' said Dot. 'The passengers. I see. So you are looking for a Raffles, a gentleman thief?'

'Apparently,' said Phryne. 'As soon as you are ready, call down and get Mr. B to phone the luggage office. Now, I was going alone, but would you like to come with me, Dot?'

Dot blushed in confusion. 'But I thought I was coming with you,' she said. 'Who's going to look after your clothes?'

'They have stewardesses,' said Phryne.

'Stewardesses,' said Dot scornfully.

'I didn't mean to just uproot you without a word, old thing,' said Phryne.

'My intended, Hugh, he's away too,' said Dot. 'I've always wanted to sail on one of those big ships.'

'So you shall,' said Phryne. 'I'll go and tell the family and you stuff a few things in a bag.'

Dot reached for more tissue paper and waited until the door was closed before she gave a brief, ladylike snort. Stuff a few things into a bag, indeed. Miss Phryne would have dances, dinners, deck games, swimming and probably climbing around ships in the dark. That needed a considerable wardrobe, and Dot wasn't going to forget anything.

Phryne walked into the small parlour and clapped her hands. Silence eventually fell. Mr. Butler had hauled Molly into the kitchen and shut the door on her. Ember had descended from the curtains and stalked upstairs, disdain of everything canine in every line of his svelte black body. Ching had been muffled in Eliza's bosom. The girls abandoned their game.

'Gentleman. Ladies,' Phryne announced. 'I have decided to accept P&O's invitation to do a little sleuthing on their new ship. Eliza will be in charge of the house, Ruth will be in charge of Molly and Jane will be in charge of Ember. Draw on my bank account for any expenses and if you absolutely must find me, you can telegraph the ship. That's all,' she said, and walked away, leaving their protests ringing in the air.

'Peace, perfect peace,' sang Phryne devoutly. 'With loved ones far away.'

Thursday

A crowded interval later, Phryne was standing at the SS *Hinemoa's* rail. Station Pier stretched out before her. The sea was blue and as flat as a plate. The sun gave a preliminary scorch, reminding Phryne that she needed the hat that Dot was carrying.

She could see her family down below. Ruth, who had a good throwing arm, flung her a bright pink streamer and Phryne caught the end. Engines thrummed. Men shouted on the dock. The great hawsers were loosed and hauled dripping into the ship. From being as stolid and unresponsive as an apartment block, the ship came alive.

Tugs tooted. Shining, glittering, as splendid and ornate as an iced wedding cake, the SS *Hinemoa* slid gently out from her mooring, and in Phryne's hand the bright pink streamer snapped. Her last link to land. Phryne and Dot waved. *Hinemoa* tried the water and liked it. The familiar faces slid astern; Ruth and Eliza and Jane and Lady Alice.

'We're away,' said Phryne on a released breath of pure excitement, and turned to see Dot dabbing at her eyes. Phryne patted her arm.

'Come along, Dot dear, we'll go and have a look at the ship,' she said briskly. Dot wiped her eyes and fell in behind.

They were accosted by a deferential older man in immaculate whites. Stripes on his sleeve informed Phryne that he was an officer. He had a short, ingeniously topiaried grey beard and stippled hair just the colour and texture of a badger fur shaving brush. He held out a hand for Phryne's and shook it heartily.

'I'm afraid that the captain is rather busy, Miss Fisher, or he would be delighted to show you our ship. He's sent me instead. I hope I'll do? Navigation Officer Theodore Green at your service.'

He had an endearing diffidence and hazel eyes like brook water, so Phryne smiled graciously and tucked her hand under his elbow.

'I'm sure that you will do admirably,' she assured him. 'Take us to our suite first, if you please, and then we will be delighted to look at your beautiful boat.'

'Ship, Miss Fisher,' he said a little anxiously as he led her through a doorway into a vaulted space as big as a cathedral. 'She's a ship. You must never call her a boat, you know.'

'Ship,' said Phryne, accepting the correction. Navigation Officer Green sighed with relief. The young woman on his arm might have looked like a *Vanity Fair* fashion plate, with her Dutch doll black hair and her Cupid's bow lips and her dark blue travelling suit by Chanel, but she had intelligent green eyes and might even prove interesting to converse with. Navigation Officer Theodore Green dreaded these guided tours. He loved the SS *Hinemoa* with all his heart and loathed the silly things that foolish persons said about her when he was trying to tell them something important.

'Oh my,' said Miss Fisher, exactly as the officer hoped she might, when they rounded a corner and the full glory of the Grand Salon burst upon them. He began his prepared speech.

'Seven screens by—'

'Tiffany,' said Phryne. 'Furnishings by Liberty and William Morris, light fixtures by La Farge of Paris, I believe. Dot?'

'I never ever saw anything so pretty,' said Dot. 'It's like a church.'

The Grand Salon was panelled with wood painted a soft ivory. The furniture was of light beechwood, curved in the Deco manner. The light fittings were of bronze, vines curling upward or downward to hold the coloured electric globes. And through seven full length stained glass windows the sun poured, patterning the floor with jewelled light. They were gorgeous, barbaric, and yet very simple. Phryne felt for a chair and sat down.

'Oh my', she said again. Dot crossed herself. Stained glass had an elevating effect on her.

'Australian and New Zealand birds and trees,' said Theodore Green, touched and gratified by Miss Fisher's reaction. 'Commissioned from Tiffany when the ship was designed. They cost—'

'Do shut up a moment, my dear Navigation Officer,' interrupted Phryne, so amiably that he could not take offence. 'Let us look at the windows. Cockies on a ghost gum on one side, balanced by fern forest with kiwis and—what's the black bird with the white ruff?'

'A tui,' said Theodore.

'A flowering gum on one side and a New Zealand tree on the other.'

'A pohutukawa,' said Navigation Officer Green very quietly.

Phryne nodded and went on. 'A flock of Darwin finches on one side and a flock of budgies on the other. Look at that marvellous chalk-blue! And the lyrebird in the middle on his mound. Gorgeous. And I get to look at them every day. Wonderful.' Phryne regained her feet. 'Onward, if you please.'

'This is the Palm Court,' said Theodore Green. 'You will see that six decks of the ship curve around this central staircase, lit during the day by the glass dome above and during the night by the chandeliers. An orchestra plays every night in the Palm Court for your dancing pleasure.'

'Will you save me a dance?' asked Phryne wickedly. Theodore Green blushed, as she had thought he would.

'Why yes, Miss Fisher, honoured,' he said. 'You'll like the orchestra. We've been able to get Mavis and the Melody Makers again. They've been with us for four cruises now. Their Melbourne engagement fell through—the theatre burned down—so we snapped them up. They're very versatile. String quartet, chamber orchestra, jazz band, dance band, and they have a jazz singer and a ballad singer—really, you will enjoy them, I think. This way, and we pass the breakfast room, and down these steps here we have the Imperial Suite.'

He opened the door. The rooms had the amplitude of a royal apartment in an expensive hotel. Theodore Green opened doors, exhibiting Dot's room, Phryne's grand bedroom, her bath and WC, her very own telephone for room service, her radio, and her own private balcony. Dot sank down on her bed, and Phryne cast her hat onto her dressing table.

'All your baggage has been stowed by your stewardess,' explained Theodore Green. 'There's really quite a lot of room in the wardrobes and so on. Now, shall I leave you to settle in? Just pick up the phone and you shall have whatever your heart desires,' he said, willing to lay the full splendours of his ship before this intelligent and aesthetic visitor.

Phryne beamed at him. 'Thank you,' she said. 'But I'm not at all fatigued and I would love to see more of the ship. If you can spare the time to conduct me?'

'Oh yes, Miss Fisher, until we clear the heads we are under pilotage.'

'Just a tick, then, and I'll brush my hair. Dot, are you coming?'

'No, Miss, I'd like to explore the apartment,' said Dot. 'And the clothes will need to be rehung.'

'Good. Order some tea for yourself, then, and start on that nice thick book which tells us how to conduct ourselves at sea. Mr. Green, what is the greatest crime which ladies are likely to commit against your ship?'

'Leaving the fresh water tap running, Miss Fisher,' he answered honestly.

'Very well. Dot, make a note for us not to do that. Back soon,' she said, blowing her companion a kiss.

Left alone, Dot stroked her bedspread, which was of rose patterned satin, and then sat down on Phryne's bed, which was very springy and covered with dark blue morocain. She had just poured herself a little water to wash her face, carefully turning off the tap, when there was a knock at the door and a tea tray came in, carried by a stocky, dark-skinned young woman in a white uniform and cap.

'Hullo-ullo-ullo!' said the tea-carrier. 'You must be Miss Williams. I'm Caroline, your stewardess. Miss Fisher not here?'

'No, she's being shown round the ship by an officer, a Mr. Green, I think.'

'Poor Teddy, how he does hate being a guide,' said Caroline, setting the tray down on the polished table without spilling a drop. 'Can I pour you a cup? Shame to waste good tea. Our tea's very good, if I say it as shouldn't.'

Dot, who had been inclined to bristle at the very idea of anyone else looking after her Miss Phryne, warmed to this downright young woman with the scoured hands and the dark curly hair escaping from her cap.

'Only if you sit down and have a cup with me,' she said. 'Miss Phryne will be hours. And she was getting along fine with your Mr. Teddy. Are you from India?' she asked delicately.

Caroline laughed. 'No, I'm a Kiwi,' she said. 'From New Zealand. I'm a Maori. Still want to have that tea?'

'Of course,' said Dot, surprised. In a household which contained, at times, lost revolutionaries, grieving Latvian widows, cane cutters, clowns, Chinese lovers and that lady from the carnival and her snake, Dot had no race prejudices left. The small number she had started with had been so comprehensively disproved that she had made a philosophical decision to take everyone as they appeared until proven otherwise. This did simplify life in Phryne's establishment. Caroline grinned a wide grin and sat down.

'This is such a beautiful ship,' observed Dot, after her first sip of very good tea.

'She's lovely, isn't she? I've been on her since she was launched. My brothers are all sailors, but they don't let women join the merchant marine, so this is the best I can do. And it's good enough. Hard work, yes. Some of them dowagers are right bitches. But here I get good pay, good company, strict discipline amongst the crew, real good food, and a new sky every day—what else can a girl ask? Have one of the little cakes. Petty fours. We carry a specialist pastrycook, you know.'

'Anything that she hasn't got?' asked Dot, a little ironically. She still had to listen hard, to sort out the strange hard 'e' and the guttural which turned every 'i' into a 'u'.

'No bad people,' said Caroline. 'More tea?'

Phryne was listening to Navigation Officer Green, because he had a very pleasant voice. She could tell, however, that she was not going to retain much of what he was telling her. Phryne had had many things explained to her which she had not retained, the chief of which was the offside rule, and she had never missed any of them yet.

'She weighs eighteen thousand tons,' he was saying, leading Phryne down a flight of stairs. 'She's five hundred and eighty feet long. Here's the Turkish bath, which is available to ladies between ten am and noon, and again between three and five pm. Hello, Hans—our masseur. This is Miss Fisher.'

Hans, emerging on a puff of steam, noticed Phryne, smirked, and rippled a few muscles for the lady. She inspected him coolly. Phryne had met muscle-bound narcissists before. She was not impressed. Not even by the white singlet.

'Very nice,' she said. Theodore Green hurried her along. 'Here is the ladies' beauty salon. Any sort of beauty treatment, though if I could venture to say it, Miss Fisher, you don't need any.'

That was a compliment. Phryne smiled. 'Thank you.'

The salon exhaled the scent of freshly corrugated hair and attar of roses. It seemed well appointed. Several young women in pink smocks smiled at her as she passed.

'Then there is the gymnasium,' said Theodore Green. It was heralded by a strong smell of goanna oil liniment. 'And the barber shop. Cleanest shave in town. The ship's shop is here,' he added, stepping back. This was where all the lady passengers of his experience had rudely shoved him aside to fall on the merchandise with cries of glee. And it was a rather good shop, he had to agree, stocking everything someone might have forgotten to bring or be expected to want on a sea voyage. Cosmetics, bathing caps, woollen socks, baby bottles, nappies, hairpins, aspirin, shawls from the Indies, dolls, books, tins of toffee, fudge and biscuits for night starvation and ducky little sailor's caps with SS *Hinemoa* emblazoned on the front.

Miss Fisher was different. She gave the shop an approving glance but did not even remove her hand from his arm. 'Excellent,' she murmured. Theodore Green was disconcerted. This lady had adored the windows. She hadn't needed a cup of tea. And she didn't want to shop. He was quite out of his reckoning. He felt he might be falling in love.

'And then along here we have the Smoke Room,' he said, indicating a pair of closely shut wooden doors. 'Gentlemen only, I'm afraid, Miss Fisher. But you are welcome to smoke in here,' he added, leading her into a room lined with bookshelves. There were long tables and low, comfortable armchairs. There were small desks for those who felt that they should write at least a postcard for the people they had callously abandoned at home. 'This is the library. You will also find magazines and games. Perhaps you might like a little refreshment now?' he asked, suddenly longing for a cup of real coffee.

'Yes,' said Miss Fisher, sitting down and taking out a cigarette case. 'This is a delightful room. So very airy and light. Might I ask for coffee, if it isn't made from a bottle with a genie on the front?'

'Leo is from Sicily. They make very good coffee there,' said Theodore Green, convinced that he had found his soul mate. He located a match and lit Miss Fisher's cigarette without dropping the box or setting fire to the lady's hair, and sat down beside her, giving his order for coffee to a passing steward.

'This ship is like a city,' she observed, watching his face.

'Just like a city,' he agreed. 'There are nearly seven hundred people to look after the eight hundred passengers. It's like one of those English manors. We do our own laundry, cook all our own food, amuse ourselves—and sail the ship, of course.'

'Indeed.' Miss Fisher sat, peacefully smoking her gasper, and did not seem to mind him to tell her any more interesting facts about the ship. In the middle of a very busy day, her company was unexpectedly soothing.

Coffee came in, with Leo's special little almond cakes which he always gave Theodore, who appreciated Italian cuisine. Somewhere a baby was crying. Miss Fisher raised an eyebrow.

'We have a few children on this voyage,' he explained as the steward poured the inky beverage. 'But none in First. In any case, they will be in the nursery mostly, and that's right down at the stern. No need to think that your sleep might be disturbed.'

'Good,' answered Phryne, sipping. 'This is excellent coffee. How about pets? Are people allowed to bring small yappy dogs aboard?'

'No pets,' said Theodore Green. 'Not even in First. We made an exception only once. That was a very famous actress and her Siamese cat Koko. A very elegant, well behaved cat, too. Purser was terrified for his silk coverlets, but Koko just liked lying on them. A bit vain, perhaps, but very civilised.'

'Cats,' said Phryne, 'are different. Ships and cats have gone together since the ark.'

'We have a few cats on the strength,' admitted Theodore. 'But they are part of the crew.'

'Very proper,' said Phryne, and held out her cup for more coffee. 'Do you think we can be overheard, Mr. Green?'

'No, Miss Fisher,' he said, looking around. 'There's no one here and the windows are too far away.'

'Good,' said Phryne. 'Pour us some more coffee, then, and tell me about the first class passengers. Perhaps that was a little abrupt. Read this letter from the company,' she instructed, putting it into his hand.

He read. It was on letterhead and he knew the signature. He looked at Phryne with a wild surmise.

'I'm your detective,' she said, and smiled. 'I'm here to find out who's pinching the jewellery. And you are going to help me.'

Theodore Green surrendered without a fight. Resistance, apparently, was futile.

'I was told that someone was coming,' he said. 'Here is your sapphire, Miss Fisher.'

Phryne accepted a wash-leather bag and undid the drawstring. Onto her palm rolled a blue stone as big as a doorknob, sparkling like ice.

'Oh,' she said. 'How very, very pretty. A very good fake.'

Theodore Green smiled.

'And here is the story of the stone,' he said, giving Phryne a small booklet. 'Call me if there is anything I can do, Miss Fisher.'

'I will,' responded Phryne.

● ● ● ● ●

To Miss Maggie May
Liverpool

Mags old girl got a good berth on a big ship. None of them coasters. Trans Atlantic. Good prog and not too bad gelt. When I get back what say we get drunk for a week?

Your old pal Jack

Chapter Two

Was this the face that launch'd
a thousand ships?
Christopher Marlowe
The Tragical History of Dr. Faustus

Dot had been conducted through all the rituals of the SS *Hinemoa*
by Caroline and was peacefully embroidering when Phryne came
back. She looked a picture, Phryne thought, pretty Dorothy
sitting in a white wicker chair with her back to the light and
the sun making a halo out of her chestnut hair. A Dutch master
would have been ravished. Dot herself never paid much attention
to her appearance, considering that the best thing that could be
said of her face was that it was clean.

'Hello, old thing,' said Phryne, sitting down on the blue
morocain sofa and lighting a gasper. 'I've just been shown over
the ship and there is an awful lot of it.'

Dot laid her work down in her lap. 'I met our stewardess,
Caroline. She's nice. I had tea. And she told me all about how
the ship works.'

'Good. Why don't you stay where you are and I'll just lie
down for a nice little snooze? I've got a lot to think about. And
you are supposed to be having a holiday, Dot dear.'

'Oh, Miss Phryne, a holiday! It's not as though I work very
hard,' protested Dot.

'Nonetheless,' said Phryne, shedding shoes. Dot gathered them up and put them on the shoe rack before she sat down and resumed her drawn thread work. The sun was at the perfect angle to allow her to count threads. And the motion of the ship was so smooth that it almost didn't seem to be moving…

● ● ● ● ●

Dot woke when someone sounded a gong. Phryne sat up and shook her hair into order.

'Ah,' she said. 'That nice officer told me about this. Come out, Dot, we're going through the heads. He said that the sea might be a bit bumpier out here.'

'Wind's cold,' said Dot as Phryne opened the French windows to the private balcony. 'I'll just get our coats.'

'I'm not cold,' said Phryne, hanging over the rail dangerously and scanning the horizon. 'Look, there we are. And now we face the rip, and here we go!'

Dot saw that the water on either side of the *Hinemoa's* elegant green sides was broken and rough, and she clung onto the rail with the one hand which wasn't caught inside her coat sleeve. The ship heaved, surged, heaved again, then there was a cheer from somewhere below and they were out into the open sea. Landscape moved away from the eye. Phryne donned her coat in one movement and was straightening up. SS *Hinemoa* tasted the waves, found an agreeably smooth path between them, and sailed on to the drum of her strong diesel engines.

'Oh, lovely,' Phryne said. 'I've never sailed in such a beautiful ship. She rides like a swan. Are you all right, Dot dear?'

'Yes,' said Dot, finally managing to get her coat on. 'She is smooth, isn't she? I brought tablets for seasickness.'

'Take one,' said Phryne. 'I'll have one too. Can't hurt and I want to enjoy my dinner. Can you see the clock from here?'

'Five thirty,' said Dot.

'Good. Then I shall have a nice bath not leaving the fresh water tap running, and then we might dress.'

'I'm in Second Class,' said Dot. 'Caroline said. All maids and valets are in the second class dining room.'

'No,' said Phryne firmly. 'You're dining with me. Second Class indeed. I did not bring you here to be patronised, Dot.'

'I might be more use with all them maids and valets,' said Dot, who really did not want to go through the ordeal of dinner in wealthy company. She never knew what to say and the gentlemen would keep paying her compliments. 'You know how the lower orders gossip,' urged Dot, trying for Miss Eliza's upper class tone.

'Hmm,' said Phryne. 'You might be right. Can you stick it, Dot?'

'Oh yes,' said Dot with heartfelt relief. 'For you, Miss Phryne.'

'That's very nice of you, Dot. I appreciate it. Then let's get on with the bathing and dressing, old thing. I wish to make an impression. I've got the bauble,' she said, producing it.

'Pretty,' said Dot. 'Looks like a Christmas decoration.'

'And what is the program for First Class tonight?' asked Phryne, shedding clothes as Dot read the ship's newsletter.

'Buffet dinner at eight,' she replied. 'Always a buffet for the first night at sea, Caroline said. Not formal dressing tonight, just ordinary dinner clothes. You're at table three with those people you know about. Then there's dancing with Mavis and the Melody Makers in the Palm Court. There's a bridge game in the smaller salon and comic songs in the Smoke Room, gentlemen only—why don't they call it a smoking room like everyone else? Drinks from the bar. What do you want to wear?'

'Blue,' said Phryne. Dot laid the dress out on her bed and went to run the scented bath without which Miss Fisher never ventured on social occasions.

'How do you want to smell?' asked Dot from the bathroom, noticing that the taps were in the shape of dolphins.

'Expensive,' said Phryne, still staring out to sea, dressed only in red washing silk camiknickers and an absorbed expression.

Bathing luxuriously and dressing slowly was a ritual which Phryne thoroughly enjoyed. When she wasn't in the mood for it she didn't do it, so it retained its opulent ambiance. She particularly liked the feeling of being dressed in all her undergarments and a dressing gown. It always made her feel like a Grande Horizontale, about to receive a new and wealthier protector.

Phryne, of course, was in no need of protection. She had an independent income, a French war pension, and a house of her own. But it was a pleasant feeling.

The bath was scented with Floris honeysuckle, which smelt sweeter for being opposed to salt air. She put on her dark underclothes and a truly vibrant dressing gown, gold figured with purple flowers like an explosion in a chrysanthemum garden. Dot joined her after a while, identically scented, in her nice warm woolly brown gown, with which she paired sheepskin slippers that kept even the ankles toasty. Dot felt the cold. Phryne smiled at them, reflected side by side in the mirror.

'We make a pair. Now, I want a gin and tonic and you want a sherry. It takes a little Dutch courage to go into new company.'

Phryne lifted the phone and expressed her wishes. In a very short time, Caroline brought in a tray. Dot introduced Phryne. Caroline looked at the scented hand in hers and didn't quite know what to do with it. Then she shook it heartily.

'Nice drop of gin,' she said cheerfully, putting a half-bottle on the small table, along with a bottle of tonic in an ice-bucket. She poured a judicious amount of the spirit into a tall, unfigured glass, and added tonic and a slice of lemon to the mixture. Phryne tasted. It was perfect. She said so.

Caroline grinned. 'Thanks, Miss. And here's your sherry, Dot. Anything else, ladies? I'm just going off duty. After me it's Nick, he's a nice bloke but he's got a heavy hand with the drinks. All his ladies get squiffy.'

'Nothing else,' said Phryne. 'Thank you.'

'I'll come back and get you at seven thirty and show you the way to dinner,' said Caroline to Dot. 'We have dinner then, too. You can sit with us if you like.'

'Thanks,' said Dot. It was a kind offer. 'I'd like that.'

Caroline went out. Dot sipped her sherry. Her family, apart from her father, were blue-ribbon teetotal, so she got a tickling feeling of wickedness from drinking even a modest glass of sherry.

Phryne drank her G and T with a distracted air. All the people at her table had been on the *Hinemoa* when the other jewels had vanished. If some unknown and exceptionally clever crew member wasn't the thief, one of them had to be. But none of them sounded at all promising. Not from the meticulous descriptions supplied by Navigation Officer Green—a man, she was sure, who noticed things, even if they weren't things that Phryne would necessarily want to know. Well, no sense in borrowing trouble, as her grandmother had said. And this was a very good gin and tonic. She laid Chaucer on her spare pillow and began to construe.

Dot, finding the ship's lights not really bright enough for complex stitching, had a bag full of detective novels. She knew that look on Miss Phryne's face. She was reading and thinking and did not want to be disturbed.

Dot put on her own dinner dress, a modest assemblage in dark oak silk with an autumn leaf pattern, and withdrew to her dressing table, where there was a lamp on a long stem. She opened her book.

She had just got to the exciting discovery of the body in the library when Phryne came to life and stood up, stretching.

'Put me into the blue dress, Dot dear, it's nearly time for your dinner. Take care, now, no Sexton Blake action. Just keep your ears open and don't take any risks. I've no idea who's involved or not so we don't say anything about the job.'

'But we can talk about the jewel?' asked Dot.

'I authorise you to positively gossip about it,' said Phryne. Dot dropped the calf length blue brocade dress over Phryne's sleek head and did up the side fastening. The dress was plain and had an almost unfashionable plunge neckline and a most respectable high back. It had been chosen to show off the jewel.

Dot fastened the ring closure and also pinned the little safety chain to the back neckline of the dress. Then she placed on Phryne's head a simple silver headband with a panache of one blue ostrich feather, which curled down to her shoulder.

'There,' said Dot. Phryne looked at the effect in the mirror. She was standing there when Caroline knocked and came in. She stood amazed.

The lady was wearing a very nice dress, but that was to be expected. What riveted the stewardess's attention was a huge sapphire on a string of smaller sapphires. The main stone blazed almost indigo, a dark fire against Phryne's ivory cleavage.

'Blimey,' said Caroline.

'Pretty thing, isn't it?' responded Phryne. 'Dot will tell you about it. I just couldn't leave it at home with all the others. It's the Maharani,' she said. 'The Great Queen of Sapphires.'

• • ● • •

Phryne walked into the Grand Salon and paused, surveying the arrangements. She located table three and headed for it, threading her way through a throng of passengers. A murmur arose in her wake and she smiled privately. That was the impression she had hoped to make. Someone so rich and so vain that they would wear a precious jewel to impress the sparse company on the first night at sea…

Table three consisted of an elderly lady in a dark red Molyneux dinner dress which she must have bought in about 1912, a tall slim man with absurdly fluffy blond curls, and a shingled young woman in the minimum of coverage allowed by the Decency Act. The gentleman stood up as Phryne approached.

'Ah,' he said, on a breath of pure admiration. 'Can it be that we have the good fortune to have you gracing our table?'

'The good fortune is mine,' said Phryne politely, holding out her hand. 'Phryne Fisher.'

'Miss Fisher,' said the tall man. 'I am Albert Forrester, a photographer. May I have the pleasure of introducing Professor

Applegate—' the elderly lady nodded affably—'and Mrs. West.'

Mrs. West was the underclad girl. She gave Phryne a soft warm little hand, limp as a recently deceased mouse, and giggled briefly. Her eyes were fixed on Phryne's bosom. So were Mr. Forrester's, but his interest, she judged, was aesthetic, or possibly biological. Mrs. West was just afire with greed.

'What a gorgeous stone,' said Mrs. West. She had a high, affected, childish voice.

'Thank you,' said Phryne.

'If you would like to come this way,' offered Mr. Forrester, 'I'll show you the buffet.'

'Please, do continue with your dinner,' said Phryne. 'I can manage. I'll be back soon.'

The buffet had been designed for slightly wobbly tummies, not yet comfortable with the sea. The soup was chilled beef consommé, the chicken was either hotly curried or in a cool aspic, the salads were crisp and offered with a vinaigrette, not mayonnaise. The beef was roasted and cold. Phryne helped herself to cold beef and salad and decided to come back for dessert. Those jellies looked so decorative, with fruit set inside them.

She returned to table three and found that it had been augmented with a worried elderly man, sitting next to Mrs. West; presumably her husband. Two solid middle aged people had also arrived: a Mr. Cahill and his wife. A retired grazier, Mr. Forrester explained. Phryne knew the type. Spent so long with his dog and his cattle that he had lost the habit of human speech and let his wife interpret the world for him. Mrs. Cahill had a comfortable figure and was wondering aloud about the constituents of the seafood in aspic that she was eating.

'There are a few more people to come,' said Mr. Forrester, consulting the card on the table. 'Mr. Jack Mason, Miss Margery Lemmon and Mr. Vivian Aubrey. Mr. and Mrs. Singer never join us on the first night out. He's got a dicey tummy.'

Phryne took a forkful of beef. It was excellent. A steward appeared, ushering an old man to the table. When he was comfortably seated, the steward whisked away and came back with a steaming dish of lamb curry and rice. The old man thanked him.

'Why do I get served and the rest of you have to carry your own dinner?' asked the old man, anticipating something which Mrs. Cahill was about to say. She primmed up her lips, disconcerted. 'You are not being slighted, my dear madam. It's just that they're afraid I might drop things. I'm not as young as you,' said the old man, smiling gently. 'And this is my seventh voyage on the *Hinemoa*. Isn't she the most beautiful ship you ever saw?'

'Rides the sea like a bird,' agreed Phryne, introducing herself. That was a really muscular curry. The vindaloo scent of it was strong enough to sting her eyes. It had certainly been specially made for the old man.

'Aubrey,' said the old man, holding her hand in an unexpectedly firm grasp. 'Vivian Aubrey, at your service. My dear Miss Fisher,' he said, drinking in the sight of Phryne with appreciation.

Phryne returned his gaze. He was a well polished old gentleman, with cherubic blue eyes and a neatly trimmed tonsure. His complexion had been coloured by hotter suns than his native Britain, she guessed, and he was almost supernaturally clean. His shirt front winked at her. She gave him an approving smile. Mr. Aubrey obviously considered himself host and carried on smoothly, including all of the group in the conversation.

'I gather you are a photographer, Mr. Forrester. What made you choose that form of art?'

'Couldn't draw,' said Forrester, brushing back his curls. 'So I had to draw with light. What was your profession, sir?'

'Old India hand,' replied Mr. Aubrey, twinkling. 'Old India bore, now, I fear. I was there for forty years, and when I came home I just couldn't settle into a nice hotel in Brighton with the same faces at breakfast until I died. Too cold, for one thing. So I just travel; a few weeks ashore at the end of every voyage, then back on board again. Always new people to talk to, always a new sea.'

'What a lovely idea,' said Professor Applegate with some irony. 'Assuming you have nothing else to do.'

'Don't want me in India anymore, my dear,' said Aubrey, taking a liberty which the professor strangely did not seem to resent. 'Memsahib passed away ten years ago. No family left except the children, and they are all married and settled down. One son in Sydney, one son in Bournemouth, one daughter in Cairo. If I travel I can see them all, and they are pleased to see me because I am not on their doorstep all the time, interrupting their lives. Oh, I must remember to get several Maori dolls for the little girls. Perhaps you would help me choose them, Mrs. West?'

'Oh yes,' squeaked Mrs. West. 'I love dolls. Don't I, Johnnie?'

'Yes,' said her husband dotingly. 'You're a living doll yourself, Jonquil dear.'

Phryne kept eating. Jonquil. Well, well. Even Aubrey appeared to have been silenced. Then Mrs. West, quivering with emotion, ventured, 'Miss Fisher…that stone…'

'Oh, the Maharani?' said Phryne. 'Isn't it just beautiful?'

'Oh yes,' breathed Mrs. West.

'It's from India,' said Mr. Aubrey. 'I think I've heard about this. The Great Queen of Sapphires, eh? Usually have a tale attached to them, the great stones. Sometimes even a curse.'

'Oh yes, there's a story,' replied Phryne. A waiter leaned over her to fill her wine glass with red wine. 'But I'll tell it another time. I have always been interested in photography, Mr. Forrester. Have you brought your equipment with you?'

'Yes. My speciality is the female form divine,' he said, gazing dreamily at Mrs. West's practically uncovered bosom. Mr. West, in a purely animal and instinctive move, slid an arm over his wife's shoulder. 'Mine!' said the arm. Mr. Forrester transferred his gaze to Phryne, who had no objections. 'I've been doing studies for the covers of fashionable magazines,' he told her cleavage.

'And you, Mr. West? What was your profession?'

'I was an accountant,' said Mr. West. 'Retired now. Made some very good investments for my clients—and for me. This is the fourth cruise I have been on. My Jonquil said I needed a rest. My children…'

Are exigent, thought Phryne, and don't approve of this new wife, who is probably younger than they are. And likely to inherit all the old man's money. Mr. Aubrey came through as the silence lengthened.

'And you, Professor, didn't I read your excellent book on Maori culture? What was it called, now, dear me, memory going at last…'

'"Moko and Maori Warrior Culture",' said the professor. 'The word means tattoo. Among other things. Do I speak to a colleague?'

'Only in the most amateur way,' replied Mr. Aubrey. 'Had to know a bit about native customs, you know, religions and so on, or one could make a frightful blunder and HO would purse the lips. Had to know the languages, too, pass all the exams, or stay down at clerk level forever. Hard cheese on chaps who just couldn't be doing with languages. There are some, you know. Nothing to do with intelligence, either.'

'Yes,' said Phryne. 'I always thought it was like being tone deaf.'

The professor awarded her an approving look. 'But not you?' she asked.

'Only French,' said Phryne. 'And a little bit of Italian and Spanish. You?'

'Maori dialects and English alone, I'm afraid. I couldn't see the sense of learning French out here in South East Asia.'

'I was an awful duffer at school,' confessed Mrs. West.

'And I never spoke any language other than English,' responded her husband. 'Never mind, Jonquil. You don't need to be clever.'

'I suppose you speak a lot of those heathen tongues, Mr. Aubrey?' asked Mrs. Cahill disapprovingly.

'Hindi, of course, and some Farsi, and a few others,' said Mr. Aubrey, his voice tightening a little. He did not like that nasty reference to heathens, Phryne observed. 'They kept moving us young chaps around and practically every new place had a new dialect.'

'In that case I must say "Namaste",' said a young woman, taking her place beside Mr. Aubrey. He pressed both arthritic hands together and returned her gesture.

'Namaste,' he said, bowing his head a little.

'Margery Lemmon,' she introduced herself to the others. 'Sorry about showing off, but I don't often get a chance to talk Hindi.'

'My niece', said Mr. Aubrey proudly.

'And how do you know Hindi?' asked Mr. West.

'Best reason of all,' said Margery Lemmon. 'Born there. Nunc said this was a lovely ship and I'm at a bit of a loose end—so I came along for the ride. This holiday is the first one I have ever taken. And it's so nice to have Nunc here. I'm allowed to share his curry, for one thing.'

'The right spirit,' approved the professor.

A young man bounded up like someone out of a musical comedy and produced the second 'hullo-ullo-ullo!' of the day.

'Jack Mason, nice to meet you all again,' said the newcomer. 'I say, this ship is a bit of all right, what?'

'And so is the dinner,' suggested Phryne. 'Get some while you can.'

'Good notion,' said Mr. Mason, and shot off to the buffet. He was tall, thin, athletic, and as far as Phryne could tell at that speed, had brown hair and brown eyes, rather like a seal's. He was sitting next to Miss Lemmon. She was tall, too, and thin, and her hair was cut short. Her air was the no-nonsense one of nurses everywhere but Mr. Mason seemed to amuse her.

'Precipitate lout,' muttered Mr. Forrester. 'He'll have that table over if he doesn't watch out.'

'He's just a boy,' soothed Miss Lemmon.

'And boys,' said Mr. Aubrey dryly, 'will be boys. Did you have a lot of difficulty, Professor, in getting the Maori to talk to you?'

'No,' said Professor Applegate, who also seemed amused at the male reaction to Mr. Mason. 'I spoke to the chiefs first, of course, and then to the shamans, the *tohunga*, and once they had passed me as not *tapu*, all was well. *Tapu* means forbidden, of course. In fact they are proud of their warriors, as well they might be. They almost beat the British, you know.'

'Impossible,' said Mr. West.

'I assure you,' said the professor. 'They fought so hard and bravely that Queen Victoria directed that there should be a peace treaty to "prevent the further effusion of blood". It's called the Treaty of Waitangi. I can lend you a copy if you like, Mr. West,' she offered sweetly.

'No, thanks,' grunted Mr. West. 'I'm on this cruise for a rest, eh, Jonquil?'

'Darling,' cooed Jonquil.

Mr. Mason returned with a plate piled high with miscellaneous meats. He managed to put it down without disaster and they watched, fascinated, as he absorbed it all, hardly stopping to chew, and then departed for a second helping.

'I used to be able to eat like that,' said Mr. Aubrey with acute envy.

'Hollow legs at that age,' commented Miss Lemmon.

'At least he'll be able to partner you ladies at deck tennis,' said Mr. Aubrey. 'A fine game…'

Phryne's attention wandered, as it always did when someone was attempting to explain rules to her. She would learn them when she had to.

The rules of deck tennis lasted through the rest of the meal. Phryne took her leave and went into the Palm Court, where she could hear a dance band tuning up.

Mavis and the Melody Makers were dressed identically in lavender satin, which had the effect of making the stouter members of the group look like well tailored cushions. The only person not wearing lavender was a short stout woman in faultless gentleman's evening dress.

They had done their best with the clothes. Two tall, slender women, one dark and one fair, so similar that they had to be sisters, had shortened their skirts and loosened their tops. The cello player had been allowed wide-cut pyjama trousers, in view of how she had to sit. The others were much of a muchness. Phryne found a wicker chair under a palm frond and ordered a gin fizz.

Phryne knew that, for all musicians, setting up was a strain and it certainly produced grumbles from the Melody Makers. One music stand slammed down repeatedly and would not stay at the right height until the trumpeter surrendered something from her mouth—under protest—to glue it into place. One sheet of the opening music was missing altogether from every copy. Mavis was sneezing, the double bass player was green with seasickness and someone had been plying the trombone with restorative brandy. She was hiccupping gently and seemed so restored as to be almost horizontal.

'Now, girls, come along,' said Mavis, a raddled woman with unconvincing brown hair and a harried expression.

'Where's Rosie?' asked the blonde sister. 'Can't play this without a clarinet.'

'Oh, bother, where is she then?' exclaimed Mavis. 'Has anyone seen her?'

'Might be back in her room,' suggested the blonde's sister.

'Oh Lord, Magda, go and see, will you? And hurry!'

Tall, slender and fair was Magda, Phryne noted, accepting and sipping her gin fizz. The trumpet player drifted over to stand a little behind Phryne, under the shade of the palms, emptying her spit valve into the pot.

'You're my Uncle Cec's Miss Fisher, aren't you?' she asked, staring artlessly into space.

'I am,' said Phryne. 'Who are you?'

'I'm Lizbet Yates,' said Lizbet, unwrapping a flat silver paper package and extracting another piece of whatever it was that she had been chewing. She had the fair colouring of the admirable wharfie and knockabout bloke Cec's Scandinavian ancestry; pale straight hair, ice-blue eyes and a humorous quirk to her mouth. She might have been twenty, perhaps twenty-two. 'Want a piece of Lumberjack?'

'Not at the moment,' said Phryne. 'What is it?'

'Chewing gum. I've got a friend who's a Yank, and they chew all the time. Keeps your mouth moist, and that's important for a brass player. It comes from Redmond, Virginia,' said Lizbet, chewing like a cow. 'One day I'm going to get there. That's where my sailor boy lives.'

'And how did Cec's niece come to be one of the Melody Makers?'

Lizbet cast a glance at her colleagues, who were still waiting for Rosie, and settled down for a good gossip.

'I drove my mum mad when I was a kid, picking out tunes on the piano, nagging her until she got me lessons. Pretty soon I knew I wasn't going to be good enough for a concert pianist so I tootled a bit on my uncle Bill's old bugle, and I was good at it. No way of getting into an orchestra, though, they don't want girls playing brass in their nice, clean orchestras. So I got a job with Mavis. Good pay, good hours. One day I'll convince 'em to let me into the Melbourne Symphony. Till then I get a lot of practice.'

'Very enterprising of you,' said Phryne, impressed. 'Tell me about the rest of the group.'

'Magda and Katrina,' said Lizbet promptly. 'First and second violins, and they both sing. Wait till you hear them playing them wild gypsy songs. They're Czech. Sisters. Annie, that's the short dark one, plays the viola and percussion. Lil is trombone. She always gets seasick first day out and says brandy's the best treatment. I reckon she's feeling no pain whatsoever.

'Joan plays the cello and the double bass. That's her in satin trousers—wouldn't be decent otherwise. Vi plays the flute and the sax, and Rosie the clarinet—I wonder where she's got to. Old Mother Mavis is going to split a gusset pretty soon. Jo's the one in the suit. She sings ballads and she can pretty much play anything, so she fills in. You on the *Hinemoa* on a job, Miss Fisher?'

'Yes,' said Phryne, deciding instantly to trust this laconic young woman.

'Uncle Cec would want me to help you,' said Lizbet. 'He thinks the world of you, Miss Fisher. Uncle Bert, too. They're really proud of working for you. You let me know if I can help. We're on every night except Sundays. Well, hooroo for now,' said Lizbet, and drifted back to the musicians.

Mavis had given up on the errant Rosie after Magda returned from the crew quarters without her. She gathered her girls, lifted her baton, and they launched into a nice, upbeat version of 'Pardon me, Pretty Baby'. Phryne sang along under her breath.

Phryne observed that Lil, the trombone player, had been propped upright against a convenient pillar. She was playing faultlessly, probably by memory. Musicians, it seemed, were like sailors; as long as they weren't too drunk to stand up they could manage their duties.

The singer was the woman in the evening suit. She had a very pleasant tenor voice, rich without being gluey. Misfits, thought Phryne, we are all misfits. Lizbet plays the trumpet which girls don't do. And that tenor Jo is good enough for the stage, though I bet she can't get a job with the Melbourne Chorale. And whoever thought that I would be a detective?

She put down her empty glass and was aware of someone hovering in her vicinity. It was Navigation Officer Green, nerving himself up to ask Phryne to dance. While this was an amusing spectacle, Phryne was not a cruel woman by nature. She cut his indecision short by walking up to him and asking sweetly, 'May I have this dance?'

'Oh, er, yes, Miss Fisher,' he stammered, taking her in his arms as though he was afraid she would break. Or, possibly, bite.

Years of sullen, compulsory attendance at Miss Gissing's School Of Dance had not obliterated his fine natural clumsiness.

But this lady seemed to know what she was doing and at least he knew the steps. And she wasn't wearing a train. He had still not got over his horror at the sound of tearing stitches, and the glacial politeness of his partner assuring him that it didn't matter at all, it was just an old dress, really.

Now the song was telling him about the red red robin going bob-bob-bobbin' along, of all unlikely things for a robin to do, and Navigation Officer Theodore Green found that he was dancing without thinking about his feet. He was aware that Miss Fisher was leading, but that was neither here nor there. The fact remained that his feet were not colliding painfully with Miss Fisher's delicate louis-heeled blue shoes and they were moving around the Palm Court dance floor in fine style.

'See, it's easy,' said Phryne, tilting her head to speak to him. 'As long as you forget what your feet are doing. Talking to me will aid this process.'

'Really, Miss Fisher?' he asked as they executed a precise turn and came back across the floor. He could have rested his chin on her sleek head and she smelt wonderful.

'I've met all the passengers concerned,' she told him. 'Mr. Aubrey is a charming man and seems wealthy enough.'

'Oh yes, Miss Fisher, I believe he's very comfortable. When we finish these little New Zealand runs, he's already booked on the round-the-world cruise. All the crew like him. He's a very nice old gentleman and has some fascinating stories about the old days in India. Really cheers up when the weather starts getting tropical.'

'Just so. Mr. Forrester couldn't take his eyes off my chest, but he wasn't looking at the gem.'

'Er, I believe that he's very successful with the ladies,' said Theodore Green reluctantly. 'Stewards always knock and wait for a count of ten before they go into his cabin. But there haven't been any complaints,' he said.

'No, he would only be interested in the ones who wanted him,' said Phryne. 'That's the secret of being a successful man about town. Make it your rule in life, my dear Navigation Officer.'

'Er…' said Theodore Green wildly.

'Mr. West is very possessive. Mrs. West is very young.'

'That's true. A couple of times there have been…well…scenes when some young man was paying her attention which Mr. West considered too familiar. Now our surgeon has fallen for her. Hook, line *and* sinker, I'm afraid. Her clothes seem to invite…er…'

'Closer inspection?' asked Phryne wickedly.

'Er, yes, Miss Fisher.'

'True. The gown she was almost wearing this evening would have made about two napkins and a small tablecloth. But that is the fashion. She would have ripped the gem off my neck if she could.'

'She has lots of her own,' Theodore informed Phryne. 'And one of hers was stolen last voyage. Cost the company a pretty penny to hush it up.'

'Greed knows no moderation,' said Phryne severely. '"These are the Four that are never content, that have never been filled since the Dews began—Jacala's mouth, and the glut of the Kite, and the hands of the Ape, and the eyes of Man".'

'Kipling,' he said. 'The "Jungle Book". You know that he made up the *Just So Stories* on a ship?'

'Yes,' said Phryne, still thinking about Mrs. West. 'If one of her jewels was stolen I think that means we should discount her. I'd say she loves those gems with a fiery passion.'

'Very likely,' said Theodore Green as they essayed another turn. This was working! Who said he couldn't dance?

'I can't see Professor Applegate stealing a stone unless it was a Maori artifact. Margery Lemmon is a possibility. So is that bouncing young man Mr. Mason. He might think that being Raffles' 'The Gentleman Thief' was jolly good sport. The Cahills haven't a particle of initiative. 'Well, we shall see. There,' she said, as the music stopped. 'Wasn't that fun?'

'Oh yes, Miss Fisher,' breathed Navigation Officer Green. 'Can I get you a drink?'

'Yes, please,' said Phryne, allowing him to conduct her to her previous chair. 'Champagne.'

The Palm Court was filling up with dancers. Mavis and the Melody Makers were doing well for a band with a missing clarinet and an alcohol-assisted trombone. They were playing a quickstep: 'Ain't she sweet?'

Jonquil West floated past in the arms of Doctor Shilletoe, the ship's doctor. The doctor was a personable young man. Phryne saw Mr. West hunched at a small table, his clasped hands before him, quivering with tension. The couple danced very well. She was almost professional. It crossed Phryne's mind to wonder where Mr. West had found his Jonquil.

She was wearing a red dress which dipped almost to the waist at the back, revealing her porcelain pale skin. The doctor's hands, perforce, were stroking the smooth torso. Mrs. West was almost purring.

There's trouble, thought Phryne, looking at the darkening West face. Why on earth would he take her on these cruises when he's as jealous as that? She's bound to dance with pretty young men. That's one of the things which cruises do for young men. Strange.

Navigation Officer Green came back with a glass of champagne. He was very proud of getting that glass across the dangerous terrain of the dance floor and safely into Miss Fisher's hands without spilling a drop. Phryne accepted it. Good champagne. In the French manner, if not actually French speaking.

'None for you?' she asked.

'Oh no, Miss Fisher, we can't drink with passengers, it's a company rule.'

'But you can dance with us?'

'Yes, we're expected to dance.' Until now this had struck him as the most dire of his duties but he was beginning to reconsider this opinion. 'Good exercise and good relations with the passengers. On sailing ships, they used to make the crew dance.

On long voyages, you know, when they were becalmed or on station. Gets the fidgets out of the legs.'

'And gives them something to do with their hands,' said Phryne lightly. Evidently nothing was going to deter Theodore Green from imparting interesting facts to Phryne. She decided to enjoy them. You never know, she told herself, when you might need a fact or two.

Mr. and Mrs. Cahill went past. They danced well, thought Phryne, as though they had danced together for a long time. Margery Lemmon was dancing with her uncle, old Mr. Aubrey. The language they spoke was not English but sounded sweet on the tongue. The professor was not dancing. She was sitting at a small table, reading a letter through pince-nez. Albert Forrester was setting up his camera and tripod.

'Come along, Miss Fisher,' he called to her. 'You'll look wonderful amongst the palm leaves.'

'I'll leave you,' said Theodore Green regretfully.

'See if you can get Mrs. West away from Doctor Shilletoe,' Phryne advised. 'Cut in on him if you need to. That might avert the scene which is presently on its way at the speed of sound.'

'Right you are,' said the navigation officer, fired with new confidence. Phryne saw him tap Doctor Shilletoe on the shoulder and possess himself of an armful of Mrs. West just as her husband was standing up from his thunderous crouch. When he saw his wife in the safe arms of an inoffensive officer of the ship, West relaxed and accepted a drink from a hovering steward. Good, thought Phryne. Scenes are so inelegant. They can, of course, be instructive, but I can bait that man at any time and this is my first night.

She posed under the fronds for Mr. Forrester. He was an unusual photographer. Instead of giving endless instructions in a faintly annoyed tone—'chin a bit higher, turn your head a little, no, not that much'—he talked amiably and then, when one was least expecting it, took the picture. He was using a camera that Phryne had always associated with Hollywood films. It had a handle.

'Yes, it's a cine camera,' he told her. 'I engineered it to take one frame at a time. The exposure is a lot faster than plate, so I can catch a passing expression. It's a bit more iffy to develop but at least I don't have to lug plates around.'

'Interesting,' said Phryne, suddenly feeling weary of people telling her things. 'Would you like to dance?'

'Delighted,' he said, clapping his lens cap in place.

Photography was his second love, after all. His first was ladies of all sizes and shapes. And this one was a very delectable size and shape indeed.

And the band played 'Walking My Baby Back Home'.

● ● ● ● ●

Phryne returned to her cabin, resisting a pressing invitation to his cabin from Mr. Forrester, and sank onto her bed. Dot was head down in the wardrobe. All Phryne could see of her were her well shod feet.

'Dot, are you looking for something?' she asked at last.

Dot's head appeared. Her face was red with effort and anger.

'Miss Phryne,' she declared. 'This room has been searched!'

'Well, well,' murmured Phryne. 'Anything missing?'

'I've just been checking. Nothing's gone, but it's all been handled, moved around.'

'You're sure?' asked Phryne, knowing that Dot was sure. She had re-arranged all their goods only a few hours ago. As she had expected, Dot nodded.

'Was your stuff searched?'

'All of it. Even...' Dot's lip quivered. 'My underthings.'

'Dot, dear, come and sit here by the window and we shall finish off that nice bottle of gin. It's not personal. The burglar was looking for information about me and had no interest in your underclothes, I promise.'

'Promise?' asked Dot, accepting a glass of gin and tonic. She sat down in the pretty wicker chair and looked hard at Phryne. Then she nodded and sipped her drink.

'I'm very glad that he or she didn't find this,' said Phryne, producing a closely folded wad of paper from her evening bag.

'What's that?' asked Dot, on a gasp. She wasn't used to strong drink.

'My briefing notes on the other four robberies. All that the burglar would have seen in here was proper: the clothes and possessions of a lady of my station. Nothing unusual. I thought this might happen so I carried all my dangerous secrets with me. Don't worry. The burglar won't be back. He or she now knows that we are just who we said we were.'

'All right,' said Dot. 'But it gave me a turn.'

'I bet it did.'

Phryne and Dot stared out at the sea. The waves were black, rolling gently, and the stars overhead were pounced silver on black velvet, like the mourning dress of a queen. Phryne drank her gin, pleased. The cabin was very quiet. Then she heard a scratching noise. Scratching noise?

'Dot, did you hear something?' she asked. Dot leapt to her feet.

'He's under your bed!' she exclaimed, grabbing up a discarded shoe.

'And he shall shortly not be under my bed. Out you come, if you please,' said Phryne. 'I am armed, you know.'

There was a pause. Then out from under the sumptuous bed came the most disreputable tom cat Phryne had ever seen. His tail was chewed to string. His ears were punched like bus tickets. He had been, probably, a very pretty silver tabby kitten, but life had been hard on him. He paused to strop a claw or two on the carpet, then picked up his burden and walked to Phryne's feet, where he sat down, staring up into her face. He had very clear, very green eyes in his pugilist's face.

'Well,' said Phryne, putting the gun back under her pillow and suppressing an urge to giggle, 'nice to meet you, sir. That's a very fine rat you have there. He must have got in when the burglar did, Dot. Now I suppose you would like me to open the door?' she said to the cat.

'Maybe we better call the steward,' said Dot. 'He's a ratter, they might be looking for him.'

Dot used the telephone, not without her usual trepidation that it might fizz sparks through the earpiece, and a voice said that he would be right there.

There was a knock some five minutes later. Phryne had managed to make a closer acquaintance of the cat, who had put down his rat to allow her to scratch him behind the ears and under the chin. He purred rustily. Whatever it was that constituted confident, easy maleness, he had it by the oodle. And Phryne had always liked aged roués. This one had certainly been well battered in the lists of love.

'Good evening, ladies,' said the steward. 'I'm the night steward, Nick Jones. What about a little late supper to stave off those bad dreams? Or perhaps another drink?' He was a stocky, personable young man with an agreeably breezy manner. 'Or maybe some tea?'

Then he noticed Phryne and the cat. He staggered. His voice went up a full octave.

'Scragger? What are you doing here?'

Scragger gave the steward a disgusted look and a deep, commanding 'mew'. Then, recalled to his duties, he shook off Phryne's hand, picked up his lawful rat and exited, sauntering past the steward with his insolent tail as straight as a taper.

'I'm so sorry, ladies, I can't think how he got in here. Does anything need…er…cleaning up?'

'No, he took his rat with him,' Phryne pointed out. 'Has Scragger been with you long?'

'He stowed away on the first voyage,' Nick replied, mopping his face with a very white handkerchief. 'Resigned his ticket on a South Sea freighter, or so they say. I know you'll want to complain about this, ladies, but could you sort of say that he didn't soil your cabin or bite anyone? We're all fond of old Scragger…'

'I haven't seen anything to complain of,' said Phryne. 'Have you, Dot?'

'No,' said Dot. 'I'd much rather he had the rat than it was still in here.'

'He might have brought it with him,' replied the steward. 'He shouldn't be up on this deck at all but there isn't a lot you can do to confine cats to quarters. Thanks very much, Miss Fisher, Miss Williams. That's really nice of you. Now, can I bring you a little light plate of something tasty?'

'Yes. Biscuits and cheese, please, and a fruit salad. What about you, Dot?'

'I had a big dinner,' said Dot doubtfully. 'But the sea makes you really hungry. I'd like a fruit salad too. And,' said Dot, greatly daring, 'another glass of sherry.'

She wasn't going to become a lush, but the burglar handling her unmentionables had shaken her.

When Nick came back, Phryne piled strong mouse-trap cheese on her biscuits, and Dot fished bits of mango out of her fruit salad. Dot loved mango. They sat for a while in silence.

'Tell me about your dinner in the second class dining room,' said Phryne.

'It was very nice,' Dot said, swallowing a piece of unexpected pawpaw. 'I met the other maids and Mr. West's valet, Mr. Thomas. He's just come to Mr. Mason, the others are old hands. The food was really good. Beautiful fried fish and chips, lovely salads, that soup in jelly which Mrs. Butler makes as well. Cold roast beef. Caroline says that the food in Second Class on the *Hinemoa* is better than First Class on any other ship. Lots to drink if you wanted beer and two drinks each for the ladies. I gave mine to Caroline.'

'A good idea,' said Phryne. 'So, what was the on-dit?'

'Miss?'

'The gossip?'

'Oh, there was lots of it. Mr. West is terrible jealous and Mrs.

West flirts a lot—and they say her dresses are more like bathing slips than something a lady would go to dinner in.'

'So they are,' said Phryne.

'They talked about the thefts,' said Dot. 'All the maids think it must be one of the crew but they can't work out how he gets the stones off the ship. The crew say they're sure it isn't them. What else? That Mr. Forrester is a bit of a ladies' man. Mr. Charles, the head steward, he's been on ships all his life, he says that he walked into the cabin and saw rows of pictures all spread out. Bring a blush to a policeman's face, he said.'

'Did you get the impression that these were—how shall I put this?—pictures of men and women together in displays of marital affection, or were they just nude ladies?'

It had been a good try at delicacy, but when Dot puzzled through the question she blushed as red as a poppy could do, after its second sherry.

'No!' she gasped. 'Just ladies with no clothes on.'

'Ah,' said Phryne. Mr. Forrester might have been taking anything from the sort of feelthy postcards one was offered in the Place Pigalle to Art Studies for the Connoisseur (ten shillings a packet, twelve different poses) or even real art.

'And what about the elderly but charming Professor Applegate?'

'They say she's nice. She's got a lot of Maori stuff in her cabin,' said Dot, very thankful to have escaped the photographer and the nudes. 'Caroline says that some of the things are *tapu* to her—she isn't allowed to look at them or she won't ever have any children—so another steward looks after the lady. Caroline was very serious about this heathen *tapu* nonsense. And she's supposed to be a Christian.'

'Never mind, Dot dear, haven't I seen you throw salt over your shoulder? Refuse to open an umbrella indoors? Say "touch wood"?'

'I suppose,' said Dot grudgingly. 'Well, let's see. Mr. Mason is the son of a famous lawyer. He doesn't get on with his dad. He's kept on a short allowance until he does as his father wants, which is to go to university and study law. But he wants to be a footballer. His father won't hear of it. Says football is low. No one knows much about the Cahills, except he's quiet and she does the talking. They say he's a nice old bushie and his wife's very moral, but all right really.'

'That was my impression too,' Phryne agreed.

'The Singers, they never go to dinner on the first night, but take a sleeping pill in case they get seasick, even though they never have,' said Dot. 'Mr. Charles says Mrs. is very wrapped up in Mr, but he doesn't care for her so much. The old man, Mr. Aubrey, everyone loves him. Always good-natured, never cross, lots of interesting stories. Mr. Charles says that the company ought to keep him on every voyage just to make things pleasant for the passengers and crew.'

'Did you hear anything about the musicians?'

'Mavis and the Melody Makers? Only that they're no better than they ought to be. But everyone thinks they are good at music. There's one of them, Jo, a woman, she always wears men's clothes, and they say—'

'I can imagine,' soothed Phryne, not wanting to watch Dot blush again.

'Anyway, that's about all. I stayed for a couple of games of pontoon, then I came back here, and I knew right away that someone had been in the room. And that's how Scragger must have got in, of course. When the burglar opened the door.'

'Thoughtfully bringing his own rat, too. I wish we could ask Scragger who our burglar was.'

'We can ask him,' Dot pointed out. 'We just wouldn't understand the answer.'

'True,' said Phryne. 'So, the hunt begins, Dot.'

Dot looked at her in comfortable dismay.

'Here we go again,' Dot agreed.

● ● ● ● ●

To Isaac Mcleod
Mull

Dear Brother
Our brother John has sent the money for the tickets and we
are sailing from Southampton on the morrow. Please comfort
our mother as well as you can John. When we get to America
it should surely not be long before we can bring her to us.

Your loving sister
Mari

Chapter Three

They hear a voice in every wind
snatch a fearful joy.

Thomas Gray
Ode on a Distant Prospect of Eton College

Friday

Morning was announced very gently by Caroline knocking on the door and bringing in a beverage tray. Dot, who had slept the sleep of the virtuous (ensuring a continuation of that virtue by locking her bedroom door and putting a chair under the handle in case the burglar came back to finger her chemises again), was sitting on the private balcony, brushing her hair. Phryne was half awake.

'Good morning,' whispered Caroline. 'There's coffee made by Leo for Miss, he made it special because Teddy says she likes that sort of coffee, and tea for you. Breakfast's on in both parlours as soon as you like, or I can bring it. Which do you want?'

'Come back in half an hour and I'll tell you,' Dot informed her.

'Right you are,' said Caroline, and left silently.

'What's the time?' asked Phryne sleepily.

'Eight o'clock and a fine morning,' said Dot, flicking back the curtains. Cool salt air rushed in through the French windows. Phryne stretched like a cat.

'I'll just have a shower,' she told Dot. 'I had the strangest dreams. Is that coffee I can smell?' she called over her shoulder, dropping her nightdress as she went.

'Italian coffee,' replied Dot cunningly. That should guarantee a swift return. Phryne loved coffee with a deep and sincere passion.

Miss Fisher was back in minutes, wrapped in a large towel. She drank a couple of cups of coffee reverently. Dot was reminded of a cat drinking milk. There was the same sense of almost religious fervour.

Dot had already dressed in a sensible beige skirt, coffee coloured blouse and brown cardigan.

'Shall I have breakfast served in here or do you want to go out?' she asked.

'At this hour?' Phryne asked, shocked at such a suggestion. 'Croissants, Dot dear, or hot rolls, with butter and jam. You go and have a proper breakfast.'

Dot who could not understand anyone who could afford to eat porridge and eggs and bacon and kidneys and mushrooms and kedgeree every morning of her life opting for flaky sort of French bread things, shrugged, smiled and went out. She left Phryne with the coffee pot. Early in the morning, the coffee pot was always Phryne's favourite companion. Not only did it yield coffee, it did not talk. Phryne was in entire agreement with Oscar Wilde about people who were witty at breakfast.

Presently Caroline brought a fresh pot of coffee, croissants which were perfectly canonical, the usual preserves and the ship's newsletter. She did not say a word, indicating either that Dot had warned her or that she knew about people who liked to approach mornings gently and by degrees, instead of vulgarly pouncing on them.

The ship's newsletter—they must have their own printing press, how enterprising of them!—was a single sheet which announced that today they were at sea, there would be a deck tennis tournament and a swimming race for those interested, that the weather was expected to be calm, that Mr. Valdeleur was taking on all comers at a simultaneous chess exhibition in the library, and the Palm Court would be open for morning tea, lunch, and afternoon tea with music from the Melody Makers.

Phryne tore a croissant apart and ate it meditatively. It was very good. A little heavy on the butter but that could be expected of a Sicilian baker with a generous southern Italian nature.

Birds glided past the windows, matching the ship's speed so exactly that they could be examined as clearly as if they were museum specimens hanging on wires. A silver gull, perfect to the pencilled red eyeliner around its bright blue eye, examined her coldly, decided that she was neither threat nor prey, and abruptly decelerated towards the aft disposal of the breakfast detritus, flicking up and back on cupped wings like an acrobat.

Phryne dressed in a lounging robe and took her last cup of coffee out to her private balcony. There she assembled a glass of water, a pencil, the packet of briefing papers, a smoker's friend and her cigarettes. To the soothing accompaniment of the water and the distant cries of passengers playing deck tennis, she began to read and make notes. By the time Dot came back she was ready to talk.

'Good breakfast, Dot?' asked Phryne, seeing that her companion was pink with food and nice fresh air.

'Eggs made in three ways, sausages and very good bacon, and lots of chafing dishes with everything you could ever want,' said Dot dreamily. Food made her sentimental. 'It was lovely. And as much tea as you could drink.'

'Good,' said Phryne. How did people eat like that in the morning? It was vaguely obscene. 'I've gone through all the notes they gave me.'

'And?' asked Dot, sitting down in the next wicker chair.

'Why don't you get your embroidery and I'll talk about the previous thefts. It helps me remember them.'

'All right, Miss. I know what you mean. When my mum sent me for messages, I used to make them into a little chant, like in church. Lard, loaf, onions, ask Mr. Johnson for some sage when you pass his garden.'

'And you were having roast chicken for dinner,' suggested Phryne absently. Dot gaped. Phryne looked up.

'It was simple, Dot,' she explained. 'They are all the ingredients for chicken stuffing.'

'It sounds easy when you explain it,' said Dot. 'But it's magic if you don't.'

'Sherlock Holmes had the same problem,' Phryne returned. 'I've definitely got to stop explaining.'

Dot fetched her sewing. Phryne settled down to expound.

'The first theft was from a young American lady with the unlikely name of Florence Van Sluys,' she said as Dot threaded her needle expertly. 'She had brought aboard a very valuable diamond necklace given to her by her doting father, a Midwest person involved in some oil enterprise, on the occasion of her eighteenth birthday. One minute she was dancing in the frolicking throng bedecked with enough ice to cut out a cathedral window, the next—poof!'

'Poof?' asked Dot, drawing a thread through the fabric.

'No necklace,' said Phryne. 'She thought that the clasp must have come undone, and the whole dance floor was searched, as was the lady in case it was caught inside her clothes. No necklace. Miss Van Sluys was put to bed inconsolable and everyone was questioned about it, but no one saw anything. And they stuck to it. Mavis and the Melody Makers were questioned but all they had seen were people whizzing past in a quickstep. Mr. Van Sluys threw a conniption of massive proportions, but nothing was ever found and P&O paid for the necklace. A pretty penny, as I understand.'

'No one saw anything?' asked Dot, picking up cross threads with a deft needle.

'Well, they saw lots of things, but none germane to the issue. At the time, the photographer was spooning with a middle aged widow on whom he had amorous designs, the professor was sitting the dance out with old Mr. Aubrey, the Singers and the Cahills were dancing with each other, Mrs. West was dancing with Jack Mason, Mr. West was dancing with someone else and the crew were doing what the crew usually does. Mavis and the Melody Makers were playing "Tiptoe Through the Tulips", though I don't see how that piece of information helps.'

'Must have been a young man,' said Dot, threading another needle without even looking.

'Why do you say that?'

'He had to get close to her to undo the catch,' said Dot, not even beginning to blush. Phryne wondered if her sojourn in Phryne's house was coarsening Dot's sensibilities. 'Dancing a quickstep he has to put his arms around her.'

'True. However, a lady accomplice, dancing closer than usual, could do the same thing,' said Phryne. 'It's not likely the catch undid itself. People who make diamond necklaces usually provide them with a Bank of England secure fastening. Anyway, the girl's maid would have checked, that's one of the duties of a maid.'

'Should I be doing that, too?' asked Dot.

'No, you aren't a maid, you're a companion,' said Phryne affectionately. 'People with companions look after their own jewellery. However, one can imagine the scene. Shrieks, wails, panic, denunciations from Papa, apologies from the company, and all this brouhaha results in—no necklace.'

'Right,' agreed Dot, tying off a thread.

'Next one was two voyages later,' said Phryne. 'Famous opera singer, La Paloma di Napoli, real name Caterina Marinara. Light coloratura, very good at baroque music. Most famous for "The Jewel Song" from "Faust". By Gounod.'

'Never heard of him,' said Dot flatly. 'Should I put another brown thread through this edging, Miss, or would gold be better?'

'What is it going to be when it's finished?' asked Phryne.

'Afternoon tea cloth,' said Dot, shaking out the folds.

'Not gold. Not for afternoon tea. Why not weave in a strand of that burnt sienna I see there? More dramatic but not vulgar.'

'Good idea,' said Dot, who always took Phryne's advice on aesthetics. Phryne might not be able to mend even so small a thing as a rent in a stocking without pricking her fingers, making ladders, and finally throwing the stocking away and buying another, but she had excellent taste. 'What does La Paloma mean?'

'The dove,' responded Phryne, lighting a gasper. 'They call her "the dove of Naples". Though if any dove unwisely alighted in the part of Naples that Caterina comes from, the inhabitants would have eaten it instantly. Like many from poor hungry beginnings, she has considerable embonpoint and the temperament almost expected of opera singers. Tears. Complaints. She was travelling with a frayed accompanist and a very stout hearted maid, once her nurse. The only person reckoned able to deal with one of Miss Marinara's tantrums was this nurse, Signora Capadimento.'

'Stands to reason,' said Dot. 'It's hard to fool someone who's wiped your bottom—and smacked it—when you were a baby. It's like trying to impress your mother with how sick you are when you don't want to go to school. Very hard to do.'

'Indeed.' Phryne stubbed out her cigarette and ruffled the notes. 'But even the signora couldn't calm the dove of Naples until P&O offered her a large sum, which she accepted, drying her tears with the hand not holding the money.'

'What was stolen?' asked Dot.

'A big ruby,' said Phryne. 'While La Paloma was busy at the salon, having her hair washed. The stone should have been in the captain's strong box, but the singer liked having it close; it reminded her of the giver, the Maharajah of Gopal. Apparently he was quite smitten. While she was out, the stone vanished from her cabin. This cabin, in fact. Everyone was questioned. The stewardess didn't notice a thing. I rather gather that La Paloma had made her work for her wages, poor girl. It was Caroline, your Maori friend. You might ask her about it. In fact, the steward-ess was Caroline in all these cases, which need not surprise us, because she looks after both Imperial suites. Anyway, fits having been thrown, as we might say in Latin, P&O stumped up and La Paloma forgave them, unbending so far as to give a recital of light classical pieces for the adoring multitude.'

'That was nice of her,' said Dot, admiring the contrast of light beige and burnt sienna. Phryne had, of course, been right about gold. Gold during the day was vulgar.

'More so because she went and sang for Second and Third Class as well. Perhaps sopranos can be forgiven a little uneasi-ness of temperament. All those high notes must rob the brain of oxygen, I expect. At the time of the theft, most of our suspects were blamelessly occupied elsewhere, the only one unaccounted for being Jack Mason, who was supposed to have been in the Turkish bath. He may have been there but the attendant doesn't remember seeing him. He pointed out that the steam was so thick that he might have missed even so fast moving a target as Mr. Mason.'

'And the third theft?' prompted Dot.

'Was of a collection of emeralds—the Attenbury emeralds, Dot, you may remember hearing about them. It was in all the papers.'

'An old man died and left the jewels to his nurse. And the family took it to court to say that he was cuckoo,' Dot recalled. 'But I can't remember what happened.'

'The family won,' Phryne told her. 'They proved that the old gentleman repeatedly walked on his hands, are only a vegetable diet, refused to see any of his relatives when they called and sent his nurse out to, for instance, buy overripe mangoes so that he could throw them against a wall. He liked the splosh, apparently. The nurse looked on these actions as harmless eccentricities but the stern majesty of the law took a different view. The mangoes alone were enough to convince the court that the testator was not in his right mind. Miss Jacobs, the nurse, was turned out without a penny and became companion to Miss Berengaria Reynolds, the elderly lady who was the principal beneficiary, being the old man's only close relative. His sister, I believe.

'Reading between Mr. Navigation Officer Theodore Green's tactful lines, I gather that the old lady was one of those poisonous bitches who make it their practice to humiliate their companion in every possible way. Especially in public. Miss Jacobs was always being sent back for things she had forgotten because Miss Reynolds hadn't told her to bring them, berated for bringing things Miss Reynolds didn't want after all, called a fool in every possible way for failing to read her mistress's mind and grudged any time out of her persecutress's claws. Presumably in case she recovered any joie de vivre.'

'I know that sort of lady,' said Dot, lips tightening.

'Me too. Not to mention the personal abuse, about how ugly she was and how unlikely to attract a man, and how she would have to spend the rest of her miserable life as a companion to such as Miss Berengaria,' said Phryne. 'Now if Miss Berengaria had been dropped overboard no one would have been even slightly surprised. There might, in fact, have been discreet applause. But instead the Attenbury emeralds went byes while Miss Berengaria was taking a virtuous afternoon nap and Miss Jacobs was in the Palm Court, drinking a gin fizz in company with Mr. Albert Forrester. And if ever a woman needed a gin fizz and some complimentary male company it was poor Miss Jacobs. Of course Miss Reynolds instantly denounced her for the theft, but it was clear that she had a perfect alibi.'

'And the jewels were never found?'

'Not so much as a glint of green glass. The last theft was from Mrs. West, the underdressed lady. It was a necklace of perfectly matched pearls. Pink ones, each about the size of a marrowfat pea. Worth untold squillions, though Mr. West settled for less than that. Again, removed from the lady while she was dancing. With, as it happens, Mr. Mason, but she dances with him a lot. Again, an increasingly stringent search. Again, not a sausage. Same cast. They must know each other very well by now.'

'Indeed,' said Dot. She stitched steadily. 'Oh, by the way, Miss, I met a musician who said she was Mr. Cec's niece.'

'Lizbet Yates? Plays the trumpet. Which I think is very enterprising of her.'

'Nice girl, though she's a bit rough and some of the other Melody Makers are rougher,' opined Dot, biting off a thread. 'The amount of drink they got through, you'd think it was the wharfies' picnic. And it's not nice, a lady drinking beer like that.'

'All brass players drink a lot of beer,' said Phryne. 'They blow themselves quite dehydrated. Or that's what I'm told—by, now I come to think of it, brass players. At least she's a good tempered creature, unlike some male trumpeters I have met.'

'Nice as pie,' said Dot. 'Very friendly. I'm having lunch with most of them. Lunch in the Palm Court only rates a string quartet so the rest of them get to sit down with us servants and crew.'

'Keep your ears…er…peeled; doesn't sound right, does it? Pay close attention, Dot dear. Who knows all about the passengers? The stewards. See if you can find anything that the victims had in common.'

'They are all ladies,' said Dot.

'Yes,' said Phryne. 'But that may just be because it's the ladies who wear the jewels. Now, I'm going to have a swim. Coming?'

'Too cold for me,' shivered Dot, who could be persuaded to venture into the shallow end of a pool only when the temperature was over the century mark and rocketing skywards. 'I'll sit here and complete this side of my sewing. Then I might have a walk around and look at the shop. The stewards say it's very good. I need some more ivory thread.'

'Then I'll see you later,' said Phryne, donning her bathing slip, putting a loose cotton dress on over it and gathering towel, bathing cap, hat and capacious bag. It was figured with Pierrot and Columbine in jazz colours of black, white and purple. It had been made for Phryne by a craft needlewoman in St Kilda, discovered contributing real works of art to the Lady Mayoress's Fund Sale of Work. For possibly the first occasion in that fund's history. Her hat had a gay panache of a jazz coloured scarf, knotted in the middle and stitched to the band.

'Miss!' hissed Dot. 'What about the…thingy?'

'Got it safe,' said Phryne, patting her bag. She stowed into it various other aids to comfort and went out.

Dot threaded another needle. Swimming! It must have been spending all that time in Europe, where it snowed, that made Miss Phryne so proof against cold. Or possibly it was her hot blood.

Leaving that topic immediately, Dot put on the radio, which played gentle dance tunes, and resumed stitching.

Sean O'Reilly
Queenstown
Ireland

God and Patrick be with you cousin dear we will be arriving on the train at eight in the morning on the seventh. Little Seamus is eager to be on the big ship. He says it is lucky because of the name of the line. Father says he will grow up to be a fisherman. Men who use the sea always watch stars, you see. I am so glad that you will be able to see us on board. We are to be gone forever and that is a weary time.

Yours, dear cousin
Fionnghula

Chapter Four

I would be the necklace
...Upon her balmy bosom

Alfred, Lord Tennyson
'The Miller's Daughter'

The water was agreeably cold and refreshing. Phryne dived in, swam a few strokes, then rolled over and lazed. This time, ten of the morning, when the day had been properly aired, was her favourite. All the fanatical early-to-rise brigade had done their grim ten laps and gone to a virtuous breakfast. It was too early for the real sybarites who never breakfasted but arose in good time for lunch. The swimming race was at three. The sky above her was as blue as lapis lazuli. She floated on her back in the dead centre of an empty swimming bath in complete luxury.

But it was not to last. A young man hurried up and flung himself almost on top of her. Phryne was forced down to the bottom, from whence she rose in wrath and fetched Jack Mason a tidy buffet on the ear.

'Idiot,' she snarled. 'Can't you look where you're diving, you clumsy lout?'

'Oops!' he said ruefully, clutching her by the shoulders and trying to rub his ear with the same hand, which had the effect of driving Phryne under again. She dived away from him and came up at a safe distance, still furious. Jack Mason, keeping out of cuffing range, said, 'Golly, Miss Fisher, dashed frightful of me! Can you ever forgive me? Let me get you a drink? I say, Steward!' he called to the swimming pool steward, a sedate older man in a white coat. 'Can you help this distressed lady out and fetch her a nice drink? And me too? I really am so very sorry,' he said again, paddling to the side like a puppy deeply conscious of a suspiciously wet spot on the Axminster.

'I'm all right,' Phryne told the steward as he reached for her. In one lithe movement she hauled herself out of the pool and wiped her face. 'Get me a Singapore sling, please. And one for the idiot,' she added.

Jack Mason leapt to her side, putting a solicitous arm around her shoulder. Phryne shook him off. She had left her bag and towel on one of the sun lounges which was, regrettably, just out of sight around a corner. But she heard the snap of metal and a soft exclamation. Slipping out of the penitent's clutch, she padded to her lounge and found that two people had joined her. They were the professor and Mr. Aubrey. The Pierrot bag was just where she had left it, under her towel. It did not seem to have been disturbed.

Phryne pulled off her bathing cap, dried her face and arms and wrapped the towel around her. It was a first class bath sheet and would have wrapped the stouter form of a matron without trouble. It went round Phryne twice.

'My dear Miss Fisher!' cried Mr. Aubrey. 'What has this young brute been doing to you?'

'Spirited attempt to drown me,' Phryne replied. 'But he's buying me a drink to compensate.'

'I should think so, indeed,' said Mr. Aubrey. He had both hands under his steamer rug, intending to snooze in the sun. The professor was engaged in reading a very thick book. Her hands were an old woman's hands, patched and blotchy. Phryne could not tell which, if either, had encountered that spring-loaded mousetrap that was the last thing she had put into the Pierrot bag. It had definitely caught someone. Scragger was not the only rat catcher on the SS *Hinemoa*. Phryne spread out the towel, lay down on the sun lounge and delved in her bag for smoked glasses, her cigarettes and a lighter. Yes. The mousetrap had been sprung.

She allowed Mr. Aubrey to light her gasper.

'I don't approve of young women smoking,' the professor said severely. 'Ah, here is your drink.'

'And your apology,' said Jack Mason, flinging himself down beside her and almost spilling her off the sun lounge. He took up one of Phryne's pale bare feet and kissed the toes. 'Abject,' he said.

'Oh, very well,' said Phryne crossly. If she didn't forgive him he would go on making awkward demonstrations of remorse all day. 'You're forgiven,' she said, taking a sip of the cherry flavoured drink.

'Anything from the char-wallah?' Mr. Aubrey asked the professor, who shook her head. 'Tea, Steward, if you please,' said Aubrey to the older man. 'Chai for me, Bob, as usual.'

'That's tea with spices, isn't it?' asked Phryne, shoving Jack Mason off the foot of her sun lounge. 'Get your own chair, Mr. Mason, if you please.'

'Since I nearly drowned you, you ought to call me Jack,' he said, grinning.

'Attempted murder does not constitute an introduction,' she told him severely, which made the professor laugh.

'Quite right, Miss Fisher. Now, let's change the subject.'

'Oh yes, let's,' agreed Phryne. 'What about the name of the ship? It's a Maori name, isn't it? Can you tell us the tale?'

Professor Applegate seemed touched. 'She's one of my favourite stories. You know that the Maori had clans, and each clan not only had a clan chief but an aristocracy, a royal family? They were given the best food and great respect, but their lives were constrained by many more *tapu* than those of the commoners, and especially the girls. Some of the princesses were required to stay in their huts, out of the sun. They weren't allowed to do things the ordinary girls did, like fish or wander the forest or take lovers. Maori girls could take as many lovers as they liked until they married,' said the professor, a little wistfully.

'But not the princesses?' asked Jack Mason.

'No. They had to stay virgins, because they were used for diplomatic marriages between clans. And by staying out of the sun their skin grew pale, which was desirable. They had servants and company and were allowed to dance and sing and so on, but it must have been a narrow life when the princess compared herself to the other maidens. Also, they were tattooed with curves and lines on mouth and chin, which is agonising.'

The professor rolled up one sleeve to reveal a dark blue bracelet tattooed on her forearm. 'The curves of the unfolding fern,' she said. 'It was a great compliment from Te Rangi and it hurt like billy-o. If it hadn't been for a good solid gulp of preparatory laudanum I believe that I might have disgraced myself by screaming. And that would never have done.

'Well, such a one was Hinemoa. She was very beautiful and very desirable, and her father was consulting with a number of chiefs as to which prince she would marry, but she had fallen in love with a fisherman. She could see him and talk to him as she sat in her seclusion, and he was the one for her. His name was Tutanekai, and he lived across the bay at a place called Mokoia. He loved her, as well. He won all the prizes at the Maori equivalent of the Olympic Games and he could also play the flute but he was of relatively humble birth and he hadn't even thought of offering for her. But Hinemoa's relatives, thinking that she spent too long talking to this pretty warrior, took the precaution of pulling all the canoes up onto the beach, and Hinemoa by herself could not move them. They are very heavy.'

'I bet that didn't stop her,' commented Phryne. 'No more than the Hellespont stopped Leander getting to Hero.'

'But this was the other way around. If her lover carried her off he would spark a war. She had to give herself away. Then it would be a fait accompli. Maori women were not forced to marry the ones their fathers selected except in very unusual circumstances. So, picture the scene. In the dark, Hinemoa sends her attendants away, saying she is sleepy. Then she gathers six gourds and ties them together to make a float. She sets off on the long swim. It is cold and dark and she isn't sure of the way. She swims for hours. Finally she beaches, cold and very tired, and rests in a warm pool in the stone now called Hinemoa's bath.'

'But how did she attract her young man's attention?' wondered Phryne. 'I gather that she isn't wearing any clothes at this point. Although a naked woman is welcome everywhere, that might not be what she had in mind.'

'As you say,' agreed the professor, rubbing one hand slowly over her knuckles. 'Fortunately Tutanekai sends his servant down to the pool to get him some water. Hinemoa asks, "Who is that water for?" and when the servant says, "Tutanekai", she grabs the gourd and smashes it. This confuses the servant, who is convinced that she's some sort of demon, and he flees to his master and says that there is a devil in the pool which smashes gourds. Tutanekai puts on his feather cloak and takes his spears and his greenstone club and goes down to interview the monster. "Who are you, gourd smasher? What name shall I put on the cup I shall make out of your skull?" he asks the monster in the pool, and gets no reply. Instead someone takes his hand. "Who is here?" he asks. She says, "It is I," and stands up out of the water as beautiful as a heron. So he wraps his feather cloak around her and takes her to his house, where they declare that they are married. The next day comes a fleet of canoes.'

'Oh dear,' murmured Phryne. She was dry enough to put her dress on but did not want to interrupt the story.

'No, there was a large celebration instead of a war, and Tutanekai's brother Tiki married Hinemoa's sister, eventually providing a blending of the two tribes. They don't all end that well,' confessed Professor Applegate. 'But Hinemoa's is a nice story, and a nice name for a ship.'

'So it is,' agreed Phryne, pulling on the cotton dress and clapping on her hat. 'Thank you for telling me. I'd better go and have a shower and wash all this salt off my skin. See you at lunch?' she said and walked off, swinging the bag easily in one hand, the towel draped over her shoulder. She was conscious of a little constraint behind her, but she kept going and did not look back.

Showered, she took herself to the beauty salon, where she was creamed and massaged and her hair was washed in three changes of water and the salon's French shampoo. Her attendant was a sparrow-like girl with a strong New Zealand accent. From her badge, her name was Rose.

'Oh, Miss Fisher, that's very nice hair,' said Rose, scrubbing at Phryne's scalp. 'Cut in Melbourne? I thought so.'

'The original cut was Paris,' said Phryne, drowsing under the deft massage.

'I'm going there next trip,' said Rose promptly. 'I'll say this for P&O, they treat you good if you want a long cruise. Most girls only want to sign on for the short ones. Me, I want to see Cairo and the pyramids and London and Paris.'

'You'll go far,' predicted Phryne. 'With those clever fingers.'

'Hope to,' said the young woman.

'I was speaking to the professor and she told me about the woman this ship is named for,' commented Phryne.

Rose grunted. 'She knows all them Maori legends. The Maoris on the ship'd do anything for Professor Applegate. They call her Kuia-paa, wise grandmother, and there's some sort of magic connected with her. *Mana*, you know. Pure superstition. I used to live near a Maori reservation,' she explained. 'I played with the Maori kids when I was a kid.'

But not when you grew up, thought Phryne. She asked aloud, 'What do you make of all these thefts?'

'It wasn't us,' said Rose instantly.

'Never thought it was,' responded Phryne. 'You looked after the ladies, didn't you?'

'Not all of them. That Miss Van Sluys, she brought her own maid with her to dress her hair. Wasn't going to have any of us touching her. Stuck-up thing! I did Miss Berengaria Reynolds' hair. It wasn't a lot of fun. There are some people who just won't be pleased, no matter what you do or how hard you try?' Her intonation rose at the end of the sentence and Phryne treated it as a question.

'I know,' she responded.

'She was one of them. Could she go crook! And the same went for that La Paloma woman. Beautiful hair, real black hair, but so fine and matted with lacquer. Needed three goes of coconut oil to start to untangle it. And she screamed and carried on the whole time, as if I was trying to pull it out by the roots. Lucky she was speaking Italian because I reckon she was calling me every name she could lay her tongue to. Looked good when I finally got it dressed, but. Her maid gave me a handful of coins and said La Paloma was sorry for screaming at me. Sorry! Hah! But she sang like an angel, they said. There's no telling about people, like my gran says. Mrs. West is all right. Never says much. Giggles a lot. Why do you ask?' queried Rose belatedly.

'Just interested,' said Phryne. 'I brought my big sapphire with me, and I don't want to lose it.'

'I reckon you ought to put it in the captain's strong box, then,' said Rose. 'Sit up, Miss, you're all done now. I'll just comb you out. You want to dry it under the machine?'

Phryne looked at the strange hooded hot air apparatus and declined. 'It'll dry just fine on its own,' she told Rose, handing over the fee and a thumping tip. She went out on a wave of goodwill.

Curious, thought Phryne as she went back to her cabin. Dot was not there. Her embroidery lay abandoned on the wicker chair.

More ivory thread, Phryne remembered. Perhaps she might just wander down to the ship's shop when her hair dried.

Before that happened, she needed a cup of coffee. Phryne phoned her stewardess. Caroline came in with a tray. She set it down and poured carefully. All her movements were very precise. Not a drop spilled on the polished surface of the tray.

'Leo says, do you like your coffee stronger than this?' she said. 'He's really pleased that someone likes that black muck. Bleach a black dog, I reckon.'

'It's just habit,' said Phryne. 'Tell the admirable Leo that I like coffee as strong as he can brew it. Espresso, tell him. Do you know where Dot is?'

'She said something about more thread,' said Caroline, noticing the half-completed afternoon tea cloth. 'That's pretty. She does very nice work.'

'She certainly does,' agreed Phryne, who was convinced that sewing was for other women. But Dot's skills were certainly useful. 'Tell me, you have had to look after some very difficult women. Miss Van Sluys? Mrs. West? Miss Reynolds? La Paloma?'

Caroline leaned a hip against the dressing table and prepared for a cosy gossip while Phryne drank her coffee. If she could take the tray away it would save her another trip. 'Well, if you'd been looking for the four to drive an honest woman out of all patience, you've named them all,' she said in her strange accent.

Phryne laughed. 'Who was the worst?'

'Hard to say. Mrs. West can't make up her mind for love nor money. One moment she wants tea, or maybe coffee, then maybe a drink, or would Johnnie mind? And all the time I'm standing there, shifting from one foot to the other and knowing I've got another cabin to mind. How her husband puts up with her I don't know, except she's very pretty.'

'Handsome is as handsome does,' said Phryne sententiously.

'Yair,' agreed Caroline. 'La Paloma was all right. She had her own maid who seemed to have her under control. Ate a lot and drank a lot but mostly she screamed at the maid, not at me, which was fine with me. Miss Van Sluys didn't give me the time of day, except when I didn't bring things fast enough to suit her fancy, and then she'd threaten to tell her papa and I ain't working for her papa, thank God. But the one that got my goat right and proper was that old monster, Miss Reynolds. The life she led her companion, it would make angels weep. Mary fetch this, Mary get that, really Mary you are a fool, no one will ever marry you. Terrible old woman she was. Some of the stokers said she was an evil *taniwhara*.'

'What's a *taniwhara*?'

Caroline's brow wrinkled as she sought for a translation. 'An evil…fairy?'

'Not a fairy,' said Phryne. 'Unless you're thinking of something small, with wings, that buzzes round flowers.'

'That's bees,' Caroline told her. 'Professor Applegate would know the right word. They're spirits which take a human body, except they belong to places.'

'Sounds like spirits of place. The Romans had them and called them genius locii. Naiads and dryads and sea-monsters.'

'Them things. That was the word. Genie. There's lots of good ones and a few bad ones. Some of the crew said she was an evil genie and Miss Jacobs was her captive. Seemed like that, and all. Well, she lost her emeralds which she shouldn't never have had in the first place, and the company had to pay for them. But I did hear,' added Caroline, collecting her tray and opening the door, 'that Miss Jacobs got away in Melbourne. Left the old bitch flat. Someone told me that. I hope it's true. Well, all this gossiping isn't getting the sheep shorn,' she added, and went out, allowing the door to close behind her.

Phryne had a lot to think about, and did so until the luncheon gong sounded and she had to find a respectable dress and some sandals. Not for anything was she going to wear stockings on such a lovely day. Besides, she had hopes of another swim, if she could arrange to have Jack Mason secured to something stout. Pity keel-hauling is quite out of fashion, she thought, and went to lunch clad in a shift patterned with parrots, a loose-weave scarlet shawl, and a pair of beige kid sandals hand-made for her small, high-arched feet.

Lunch was delightful. The soup was a delicate consommé, the fish had clearly died willingly for their ultimate destination as sole bonne femme, and the salads were appropriately crisp: cucumbers and lettuce with a vinaigrette, and cooked potatoes under a velvet blanket of mayonnaise. There were vases of fresh flowers on every table and the string quartet played selections from light classics. Rather stressing the Brahms, but Phryne could tolerate Brahms in a good cause.

The table had the usual cast: Mr. Forrester, both Wests, Professor Applegate, the Cahills, Jack Mason, Mr. Aubrey and Miss Lemmon (the last two in close conversation in a foreign tongue). A fiftyish, stocky, bald stranger had joined table three. He rose and introduced himself as Mr. Singer and a fluffy woman in a pink cardigan as Mrs. Singer. He had been, it appeared, a fabulously successful man in the sheet metal business and was now retired and, Phryne thought, on some sort of mission of exploration. Mrs. Singer remarked brightly that this was their fourth cruise for the year. Mr. Singer ate potato salad with his cold ham and grunted an assent when she appealed to him.

'Oh yes, we've been round the world twice,' she said. 'Haven't we, dear? Always on P&O, they're so reliable. Mr. Singer always checks the crew manifests and the stewards to see if there are any undesirables amongst them, don't you, dear?'

Mr. Singer grunted and gestured for a steward to fill his beer glass.

'He won't find any undesirables on this line,' put in a young man. Unlike Jack Mason, he seemed content to sit still. 'Nice to meet you, Miss Fisher, I'm Doctor Shilletoe. Feel the faintest qualm, give me a call. Always at your service,' he said, his eyes widening as he took in Phryne's attractions, and she did not doubt his sincerity. 'Even just a headache should be treated right away,' he added hopefully.

'You must lead a very interesting life,' said Phryne. She recalled the doctor. He had danced so close to Mrs. West that they were almost sharing the same gown. 'Professionally, I mean.' She smiled artlessly into the big brown eyes of the charming young man. He hurried into speech, anticipating Albert Forrester, who had not given up on Miss Fisher.

'Oh yes, well, there're the usual injuries amongst the crew, broken bones from falls and burns from the engines. I've had to deliver a few babies and we're always available for messages from the merchant fleet. I got one today from a small cargo vessel about a man with abdominal pain, and—no, perhaps not at lunch,' he said, intercepting a glare from Mrs. Cahill. 'I'm free until three,' said the young doctor. 'Perhaps we might continue this conversation in the Palm Court later, Miss Fisher?'

'Indeed,' Phryne said, smiling. 'But you were saying about undesirables?'

'Oh, it's hard to get a job on a P&O ship, and the captain is very choosy about who he signs on. No criminal records, no problems in their previous berth. He calls this a happy ship and he aims to keep it that way.'

'Good,' said Phryne. 'I like calm. And peace. And isn't it just the most beautiful day?'

'Enjoy it while you can,' said Mrs. Cahill with a spurt of venom. 'Tomorrow it will be cold. We're going down to Fjord land, and it's always cold there. Glaciers. Ice.'

'Then, my dear doctor, if you have finished, perhaps we might go up on deck and enjoy it while it lasts?' suggested Phryne, and Doctor Shilletoe bolted the rest of his lunch so speedily that Phryne feared for his digestion. Phryne ate a crème caramel with just the right amount of burned sugar on the top, drank a cup of pale coffee—not a patch on Leo's—and excused herself.

The young doctor led her up onto the sun deck and found her a chair in the shade. He suddenly looked very tired and swayed perilously.

'Do sit down,' said Phryne. He sank down beside her. 'What happened to the man with the abdominal pain?'

'It sounded like a dicky appendix, so I told them to put into the nearest port and take him to hospital. But they were too far out, so I talked the ship's barber through the op. I was so worried about them giving chloroform—you can kill someone really easily with chloroform and the idiots had been keeping it in a warm place so I didn't know how strong it was, and it wouldn't do for the poor fellow to wake up. The actual operation isn't too hard if you keep your head. I have never had to describe an op over the radio in morse code. Sparks kept going green on me. I was matching him by the end of it. It was really horrible.'

'Steward,' said Phryne to one of the ubiquitous white coated men—did they get them from a factory?—'a stiff brandy. Make it a double,' she added. Doctor Shilletoe, given a sympathetic audience, had all of a sudden fallen to pieces. Phryne was entirely familiar with the nervous reaction which had a nasty habit of socking one over the occiput after one had done all the proper things and dealt with the emergency. She suffered from this delayed shock herself. She leaned the young man's head back on her arm and shoved a pillow behind him.

'Can't drink with the...' he murmured.

'Nonsense,' said Phryne bracingly. 'I will explain to the captain, and so will—er...sorry, I don't know your name, Steward.'

'Roberts, Miss,' the steward informed her. 'They say he saved that sailor's life,' said Roberts stoutly. 'Poor Sparks is still in the head, throwing up. Drink this, sir, do,' he urged, putting the glass to the young man's lips.

Doctor Shilletoe sipped, coughed, and drank the brandy off. Then he shuddered. Not a young man given to hard liquor, Phryne noted with approval. Roberts went back to the bar and returned with a tall glass full of ice and a sparkling mixture.

'Shandy,' he explained. 'Just lemonade and sherry. He'll be thirsty after all that booze.'

'Very astute of you, Roberts,' said Phryne. Doctor Shilletoe accepted the glass and took a long gulp. Then he sat up and wiped his eyes.

'I'm so sorry,' he said. 'And I meant to make such a good impression on you,' he added with the suspicion of a chuckle.

'So you did,' Phryne told him. 'Have you ever done that before? Talked someone through an operation on a radio?'

'No, never. It was grotesque. And so slow! I'd say something, Sparks would put it into morse and telegraph it, then their sparkie would decode it, then the answer would come back the same way. It was like long distance chess, with lives. What did you give me to drink?'

'Brandy,' said Phryne. 'And you need to reassign your three o'clock surgery. Give it to your assistant, who will be delighted if I know assistants, and get some rest. I know about shock. So do you, if you'd think about it.'

'I suppose I do,' he said faintly.

'And I will be delighted to talk with you another time,' she concluded, putting a hand under his arm and assisting him to his unsure feet. Something fell from his pocket and he was too shaky to pick it up before Phryne saw what it was. It was a photo of Mrs. West, simpering. The doctor grabbed it and thrust it into his inside pocket. Phryne did not comment but exclaimed, 'Oh, I forgot the drink chit.'

'No need, Miss,' said Roberts approvingly. 'Medical expenses.'

Phryne saw the doctor to his rooms on the third deck down and then found herself rather at a loss. This did not last.

'Miss Fisher?' asked Albert Forrester, catching her as she came back into the light well of the Grand Staircase. 'I wonder if I could interest you in some photographs?'

'Of course,' said Phryne, and went willingly.

T'ang Lee
San Francisco

The younger brother sends respectful greetings to the respected elder brother and advises that Chang and his wife and son will be with you soon. They are overwhelmed by the elder brother's kindness in sending them tickets for this voyage. If the elder brother will condescend to telegraph their safe arrival to the younger brother, he will be greatly obliged. The omens here are not hopeful.

The younger Lee brother says farewell with many thanks.

Chapter Five

Children's voices should be dear
(call once more) to a mother's ear
M Arnold
'The Forsaken Merman'

The interesting thing about Albert Forrester was that he was a really good photographer. Phryne looked at the wealth of pictures laid out on his bed in First Class and approved.

Not lewd pictures to sell to tourists to astound their friends in Sydney or Toronto about what you can do with a really cooperative donkey. Not even the slightly fogged art studies of bored naked whores in a cold studio somewhere in Montparnasse. These were really good. Phryne sat down to inspect them.

Mr. Forrester, who felt that his day had vastly improved from that bad moment when Miss Fisher had gone off with the doctor, sat down in a chair and watched her face. She was really looking at the pictures, and she was showing—regrettably—no sign of sexual excitement. He was an expert at detecting the rising flush, the faint bedewing of delicate perspiration, the suppressed wriggle as various organs made their presence known. No. Not, so to speak, a sausage. Philosophically, he settled for her enthusiasm for his artistic skill. Mr. Forrester got his pleasure wherever he could in whatever form it took, and was consequently a happy man.

'These are very good,' she commented. 'I love the barred sunlight, all those straight lines across the curved nude. You were thinking of Picasso, perhaps?'

'I was,' he responded.

'And these Turkish bath ones are Ingres. I never liked his nudes. Yours are much better. They look happy.'

'It was ladies' day and I persuaded my ladies to let me watch,' he said, smiling at the memory. 'They were very stiff and uncomfortable for about ten minutes and then they forgot about me and began to have fun. The thing is to stay still, not to stare directly at anyone, and not to touch. Same as wildlife photographers and bird watchers.'

'They're very innocent,' said Phryne. 'Not all young women, either. That's unusual.'

'Young women quite often haven't grown into their bodies, and they think about them all the time,' he said, picking up one of the photos. 'Older women are used to their nakedness. This is my favourite of the bathing beauties.'

Phryne examined the photograph. Against a dark wall stood four females, ranked in line with their arms around each other. They were laughing. One was an old woman, withered but strong. Next to her was a rosy plump mother with rounded belly and ripe breasts. Next to her was a thin young girl, just entering puberty, with a down of new pubic hair and budding breasts. In front of the mother stood a small girl, thumb in mouth, staring straight at the camera.

'They're my family of artist's models,' he said with satisfaction. 'This is at the Montparnasse baths, of course, you couldn't do this in England. They've been living there since Great-Grandmother came up from Brittany and established a gallette—you know, those little shops where Breton pancakes are cooked on a round charcoal stove.'

'Yes,' said Phryne reminiscently. 'I once knew Montparnasse very well. Where was the gallette?'

'Near the station, in the Rue Veuve. You really are the most amazing person, Miss Fisher.' He paused to drink in the sight of Phryne in her cotton dress cross-legged on his bed, considered how very aesthetic she would look under the covers, sighed, and resumed his story.

'Well, Grandmother Odette sat for Monet. Bella for Picasso. They have great hopes of Chrissie, who has a modern figure, sitting for the Moderne or the Fauves. Wonderful women. They can sit like a rock and never complain. And they like photographs. They're instant. They might take a lot of setting up but once the light flashes, they're free to move. I got them and a few of their Bohemian pals to do the Turkish bath scenes. They haven't any false shame.'

'None at all,' said Phryne. The four ages of womanhood laughed back at her. 'This is a wonderful picture,' she told Mr. Forrester. 'Can I buy a print? And have you any more for me to see?'

'Certainly,' said Mr. Forrester, abandoning seduction for the moment and hauling a suitcase from under his bed. He spread the pictures out. Phryne was surrounded by naked women, smiling, sombre, coy, bold, sleeping, dancing, wreathed in vines, draped in shawls. She pounced on another. A peasant woman suckling a child. Her head was bent so that a wing of hair fell forward over the side of her face and shaded the plump, kicking baby. Her work-worn hands cradled the delicate child reverently.

'You are selecting my favourites with amazing accuracy,' smiled the photographer. 'That's Tante Marie with little Angelique.'

'How many studies did you take to get that picture?' asked Phryne.

'Ten. Luckily the baby was hungry.'

What was clear from the collection was the pure, uncontaminated passion of Mr. Albert Forrester for women of any type, class or age. Phryne felt flattered on behalf of her gender. It was nice to think that someone liked women so much, when there was such a lot of misogyny in the world.

'Perhaps you might pose for me?' he asked a little tentatively.

'Perhaps I might,' said Phryne. 'Were you never tempted to photograph La Paloma? She had an abundance of flesh.'

'A Rubens rather than a Renoir,' agreed Mr. Forrester. 'But a most unpleasant woman. Do you know, she had a child when she was twenty, during a brief marriage, and she just left it with her mother in some benighted Neapolitan slum and swanned off, not even paying properly for its maintenance? The character of the sitter does tend to emerge in photographs, you know. I wouldn't have cared to have her in my collection.'

'Or Mrs. West?' asked Phryne idly, picking up a photo of a sleeping odalisque, lying on her side, the fall of her hip and shoulder perfectly outlined against a hidden light.

'No, because to take photographs I need both my hands attached to my wrists and my head in its right place on my neck,' he said, grinning. 'West, as you will have observed, is a jealous brute.'

'I noticed,' said Phryne. 'Why on earth does he bring her on these cruises, she being what she is and he being what he is?'

'There you have me,' confessed Mr. Forrester. 'I have wondered the same thing myself. I suppose the lady insists. She may look like butter wouldn't melt in her mouth, but as they said in the eighteenth century, I'll warrant that she wouldn't choke on cheese.'

'Well,' said Phryne, getting up. 'Thank you so much for showing me your pictures. They are superb. Shall I see you at dinner?'

'Certainly,' said Mr. Forrester, and Phryne took her leave, considering his offer. It was certainly more comfortable on the *Hinemoa* than it had been in the freezing studio where she had last been an artist's model. She might well decide that a nude of Phryne Fisher would be in good company amongst Mr. Forrester's ladies.

She was so engrossed that she walked right into a steward, almost invisible behind a pile of towels. They spilled and Phryne helped him gather them up.

'I'm so sorry, I didn't look where I was going,' she said, stuffing towels into his arms.

'And I couldn't see where I was going,' he answered, dragging a cart forward and refolding rapidly. 'Like my mum always said, make two trips. Not your fault, Miss. You're Caroline's Miss Fisher, aren't you?'

He was another of those stocky middle aged men with which the ship seemed largely staffed. This one had thinning brown hair and blue eyes.

'That's right,' said Phryne, wreathed in towels.

'She's been telling us about you. Allans remembered seeing an article about you in the *Age*. You're a private detective, aren't you, Miss?'

'Yes, but I'd rather it didn't get about,' she said, hushing him with a gesture.

He nodded ponderously. 'Won't get about from us, Miss. You're trying to find out about the jewels?'

Phryne hustled him into her stateroom, towels and all.

'And if I am?'

'Well, we'll help,' he said. 'It wasn't us,' he said, in identical tones to the attendant Rose in the beauty salon. 'But the company can't help wondering if it was. Makes for trouble. This is a happy ship, Miss. Lots of us turned down higher wages and so on to stay with the *Hinemoa*. We want to know who did it. By the way, Johnson's my name.'

Phryne shook his hand.

'Nice to meet you. I do want to find out what happened to those gems,' said Phryne, giving up. It was no more use trying to keep secrets on a ship than in one of those small villages beloved by Agatha Christie. 'But since I have my suspicions already and they don't involve the crew, I need you to stay schtum, understand?'

He nodded. 'Anything you want, Miss. Just you ask.'

'Caroline looked after all the victims, didn't she?' He bridled and she patted his arm. 'I don't suspect Caroline of anything. But if she wants to help, she can help. Ask her to rack her memory about any visitors to the victims before they were bereft of their gewgaws. Who came to see La Paloma and Berengaria Reynolds? Who comes to see Mrs. West when her husband isn't there? Get Caroline to talk to my companion Dot and we shall see what we shall see,' she said, with emphasis.

'All right, Miss,' he assented, folding the last towel and placing it on the ziggurat. He put a heavy hand on top of the pile to prevent it from toppling.

'And anything else you find out, tell me or Dot, and take care that we aren't overheard,' she said.

'You want to look at them musicians,' he whispered, leaning so close that Phryne could smell the mint on his breath. 'They're no better than they ought to be, them Melody Makers.'

'I shall,' she promised, and let him and the towels out into the corridor.

Since her hair was now dry, Phryne reassumed her bathing dress, took up her impedimenta and went back to the pool. Before she left, she carefully reset her mousetrap. And this time, Jack Mason was safely on the sun deck, playing tennis, and she got her swim in peace.

When she returned to her suite, Dot was there too, calmly sitting on the floor and scratching a disreputable cat behind his nibbled ears.

'Hello, Scragger, I didn't see you come in,' said Phryne, tossing her hat onto her bed. 'You must have been under the laundry cart, you clever old puss. Or in it, perhaps. Nothing like a soft bed of fresh towels after a hard morning's ratting. What have you been doing, Dot?'

'I've been walking around the sun deck with Maggie and Mr. Thomas, that's Mrs. West's maid and Mr. Mason's man,' responded Dot, getting to her feet.

'And gathering gossip like the flowers in May?' asked Phryne. Dot pinkened.

'They told me you went to Mr. Forrester's cabin,' said Dot accusingly.

'Did they? So I did. Only, as it happened, to look at his photographs, and they are very good, Dot dear, nothing in them that would bring a blush to a bishop's countenance,' said Phryne, a little severely. 'And if I decided to engage in a shipboard romance, it would be none of your business, Dorothy. I sent you to listen to gossip about other people, not about me. You must know all about me by now,' she added, stripping off the cotton dress. 'I must wash all this salt off. Find me a robe, will you, old thing?'

Dot found her a robe without another comment. Scragger, alerted perhaps by the sub-sonic noises of rodents elsewhere in the superstructure, mewed at the door and she let him out into the corridor. He wound appreciatively around her ankles a couple of times and stalked out.

Phryne emerged from the shower dripping, rubbed herself dry and donned the robe.

'Well, what news on the Rialto?' she asked. 'I've got some to swap.'

Dot gave up. Phryne's morals, as always, were her own. 'They told me a lot about the other passengers, though they wouldn't talk about their employers much,' she informed Phryne. 'Except Mr. Mason's man says that he's worried about him. He used to do all these sports, you know, football and mountain climbing and cricket, but since his father made him promise not to be a footballer, he's just been a fribble—that's what Thomas calls him. You know, a young man who wastes his time on dancing and ladies and drinking.'

'Perhaps it's a tantrum,' suggested Phryne. 'An "Oh, very well, Pater, I won't be a footballer, but I'm dashed well not going to be anything else you want me to be". Young men are tiresomely prone to demonstrations like that. Is his father likely to be impressed?'

'Thomas doesn't think so. He says that old Mr. Mason is a

formidable character, one of those iron-jawed men, and he's content to wait his son out.'

'And meanwhile youth is wasting away.'

'Something like that,' agreed Dot.

'Has the young man any idea of a profession? With all that robust energy and muscle, why isn't he exploring unknown reaches of the Amazon and having his picture taken with a lot of grinning headhunters for *National Geographic?*'

'Nice,' said Dot. 'I'll suggest it to Mr. Thomas. Though I don't think he'd like the Amazon. He knows all about wine and was telling us that this ship has the best seagoing cellar since the *Titanic*. Anyway, they think the attraction is Mrs. West.'

'Aha,' said Phryne, lying back on her bed and blowing smoke rings at the ceiling. 'Cherchez la femme, and she is a trouble-making young woman if ever I saw one. Mr. Forrester was hinting that she had the power in that partnership.'

'Well, yes,' said Dot primly. 'When he really dotes on her and she just puts up with him, then anything she says goes because he's so afraid of losing her.'

'That can backfire,' commented Phryne, blowing another smoke ring. 'For a start, being the focus of a strong-minded man's obsession isn't all it's cracked up to be, Dot. If the object is a nice, compassionate person, she will endure and endure until she finally breaks and runs away with the milkman or retreats into a convent. I have known cases, don't laugh.'

'And if the object isn't a nice, compassionate woman? Because I have to say, Mrs. West gives her maid a very hard life,' said Dot.

'Then the object becomes desperately bored, driven to affairs, and may well provoke the obsessor to extreme action.'

'Suicide?' gasped Dot, crossing herself.

'Or homicide. Or both. If Mrs. West is playing with her husband's affections, she may well get those pretty pink fingers burned. Just because he adores her doesn't mean he isn't the ruthless businessman he's been all along.'

'There's a nasty story…' Dot began.

'Do tell,' encouraged Phryne.

'Mr. West found out that Mrs. West was close to a young salesman in Mr. West's office, before they started all this travelling.'

'And he ruined him?' asked Phryne.

'Yes. The company was told to look at him and they went through his accounts and found that they were wrong and a great deal of money had been paid into his bank account. He said he knew nothing about it, but he went to jail for six months anyway and when he came out he couldn't get a job and the grog got him. Or so Thomas says.'

'Nasty,' said Phryne with a slight wince. 'That doctor and Jack Mason had better look out.'

'I suppose the doctor's safe because he's a crewman, and Mr. Mason's safe because he's already in disgrace,' commented Dot, picking up her embroidery again.

'Nothing to stop Mr. West hiring a couple of brawny stokers to beat the soul case out of him when we get to a port,' said Phryne. This time Dot winced. 'But he might even have tried that. Mason is a strong young man who probably studied boxing, and might never have made the connection between a sudden assault and Mrs. West. Hmm. I shall see if I can find out.'

'The crew don't like the musicians,' said Dot, threading a needle with dark brown thread.

'So I am told.' Phryne recounted her conversation with Johnson amongst the towels. 'I need to talk to them, Dot dear, but they always seem to be on stage. Is there any time off for the whole gang of them?'

'Sunday,' said Dot. 'On Sunday there are amateur singers in the Smoke Room and just a gentleman playing a piano in the Palm Court. They'll all have Sunday off. Do you want to, I don't know, meet them by chance, or do you want to do this openly?'

'By chance to begin with,' said Phryne.

'They have a room to themselves, for rehearsing,' said Dot.

'The crew say they all gather in there to drink and play cards. They think that's not nice. But, of course, it's the only time they all get off together and no one else likes them. That niece of Mr. Cec's, she might get you in.'

'Lizbet Yates. Yes indeed. I shall angle for an invitation. Now, what else? La Paloma isn't in favour with the female-fancying Mr. Forrester because she is a bad mother. She had a child when she was very young, abandoned it with her mother in dire poverty in Naples, and went off to become a diva, leaving Grandma and Baby in straits. And let me tell you, Dot dear, Neapolitan dire poverty is pretty close to extinction.'

'What an awful thing!'

'There might have been reasons,' said Phryne. 'She might have hated the father and by extension hated the baby. She might have hated her mother, too. She might even have had reasons for such hatred. Life is perilous for a pretty, talented girl from a background like that. Mothers have sold their daughters for a small fee if the alternative is starvation.'

'Even so,' said Dot mulishly, biting off a thread with a snap of her white teeth. 'It's not right to leave the baby. Mothers shouldn't do that.'

Phryne shrugged. 'I haven't found out anything else,' she said. 'Nothing about the Cahills or the Singers. But Rose in the salon told me that Professor Applegate is a special person for the Maoris.'

Dot nodded. 'That's what they say. A grandmother. A wise woman.'

'She's even got a tattoo on her forearm and she says it was agony,' Phryne said.

'A tattoo? That nice respectable old lady?' Dot's needle unthreaded with the involuntary jerk of her hand. 'Drat,' she added.

'A Maori tattoo. It probably has something to do with rank. She's still a nice respectable lady, Dot. And the mousetrap was sprung,' said Phryne with satisfaction. 'Either old Mr. Aubrey,

Professor Applegate or someone they knew rummaged in my bag while I was being jumped on by that muscle-bound idiot Jack Mason.'

'Did anyone have a bruised hand?' asked Dot, re-threading the needle.

'I couldn't tell. I didn't see the actual incident, just heard the snap. Mr. Aubrey had his hands under his rug and the professor has such blotchy hands that I couldn't decide. But we are attracting attention, Dorothy, the right kind of attention. Now I am going to have a nap until it's time to dress for dinner. All this detecting is tiring work. And why, Dot, is there a teddy bear on my bed?'

It was a newish bear, sitting jauntily alongside one of the *Hinemoa's* plump brocade lounging pillows. He looked more than a little out of place.

'There's a child in Third Class that forgot her favourite toy,' said Dot, 'And they tried giving her a new bear but he was too new and she just cried some more. So I said that we'd squeeze the newness out of him. I've already loosened his right ear and re-stitched his eye. He just needs to be hugged,' explained Dot. 'I'll take him tonight.'

'Oh,' said Phryne, touched. 'How very nice of you, Dot. Come along, Teddy.'

She lay down comfortably, clutching the teddy bear to her curves, and shut her eyes. She was asleep in moments.

Dot stitched steadily. If she kept on at this rate, she would finish her tea cloth before the enforced rest of the Sabbath.

Richard Van Geer
Diamond cutter
Amsterdam

This is to advise you that our representative, Mynheer H Brugge, will be sailing to America soon to convey greetings

and confidential reports to our home company in New York.
He will be pleased to carry any of your merchandise or letters
which cannot be entrusted to the ordinary post.

Brugge and Associates
Haarlem

Chapter Six

Pack, clouds, away, and welcome day.
With night we banish sorrow:

T Heywood
'Pack, clouds, away'

Phryne woke and found that she had buried her face in the teddy's soft fur. She sneezed. Dot was still stitching. An hour had gone by. An explanation for the jewel thefts which was so totally preposterous she could really only have thought of it while her usual critical faculties were disabled, bloomed in her mind and she laughed aloud. Dot looked up.

'Call for a small pre-prandial nip,' Phryne said, still laughing. 'Gin for me and sherry for you. Full dinner dress this evening. I shall wear the charcoal with the sable stole. No, it's too warm for sable. The silk shawl with all those gold beads. I've just had the oddest notion, Dot. So odd that I'm really not going to tell even you, in case you call Caroline to bring a nice straitjacket with the drinks tray. But what an idea, eh, Teddy?' She punched the teddy in his rotund tummy and was rewarded with a growly noise.

Dot called Caroline, who bustled in with her tray. 'Had a nice day, ladies?' she asked. 'Roberts says you swim really good, Miss Fisher. They're having a race on Monday, you want to be in it—the prize is a bottle of the best bubbly, corker stuff, they say, though I prefer beer myself.'

Phryne took the glass containing the perfectly mixed gin and tonic. Should she mention Mr. Forrester? Johnson had seen her come out of his cabin. Should she start explaining herself to a censorious crew? No, no, a thousand times no. They could put up with it and like it or not depending on personal preference. But it appeared that Caroline had something else on her mind.

'They told me what you do, Miss,' she said to Phryne. 'You let me know and I'll tell you anything you like.'

'Good,' said Phryne.

'It wasn't us,' said Caroline, echoing Rose and Johnson.

'I know,' said Phryne.

'Well, I'll come back later,' said Caroline, and trundled out with her tray, leaving Phryne with the half-bottle of gin and Dot with a fresh glass of sherry.

'I didn't tell them,' said Dot.

'I know,' said Phryne again. 'You can't keep secrets in a village. Someone called Allans saw my picture in the *Age*. We just don't tell the passengers and all will be well. Now for the dress,' said Phryne. 'And can you disinter the bijou?'

'Right away,' said Dot, getting out the embroidery scissors.

Dressed in the subtle, not-quite-black silk, unique because it was part of Lin Chung's haul from a silk buying trip. The colour was produced by an error in the dyeing. Phryne caught the eye. So did the sapphire, depending from its carefully securable collar.

'Two ladies lost their gems while dancing,' Phryne told Dot. 'Is there any other way you can fasten the thing, apart from that little chain and pin?'

'Oh yes,' said Dot, drawing small stitches through the high neckline of the dress. 'It's now sewn on,' she said, breaking off the thread. 'You can't see the stitches but they won't get that jewel off without taking off your dress,' Dot told Phryne, and blushed.

'And I shall wait until you do that, later in the evening,' Phryne responded. 'Have a nice dinner, Dot dear. I'm going to sit out here and watch the sea,' she said, and sat down on the wicker chaise longue, a slippery, glittering, night-black vision out of a shipwrecked sailor's dream.

She watched the sea for an hour then shook herself, put on the decorated shawl, and went to dinner.

Table three had the usual faces around it. Mrs. Cahill was complaining that the beef curry was too hot, Mr. Aubrey was explaining that you wouldn't get beef curry in India, because cattle were sacred, and Mrs. Singer was asking for a plain omelette for Mr. Singer, who, she explained proudly, was a martyr to dyspepsia.

'Always comes on late in the afternoon,' she told the table at large. 'Doesn't it, dear?'

'Don't fuss, Lily,' grunted Mr. Singer, massaging his upper belly.

'Now, I can eat anything,' said Mr. Mason heartlessly. 'Even tried some of Mr. Aubrey's volcanic curry once. A triple vindaloo called a *pali*. Mind you, steam came out of my ears and I drank the water jug dry in one hit.'

'And I told you it wouldn't work,' said Mr. Aubrey. 'You need milk to kill the spice. Young idiot,' he said, half affectionately. 'Young men! Always wanting things they haven't earned! Twenty years in India I had to spend before I could really relish a proper vindaloo.'

'And I never will,' Phryne told him. 'How can you taste anything else? Like, for example, this excellent lobster thermidor that I am eating?'

'Can't,' confessed Mr. Aubrey. 'I am afraid that once the tongue gets used to the really strong curry, everything else seems tame.'

'Curry!' shuddered Mr. Singer. 'Where's that damn omelette?' he asked the steward abruptly.

'On its way, sir,' said the steward. He edged around the table to refill Mr. Singer's glass, possibly with the idea that getting a bit more beer into the grumpy gentleman might ameliorate his temper, if not his indigestion.

'I never got used to vindaloo,' said Miss Lemmon. 'I always thought that eating it was some sort of mortification of the flesh. But they make lovely curries in Madras with coconut milk and butter. Such an array of spices! I remember going into the spice market and being almost knocked over by the scent.'

'Ah, yes,' said Mr. Aubrey reminiscently. 'Cumin, coriander, cinnamon, cloves, chili…'

'And that's only the Cs,' said Phryne, taking up a forkful of cream sauce and lobster.

Mr. Aubrey chuckled. 'There's also cayenne in C,' he told the table at large. 'And ginger and garlic in G.'

'And fenugreek and fennel in F,' added Miss Lemmon, delighted with the word game.

'And mustard, turmeric and saffron in the other letters. Not to mention O for onion,' capped Mr. Aubrey.

'And I for inedible foreign dago muck,' growled Mr. Singer.

Phryne felt that she was not going to like Mr. Singer any time soon.

'No, that would be under M for muck,' she told him coldly. 'And under I for impolite. Here comes your omelette, Mr. Singer.' She did not add 'and I hope it chokes you', but the wish could have been inferred by the alert listener.

Most of the listeners at the table were alert. They smiled upon her. There was the faint clank of ranks closing.

Professor Applegate said, specifically to Mr. Singer, 'You couldn't have afforded a digestion like that in Maori society, you know.'

'Why?' asked Jack Mason innocently.

'Well, it was a healthy enough diet, lots of fish and vegetables. They made bread out of the fern root and ate a lot of the local berries and fruits,' said Professor Applegate. 'But after the moa were killed off, and before the white man brought pigs to New Zealand, the only mammal apart from dogs, large enough for a really good hangi was…'

'Men?' asked Mrs. Cahill, catching her breath in excitement.

'What's a hangi?' asked Phryne.

'An earth oven. You get your slaves to dig a nice deep pit and build a fire at the bottom, and when it's burned down into coals, you lay clean stones and then parcels of meat, fish and vegetables on it, wrapped in flax. Then the servants pile all the earth back and it cooks very gently all night so that when the pit is opened, the aroma is superb.'

Mr. Singer was greening quite satisfactorily, Phryne thought, and threw in another question.

'So if we had a Maori Mrs. Beeton, the recipe would start, take one freshly killed enemy…?'

'Yes. In New Guinea they called men "long pig". Several of the old hands I met told me the taste was superior but very similar to pork—'

'Please,' said Mr. Singer, showing his first sign of humanity. Professor Applegate, evidently, was not going to let him get away with the dago comment too easily.

'And in Northern Queensland the cannibals preferred to eat the Chinese, because they ate rice and their flesh wasn't so salty,' said Mr. Cahill unexpectedly. 'Lots of Chinese up there on the River of Gold. What's the matter, Singer? Omelette not up to scratch?'

'What sort of people are you?' demanded Mrs. Singer indignantly.

She was about to become shrill and Navigation Officer Theodore Green, who had joined them for dinner, interjected with a desperate non sequitur. 'You were asking me about mysteries of the sea, Miss Fisher.'

'I was,' said Phryne, who was quick on the uptake. 'And you were saying that there was a ship once which got caught in the ice. The *Mignonette*, was it?'

'No, Miss Fisher, that was quite another matter. I was referring to the *Jenny*, which was encountered by the whaling schooner

Hope just south of Drake Passage in Antarctica. The whaler's lookout had signalled an iceberg and *Hope* clewed in to look at it when the iceberg split down the middle—calving, they call it—and out came the *Jenny*, battered, sails in tatters, but still more or less intact.'

'I've seen those photographs from the Shackleton expedition,' scoffed Mr. Cahill. 'The *Endurance* was just plain crushed by the ice.'

'But the *Jenny* was not,' insisted Theodore Green politely. 'Ice is a mystery and no one has quite worked out how it does things. Ice can creep up as gently as a mist or—as in the case of the *Endurance*—pierce and claw the ship to pieces. *Jenny* was a topsail schooner and of course made all of wood, which flexes and moves, not like rigid steel. Perhaps that made a difference.'

'Never mind the science, what happened?' demanded Jack Mason.

'The cold had preserved the ship perfectly, and the bodies of the crew. They had just frozen to death where they sat or lay.'

'I've seen soldiers who have fallen and died of exposure like that,' commented Phryne. 'Seemed a gentle death. They looked like they were asleep.'

'The *Hope* brought back the log of the *Jenny*,' said Theodore Green, giving Phryne a very puzzled look. 'The last entry said "no food for 71 days". And from the date it seemed that the *Jenny* had been caught in the ice for…' he paused for effect. 'For thirty-seven years.'

'I wonder if that's how the legend of the *Flying Dutchman* got started?' asked Mr. Aubrey. 'I've always wondered about that.'

'Ghost ships,' said Theodore Green. 'Plenty of room on a big ocean for ghosts. No need to scoff,' the navigation officer told Mr. Singer. 'The present king and his brother saw a ghost ship when they were naval cadets. Entered into the log.'

'And if it's entered into the log, it's fact?' asked Phryne mischievously. Mr. Green's earnestness was an almost irresistible provocation.

'Certainly, Miss Fisher,' replied Mr. Green, looking affronted. 'If you can't rely on the log, what can you rely on?'

'Indeed. Surely the *Jenny* can't be the only ship to have been trapped in the ice?'

'No, there was the *Octavius*,' he said instantly. 'Bound for China out of Portsmouth in 1761. Thirteen years later she was discovered drifting in open water off Alaska by the whaler *Herald*. Everyone was on board. All frozen and somehow perfectly preserved by the cold. Unfortunately the captain's crew were so panicked by what they saw that one dropped the log into the sea. All that Captain Warren had was the last page. It said "we have now been enclosed in the ice for seventeen days. The fire went out yesterday". Then nothing more.'

'How terrible!' Mrs. West gave an exaggerated shrug of one white shoulder which dropped her neckline to a depth which would have provoked the censor into banning the film. Mr. West reached out for the shoulder strap and replaced it, leaving his hand on her upper arm. She slipped out of his grasp and pouted. 'I am amazed that anyone is brave enough to be a sailor,' she cooed at Theodore Green. Phryne interposed her body. This dinner was proving to be something of a social minefield.

'Much less dangerous than it was, eh, Mr. Green?' Phryne prompted. 'With telegraphs and engines and so on.'

'Oh yes, much less dangerous. Indeed some men grumble that the sea doesn't have the mystery it used to have. Young men, mainly,' he said, smiling indulgently. 'We like to keep the mystery down to a minimum on P&O, actually. If you'd come up to the bridge one day, Miss Fisher, I'd be delighted to show you our navigation systems, charts, radio and so on. I do think that the Marconi telegraph is the most important invention, though. A cargo ship can get, for instance, instant medical advice from our doctor, as we saw today. A small boat can radio SOS and be heard and found when it's buried in thick fog or a dark night. Makes a great difference, the idea that one can call for help in all this wide waste of waters. If there had been two Marconi operators on the *Californian*, for instance, instead of only one who had very properly gone off duty, the loss of life from the sinking of the *Titanic* could have been greatly reduced.'

'How many telegraph operators are there on this ship?' asked Mrs. Cahill nervously.

'Three,' said the navigation officer. 'The radio-telegraph is manned round the clock, Mrs. Cahill, have no fear.'

'I've had enough of all this talk,' grunted Mr. Singer. He stood up so fast that he caught a fold of tablecloth and had to be extricated, fuming, by his worried wife. She clucked after him as he strode away.

'Indigestion does awful things to the disposition,' commented Mr. Aubrey.

'If he has dyspepsia then he shouldn't be drinking,' said Professor Applegate acidly. 'He had three glasses of beer and only ate part of his omelette. I'd say it was temper,' she diagnosed.

'And a nasty temper at that,' agreed Mr. Aubrey. 'Never mind. He's gone. How about some dessert, ladies? I can entirely recommend the ice cream.'

Phryne decided on hazelnut ice cream and pursued the topic of telegraphs. 'Why was there only one operator on the *Californian* and what difference would it have made to the *Titanic*?' she asked. Mr. Green seemed to be regretting his rash words.

'Well, you see, when the *Titanic* was sinking, the *Californian* was the closest ship, but it was proved at the inquiries, both of them, that the sinking ship couldn't be seen, and ships then were only required to have one operator, and the operator on the *Californian* had gone to bed. The *Carpathia* only got the distress signal from the *Titanic* because her operator was lying in his bunk and lazily scanning the airwaves for someone to talk to. Sheer luck, if you can call it that. Now, we really ought to talk about something else.'

'Very well,' said Phryne. She smiled brightly on Mrs. West.

'Who's your dressmaker, Mrs. West?' she asked, with a view to avoiding the woman at all costs. Such extremes of fashion as the purple shift dress which Mrs. West was almost wearing was not for Phryne. She preferred her personality to supply the outrageous edge to her appearance, not her exposed bosom.

'Brunton's in Collins Street,' replied Mrs. West. 'Of course, they're terribly expensive.'

'An awful lot of money for not a lot of cloth,' grunted Mr. West, in what was almost a joke. Mrs. West giggled.

'Madame Suzette makes most of my things. What about you? That's a very beautiful piece of silk.'

'Madame Fleuri,' said Phryne. 'The silk is from China. It was dappled in the dyeing process. The silk buyer was about to throw it away until I grabbed it.'

'And you were going to tell us about the sapphire,' said Mrs. West, her hungry eyes devouring the jewel.

'So I was. Let's take our coffee in the Palm Court and I'll tell you all about it.'

Phryne wanted to give the rest of the party a chance to slide quietly away, but none of them did. Mrs. West finished her double serve of sorbet de cassis and licked her soft red lips with her little red tongue, coloured with blackcurrant juice.

● ● ● ● ●

Seated in the Palm Court at a suitable table, Phryne took the chair facing the orchestra. At this early hour the musical entertainment consisted of Mavis at the piano, playing anodyne pieces designed not to offend. More bloody Brahms, thought Phryne.

'This stone comes from India,' she told the table at large. 'It was one of two identical stones: the sapphire eyes of Krishna in a big important temple. Then the Indian mutiny came and war swept over the area. The priests fled or were killed. An English soldier broke into the temple and dug out one of the eyes of the idol.'

'Why not both?' asked Mr. Aubrey. 'Nothing to stop him. Lots of loot got taken during the mutiny.'

Phryne shrugged. She had spent a lot of time on this story but she hadn't expected to have to tell it to an old India hand. 'The story says that he went mad and ran away,' she said. 'He ran back to his comrades and that night developed a very high fever and died. The men preparing the body for burial prised open his hand and claimed the jewel.'

'Corpse robbing,' said the professor dryly. 'Never a fortunate profession.'

'It wasn't for them,' said Phryne. 'They were caught by their sergeant and put on charge and the stone went to their commanding officer. He was arranging to have it returned to the temple—the war was almost over by then—when he went down with malaria and his batman stole the stone. He sold it in the market in Bombay for one-tenth its worth. Enough for him to go home and live like a king, though, if he hadn't—'

'Been bitten by a snake?' suggested Mr. Aubrey.

'You've heard the story?' asked Phryne, raising her eyebrows.

'I believe that I have.' Mr. Aubrey was smiling.

'The stone was sold by the Bombay merchant to a maharajah, who presented it to his principal wife and called it the Maharani, the Great Queen. Then the maharani gave it to her son, who presented it to my grandmother. She was rather a wild beauty in her time, I believe. And when she died it came to me,' Phryne concluded.

'A remarkable story,' said Mr. Aubrey. 'I believe that I did hear of this stone, indeed. And the curse does not worry you, Miss Fisher?' he asked, taking more sugar in his spiced tea.

'No,' said Phryne. 'If I knew where the temple was, I'd send it back to them, but it's not known where it was. It's the same as a rather beautiful statue of Kwan Ying which I have, which one of my disreputable relatives pinched during the Boxer Rebellion. I'd give it back, but there isn't a real government in China to give it back to. The Maharani is safe with me,' she said, stroking the stone.

All eyes were fixed on it. It was a cabochon, no facets, and in the heart of the indigo blue curve there dwelt a bright, star-shaped light. Mrs. West tore her eyes away.

'What a story,' she said in a discontented tone. 'I wish I had something like that.'

'But you had a necklace of perfectly matched pink pearls,' said Phryne. 'Or so I understand. Wasn't there a story attached to them?'

'They belonged to some old lady who had once been a courtesan,' said Mrs. West. 'They were supposed to have been a present from the Prince of Wales. But they're gone,' she said, sadly. 'I'm going for a walk in the fresh air,' she said to her husband.

'I'll escort you,' said Mr. West.

She patted his cheek. 'No, I shall have…' She scanned the available male talent. Her gaze lingered on Jack Mason, and the ambient temperature at the table rose markedly. Doctor Shilletoe smouldered angrily. Mrs. West smiled. Phryne could have slapped the little minx. 'Mr. Green,' she decided. She crooked a finger, and Mr. Green rose reluctantly. He was enjoying the conversation.

'And I shall join you,' said Phryne. Professor Applegate rose at the same moment. 'A turn around the sun deck, Mr. Aubrey?' she asked.

'Delighted,' he said.

Miss Lemmon slipped a hand through Mr. West's arm. He gave her a brief distracted smile, but it was a smile within the meaning of the Act.

'Perhaps you would accept my escort, Miss Fisher?' asked Mr. Mason.

'If you trip me, fall on me, or step on the hem of my dress it will go hard with you,' warned Phryne, taking his arm. It was an agreeably muscular arm. The young man smelt of salt water and soap, a nice clean smell. The Cahills and Mr. Forrester fell in behind as Mrs. West and Mr. Green, now reconciled to his fate, paraded up the Grand Staircase to the lido.

No sun on the sun deck, but a cool fresh breeze and a remarkable number of stars. They were as close as lanterns, blazing bright.

'When this breeze drops it will freeze,' commented Mr. Green. 'We're going south, d'you see, Mrs. West? Then across to New Zealand. The further south in these latitudes, the colder it is.'

'Until you reach the ice,' said Phryne.

'Yes. Most of Antarctica is land, did you know? It doesn't melt down to a reasonable size in the summer like the Arctic when the pack ice shifts. It's just permafrost and very chilly. Does any lady need a shawl?'

'No,' said Phryne, Mrs. Cahill, Miss Lemmon and the professor.

'Yes,' said Mrs. West. 'Johnnie, can you get it? The dark grey cashmere one. Maggie will know where it is.'

Phryne watched Mr. West disengage himself from Miss Lemmon and stalk down the stairs, and wondered what strange and possibly perilous game Mrs. Jonquil West was playing. She nudged Jack Mason to draw her closer to the young woman and laid a hand on her arm. Bracelets slid under her touch.

'Constellations,' she said to Mr. Green, meaningfully. 'Tell us all about the stars, Mr. Green, you're a navigation officer, you must know about stars.'

'The Maori say that the sky father came from there,' said the professor, pointing to a roundish black gap in the Milky Way.

'From the Coalsack nebula?' exclaimed Theodore Green. 'How very curious. The astronomer chappies are saying that the Coalsack is a very old universe which has collapsed in on itself. A black hole, they say.'

'Really?' asked Phryne. 'So the father god came from outside. Makes perfect sense. And the earth is the mother goddess?'

'Oh yes,' said the professor. 'Why does it make perfect sense?'

'Because I bet the Maori are exogamous,' said Phryne, who had not wasted her time since she left school. 'Therefore fathers always come from outside the mother's tribe.'

'Very nice,' approved the professor.

'You can make a sky map,' said Mr. Forrester, 'with a photographic plate exposed all night. Not here, of course, the ship's lights would overexpose it. The stars blaze trails across the sky. Very decorative.'

'Have you got one to show me?' asked Phryne.

'I believe so,' he said, smiling at her. 'I'll look it out.'

Mr. Green was assisting Miss Lemmon to sight along his arm to locate the pointers to the Southern Cross.

'Our skies aren't nice and neat like the Northern Hemisphere, where there is a star right in the middle of the sky,' he told her. 'To get the celestial pole you have to go up and across a bit. See the cross? Alpha, Beta, Gamma, Delta and little Epsilon Crucis.'

'It's very beautiful,' said Mr. Aubrey solemnly. 'I have always found the stars most uplifting. I remember being ill—a bad go of malaria—in a hospital in Poona and nothing to do but look out the window, and the stars comforted me very much.'

'I know,' said Phryne. 'They are such a long way away from human pain and misery. And cruelty,' she added. 'And war.'

'I'm tired of standing still,' said Mrs. West pettishly. 'Let's walk some more, Mr. Green.'

'In just a moment, Mrs. West, when I finish showing Miss Lemmon how to get to the pole. See, there is the ecliptic, where the zodiac dances around.'

'And there is Jupiter, a planet, from the Greek *planetos*, meaning wanderer,' said Phryne.

Mr. Green gave her a slightly startled look, perhaps wondering if he was being mocked, but her face was perfectly innocent of a smirk. 'Just so,' he agreed.

Mrs. West stamped her foot. 'You take me, Mr. Mason,' she said.

'Very well,' said Jack Mason. He was about to lead Mrs. West away when her husband came hurrying back with a shawl.

'It's the wrong one,' she told him crossly. 'Go back and get the right one.'

'It will do,' he said, with an appearance of mastery. He wrapped her in the soft grey folds and led her away, protesting. Phryne suppressed a grin and caught the professor with an identical expression and her hand at her mouth.

'And this is Karina, the keel of the ship Argo,' said Theodore Green.

● ● ● ● ●

Mr. Michael Johnson
New York

Hi Mike, this is to tell you that Julia and the girls will be sailing tomorrow on the new ship. Isn't it amazing how fast progress goes? I remember when it took all of two months to get across the Atlantic. I must be getting old though Julia tells me I'm not, because she's the same age as me, I guess, though don't tell her I said that. I'm staying in London for a few more weeks to deal with that Michigan steel export problem. These Brits drive a real hard bargain but they're no match for Yankee ingenuity in the end.

Best
Joe

Chapter Seven

Yet for disport we fawn and flatter both
To pass the time when nothing else can please.

E De Vere, Earl of Oxford
'A Renunciation'

When they came back to the Palm Court the Melody Makers had limbered up and were playing 'Walking My Baby Back Home' rather well, with a jazz edge to the traditional tone. Phryne walked into Mr. Mason's embrace and they danced away.

'What are you doing, wasting your life, Jack?' she asked, hoping to shock him into a reply. 'Is it the charms of dear Jonquil? That won't answer, it won't answer at all.'

He was duly jolted, missed his step and almost ran Phryne into a palm tree.

'What did you say?'

'You heard,' said Phryne grimly, signalling a steward and ordering two gin slings. She pinned Jack Mason against the palm so that he could not easily move until the drinks came and she allowed him to sit down in a wicker chair.

'You see, I came on this holiday for a rest,' she told him, 'and I am finding the whole West, Mrs. West and Mason imbroglio enervating. So before I change my table and find some sane people to sit with—though they will be sadly boring—I'm giving you a chance to explain. What is going on? Are you madly in love with Jonquil?'

'Don't say her name in that soupy way,' he protested.

'It's hard to say the name Jonquil any other way,' she pointed out, reasonably.

'I suppose so,' he said. Like many a young man in torment, Jack Mason stretched, flung out his arms (narrowly missing a passing steward, who saved his tray of drinks with an adroit zig to the left) and stuck out both legs in front of him (narrowly missing a dancing officer, who saved his partner's stockings with an adroit zag to the right).

'You're a hazard to navigation,' said Phryne amusedly. Jack Mason drew in his limbs, drank his drink, and began to explain, though he was hanged, he told himself later, if Miss Fisher was due any explanation or had any right to ask for one. Much less demand one.

'I'll tell, but this is a dead secret, all right?'

Phryne nodded.

'My father—well, I'm a disappointment to my father. Which is fair enough, because he's a disappointment to me. He wants me to go to the varsity and be a lawyer like him. Well, I tried it to please him, and I was so bored by the end of six months that I had to throw it up or die. I've always been a big hearty chap, good at games, and I wanted to be a professional athlete, but he wouldn't hear of it. So we can't agree on anything. He said he'd cut off my funds unless I gave up sport, so I gave it up. He's on the board of P&O so I can travel as much as I want. He thinks I'm going to give in, but I'm not.'

'With you so far,' Phryne assured him.

'I was at a loose end, you see, so me and a few of the football chaps at the shop—the university, you know—went to a dance place in Richmond one night. Professional dancers, you know, shilling a dance?'

'I know the sort of place,' said Phryne, who did. Weary, overly made-up girls in much mended frocks circling the floor in the arms of people who held them too close, panted over their charms, and stood on their feet. Matched, of course, by tight-waisted young men in threadbare evening dress, bright eyes and dirty necks, ready to whisper sweet nothings into any female ear, be she never so ugly. Phryne avoided dance halls. They were sad and sordid.

'So there I met—'

'She was a professional dancer?'

'Yes, and she was different from all the others. I picked her out at once. Same war-paint, same old dress, but eager eyes, not cynical like all the other old boilers. I bought her whole evening and went back the next night.'

'And the next,' prompted Phryne.

'Then—well, you know my situation. I haven't enough to marry on and anyway...'

'She isn't the kind of girl you take home to your stern papa,' said Phryne.

'Er, no, she isn't,' confessed Jack Mason. 'Then some bounder attempted to warn me off,' he said indignantly. 'Told me to stay away from her as though he was one of those American gangsters. The idea!'

'We have produced some very nasty home-grown brutes,' said Phryne, speaking from personal experience. 'What happened then?'

'I kept going to Richmond and then one night a sneering bastard called me over and told me that unless I left "their girl" alone, my father would be hearing about it.'

'And you told him to publish and be damned,' said Phryne, trying to move the story along a little. Behind her, the piano struck up and a woman began to sing a blues song. Not a voice with a great range, or great steadiness, but huge expressiveness and a strangely coincidental choice of song. It was, Phryne

ascertained, Magda, the first violin, accompanied by her sister
Katrina. Magda was clad in a long, bright red dress of immodest
cut, made by the same hands that had fashioned the bright blue
one which her sister was wearing. Both dresses glittered with
sequins. The sisters were very decorative.

'Ten cents a dance, that's all they pay me,' mourned the deep
voice, with no trace of accent. 'Gosh, how it weighs me down.
Ten cents a dance, sailors and tough guys, rough guys who tear
my gown...'

'Well, no, that is, I didn't quite,' squirmed Jack Mason.
'Jonquil herself told me to go away, that I was getting her into
trouble with her boss, and if I couldn't marry her she'd have to
find someone else who could. So, well, I went away.'

'I see,' said Phryne.

'I suppose you think I'm a cad,' he said miserably.

'No, I don't,' Phryne told him. 'You didn't love her, so why
stand in someone else's way? You behaved sensibly, probably for
a change.'

'Though I've a chorus of elderly beaus,' sang Magda, 'stockings
are porous with holes at the toes...'

'Anyway, I don't know what she wants,' said Jack Mason. 'I don't
know if she wants me or not. She complains about her husband all
the time but Blind Freddy can see that he's crazy about her. And
I'm still sorry for her, poor little rich girl, flirting with the officers
like that Doctor Shilletoe, she has him hung, drawn and quartered,
poor chap, and driving West mad with jealousy.'

'That is such a good rhyme,' commented Phryne, momentarily
distracted. 'Porous and chorus. Sorry. Did you, in fact, have an
affair with Mrs. West when she was a dancer?'

'No,' said Jack Mason flatly. Here he was, pouring out his
soul, and his interlocutor was listening to a singer. 'Women!'
about summed up his attitude to the sex.

'I really can't advise you as to what Mrs. West may be intending,' said Phryne, leaning forward to allow him to light her

cigarette. 'She might be thinking of an adulterous affair, but she might also be aware that her husband would probably kill her if she did. That's an obsessive man. She's playing with fire. I think that you should find a career, Jack. Why aren't you climbing unclimbed mountains? Exploring the far reaches of unknown rivers? You'd be very good at that.'

'You think so?' A spark lit itself in the young man's lack-lustre eyes.

'I do,' said Phryne. 'You could accompany an archaeological expedition to Mayan ruins and stop the scientists from being eaten by tigers. Or possibly jaguars, in South America, come to think of it. You're wasting your life. And if you are wondering whether Mrs. West will run away with you, I'd say that is improbable. She likes you, but she likes her luxury and new dresses and jewels and three meals a day more. Which is to be expected, working as hard as she worked and being as scared and cold and miserable and bullied as she must have been.'

'I suppose,' he said reluctantly.

'And you're not in love with her, so why keep on with this half-hearted charade?'

'I do, I do…love…her,' faltered Jack Mason.

'Not enough,' said Phryne. 'She's an excuse so that you don't have to go on with your life, make any decisions—and also to punish your father,' she dissected ruthlessly. 'None of those are the ingredients of love.'

'You're not the first person to tell me this,' he said ruefully.

'Professor Applegate, Mr. Aubrey and probably Mrs. Cahill,' Phryne guessed.

'Bang on, all three,' he said. 'And Thomas, my man. And my father. But I might take notice of you,' he said insinuatingly. 'You're young, like me.'

'No, I'm not, my boy,' said Phryne firmly. 'I don't think I was ever young like you. Come along. We're wasting valuable dancing time.'

'I'm here till closing time,' proclaimed Magda. 'Dance and be merry, it's only a dime!'

The dance floor was full. Phryne found herself too compressed to do more than the standard 'nightclub shuffle,' which consisted of moving gently in whatever direction there was room. They circled slowly. Possibly because of all that dance hall practice, Jack Mason was a good dancer.

Phryne had carefully not brought any dresses with trains. They were just pure provocation to a certain kind of lead-footed man.

She was being turned near the bandstand when she felt a sharp tug at her collar. It was instantly released. Phryne looked around at once and could see nothing unusual. The Melody Makers were tooting, thumping, plucking or sawing as to preference. Her nearest neighbour was Mr. Cahill and, on the other side, the Wests. She put a hand to the jewel. Dot's stitches had held. It was still there.

But where had that pull come from? Left, right, behind, before or—intriguingly—above? Phryne looked up. Nothing above her now but chandeliers and strings of the famous Tiffany coloured lights, festooned in garlands, red and blue and claret and yellow, figured with vine leaves and grapes and flowers.

Thoughtful, Phryne finished the dance and excused herself. She needed another drink and time to think. She sat down against the wall, ordered a double cognac, and watched the dancers.

How had it been done? Just a sharp tug from—as it might be—behind, and there went the lolly? Phryne shook her head so firmly that the drinks steward, Pierre, came hurrying over to inquire if the cognac was to the lady's liking. Not many women, in his experience, drank cognac, and the ones who did knew what they were drinking. He was terrified that harm had come to his champagne fines cognac, and was reassured by the lady in such fluent and appreciative French that he brought out his special bottle of Grandes Armagnac des Ducs and poured her a glass.

She savoured it in the proper fashion and favoured Pierre

with more appreciative comments. He made a mental note that table three should have the good burgundy with their boeuf en croute tomorrow. He could pass off the inferior bottles on tables seven and four. Table seven knew nothing of wine, sending back a bottle of riesling as "corked" because it had bits of cork in it, the imbeciles. Table four had gulped down a very special old pale brandy as though it was common wood alcohol, which was probably what they had been drinking because they had said that his brandy lacked bite. They deserved inferior burgundy. The bottles that had been stored too close to the stove might have enough bite by now for table four. A wine waiter's revenge may be long in coming, but it arrives in the end.

Pierre left the charming lady, plotting quietly to himself and wondering why she had kept that Parisienne accent when she had clearly mastered French and could have abolished it in favour of an attractive accent, like as it might be, his own, Normandy tones.

Cognac always had a good effect on Phryne's thought processes. The superlative Armagnac rather unhinged them. Unhinged might be a good place to be, Phryne thought. Rational deduction wasn't doing her any good. Information received told her that neither of the ladies who had lost their gems while dancing mentioned any touch. They would have noticed a sharp tug. Right. Therefore the jerk was produced because Dot had stitched the sapphire necklace to Phryne's dress. Someone had tried to steal the sapphire and had been foiled. Twice, so far, if the person with mousetrap fingers had been looking for the sapphire in Phryne's Pierrot bag, instead of where it actually was, sewn into the knotted scarf on Phryne's hat.

Perhaps the mousetrap had made him or her clumsy. That was a nice thought. The dancers blurred past Phryne's eyes. It was time to go to bed. Mr. Forrester danced along with Miss Lemmon. Everyone seemed to be having a good time.

Magda concluded, and bowed. The applause was general. She was really good. Jazz and blues required a precision control of dissonances: too many and the singer sounded perpetually off-key, not enough and she sounded too much like a parlour contralto singing drawing room ballads. Magda had fire and her sister's accompaniment was positively uncanny in its anticipation of the singer's changes of key.

The Melody Makers started playing the Maori Farewell, 'Now Is the Hour', as the last dance assembled, and Phryne trailed away towards her cabin, thinking such deep thoughts as were possible after three glasses of very good cognac.

Dot wasn't there, which was unlike her. Phryne managed to wriggle out of the blue dress and, unwilling to try unstitching the necklace, decided to tuck the dress into bed with the teddy bear. She cleaned her face and assumed her nightdress and dropped into the dreamless sleep of the slightly shickered.

Phryne woke feeling cold. She snuggled down into the eiderdown provided by P&O for the chills of the first class passengers, rolled over and became fully conscious.

The French windows were open. A very cold wind was blowing in. And someone was tapping at the cabin door. Phryne reacted fast. She grabbed and donned her gown and retrieved her little gun from under her pillow. Then she turned on all the lights and opened the door.

'Hello,' she said. A dishevelled Caroline gestured to a huge overalled young man who loomed behind her, filling up the corridor. He might not have been nine cubits and a span, but he would have run Goliath of Gath close.

Caroline spoke sharply. 'Bring her in here, Tui. Lay her down on her bed.'

Tui, his head scraping the roof, hulked inside and laid an unconscious Dot on her bed. He stepped back, looking bashful.

'Good boy, Tui,' Caroline told him. 'Now cut along and don't say a word to a dog.' The giant vanished with no noise at all.

Phryne, holding a gun and, for some reason, a teddy bear, stared at the closed door and said, 'Well?'

'I don't know, Miss.' Caroline wrung her hands. 'She came to dinner with us and we talked for a bit and then she said she was coming back here, and then hours later Tui came to get me because he found her on the companionway down to the engine room. I thought I'd better bring her back here.'

'Is she hurt? Concussed?'

'I can't see anything, Miss, and she hasn't got a bump on her head. She just seems to be asleep.'

'That doesn't look like ordinary sleep,' said Phryne grimly. 'Go get Doctor Shilletoe, without waking anyone else.'

There was no possibility that anyone would disobey Miss Fisher in this imperative mood. She had paled to the colour of porcelain and her green eyes were as cold as age-old ice. Caroline went.

'Now, Dorothy,' said Phryne gently, putting down the gun and the teddy bear, 'let's just close these windows and have a look at you. What have you been doing, eh?'

Phryne shut and bolted the French windows. The suite began to warm. Dot murmured in her sleep. Her forehead was cool, her hands limp, her pulse slow. Phryne examined her gently, tucking her skirt around her and pulling down the rumpled shawl. No sign of sexual interference, no torn seams or lost buttons, all her underwear in place. That was fortunate—for the attacker, Phryne thought. Had anyone molested Dot it would have been necessary to kill him and that was always difficult. No bruises, bites, no bumps under the soft hair. No skin under the short fingernails, no sign of an affray. Dot had been drugged. Why?

To allow someone to break in through those pestilential French windows and find that thrice-cursed gem. Phryne went back to her bed and pulled out the blue dress. The stitching was still intact and the sapphire gleamed balefully at her in the three in the morning electric glare. Phryne swore at it, found the embroidery scissors and unpicked the stitches, then stowed the gem in its little pouch, slung it on a ribbon to go round her waist. She tied it on. Better get dressed, she thought, some investigation was going to be necessary.

Phryne put on underwear, trousers, a jumper and soft shoes. She put her little gun in her pocket. She was more awake than she had ever recalled being. Where to begin? Where that behemoth had found Dot, on the companionway down to the engine room. And then, Phryne thought, to wherever she had lost her shoes. For Dot's stockinged toes were in evidence. Somewhere she had lost both of her sensible, low heeled evening shoes.

And now the matter was wide open again. It was no use the crew continually telling Phryne that it wasn't them. If it wasn't them, who had drugged Dot?

Doctor Shilletoe was conducted into the cabin by a distraught Caroline. He was surprisingly brisk. Phryne supposed doctors got used to being called in the middle of the night.

'No concussion,' he said, after making a careful examination. 'But her pupils are shrunk to a pinpoint. Drugged, Miss Fisher, with an opiate—laudanum, maybe. Not a dangerous dose,' he said. 'She doesn't take sleeping draughts usually, I expect?'

'She has a moral struggle with taking aspirin,' said Phryne.

'Right. Someone has slipped her what people now call a Mickey Finn.' The doctor put down Dot's hand. 'What's going on, Miss Fisher?'

'There you have me,' said Phryne. 'So the best we can do for Dot is to let her sleep it off?'

'Well, yes. Her respiration is fine, no trouble breathing, she just needs to sleep. We could wake her to pump her stomach but I don't believe that's necessary and would just cause her distress.'

'She is feeling no pain at present,' Phryne agreed. 'All right. Thank you very much for coming out. I know that I'm keeping you from your rest, but can you stay here with Dot for a little while longer?'

'I'm awake now, anyway,' commented the doctor. 'I'll just sit down in this nice basket chair and have a snooze. I'll wake if she calls. Why, what are you going to do?'

'A little recce,' said Phryne and, taking Caroline by the arm, led her out and shut the door.

'What do you want me to do, Miss?' asked Caroline. Miss Fisher was making her very nervous. Dot had hinted that her employer was a strong-minded woman but Caroline had discounted this. Miss Fisher was rich, and rich women were soft. This opinion was now undergoing rapid revision. Phryne was set-faced, very quiet, and that was a real pistol in her perfectly steady hand.

'Take me to where Tui found Dot,' she said, and Caroline complied.

The residential part of the ship at night was lit only by dim lights along the walls. Phryne followed Caroline down the back staircase to the decks below Third Class, where the crew lived, where the engines throbbed, and where the complex preparations for feeding, clothing, washing and conveying all those passengers largely went on.

Deeper still and deeper. The walls changed from decorated to plain to smeared with grease. The stairs went from carpeted to lino to American oilcloth to bare metal and got progressively steeper.

'Engine rooms are down here,' whispered Caroline. 'Out of bounds for all of us. I'd be sacked if they found me here.'

'Being sacked is the least of your worries,' Phryne told her. She could smell a heady mixture of heated metal and grease with overtones of petrol and—frying?

'Stokers live down here,' Caroline told her.

'But these engines are diesel, they aren't stokers any more,' said Phryne, to whom this had just occurred.

'It's just what they call them, Miss,' said Caroline, whose patience was fraying. 'They've got a little cubby here and they do some cooking in it, even though they aren't allowed to, because it's such a long way up to the kitchen. No stewardess service down here,' she added sharply.

'They may fry anything, up to and including a full sized shark,' said Phryne. 'It is no concern of mine. Where did Tui find Dot?'

'Tui?' called Caroline. There was a stirring in the cubbyhole and the massive man shouldered his way out. Phryne could imagine that he had to spend quite a lot of time hunched over. Ships just weren't built for large economy sized Maoris.

'Where did you find the lady?' asked Caroline.

Tui lumbered seven paces to the steep companionway which led up to the third class kitchens.

'Here,' he said simply. 'I was going to the head,' he added. 'She was all limp. I reckon they might have rolled her down the steps. But she wasn't hurt or broken and I took her to Caroline.'

'Did you see anyone around? Hear anything?' asked Phryne.

Tui's brow wrinkled. He nibbled at a massive thumbnail with a surprisingly delicate movement. 'Nothing,' he concluded. 'Except this thud. I reckon that was the lady. And here's her shoe,' he said, producing it. 'I could see she was one of Caroline's ladies, I seen her with Caroline before, so I took her to Caroline.'

'Fair enough,' said Phryne, stuffing a banknote into the huge fist. 'You did very well and I'm very grateful. Anything else you remember, tell Caroline. Now, let's have a look at those stairs.'

Caroline accompanied Phryne up the steep companionway. At the top lay the other shoe. Also on the floor was a piece of cloth which might have been a muffler or a sling, knotted with a hard knot in one corner. Phryne picked it up.

'What's along there?'

'Third class kitchens and dining room,' said Caroline. 'What was Dot doing down here?'

'I don't think she had a choice,' said Phryne grimly, climbing another staircase. 'I think she was nabbed just outside your dining room, Caroline, and carried down here.'

'But why throw her down the stairs?'

'I don't think they did. I think they left her at the head of the companionway for some reason, and she struggled in her sleep and tipped herself down the steps. By the time they came back for her she was gone. This is a nice, quiet, dead place, isn't it? Not overlooked by anything. I think she was taken because she decided to go to bed early, while I was still dancing. The French windows were open when I woke.'

'The sapphire, was it taken, Miss?'

'No,' said Phryne. 'And now this is personal. When I find out who did this they are going to repent it sorely.'

Caroline believed her.

They retraced a possible route through the ship which Dot's captors might have taken, but found nothing useful. They returned to the Imperial Suite and at the door Phryne said to Caroline, 'You've been very kind, thank you. Do something else for me. Don't tell anyone about this, and make sure that Tui doesn't tell, either.'

'We ought to tell the captain,' said Caroline, troubled. 'Ladies drugged! I never heard of such a thing! And they'll blame the crew again, sure as eggs is eggs.'

'Leave it to me,' said Phryne. 'And when it is all sorted out, the captain will be told exactly what happened.'

'All right, Miss,' said Caroline reluctantly. 'I'll go back to bed, then. I'll call at eight with the breakfast. Miss…?' she asked tentatively.

'Mmm?' Phryne replied.

'Is that gun loaded?'

'What use is an unloaded gun?' asked Phryne. She unlocked her door and slipped inside. Caroline looked at the closed door for a while, then went back to her own cabin.

Phryne found Dot asleep in her bed and Doctor Shilletoe asleep in the chair. She added herself to their number and fell asleep in her own bed, still wearing the Maharani around her waist.

Mustafa Ali
Casablanca

Salaam aleikum. The blessings of the prophet be upon your house and the houses of your sons. I report that I have expended my master's gold in buying tickets for the master's two cousins on a very good ship to America. I have sent them to Cherbourg in the care of a very reliable servant of this house. This emigration will remove them from the reach of their enemies and should ensure the further prosperity of my master's house, for which his servant duly prays.

Chapter Eight

As idle as a painted ship
Upon a painted ocean

ST Coleridge
The Rime of the Ancient Mariner

Saturday

Phryne Fisher woke as Caroline came in with the coffee. Dot was sitting up in her bed, rubbing her eyes.

'It must have been that extra glass of sherry I had,' she said woozily.

'I know you don't like coffee, Dot dear, but Caroline will give you a cup and you should drink it all,' said Phryne, sitting up and revealing that she was wearing undergarments instead of her nightdress. 'And I'll tell you all about why in a moment.'

Dot did as she was told. The coffee was Leo's finest and would have drawn a shocked gasp from an Egyptian mummy. Caroline brought in Phryne's croissants and departed without a word. Doctor Shilletoe had left Phryne a note which said that if Miss Williams experienced any nasty after-effects she should call him immediately. Phryne read it as she stripped off her underwear, dropped the sapphire into Dot's hands, and went to take a shower. It had been a nervous night.

Reclad for a cool morning, Phryne explained to Dot what an adventurous night she had had. Oddly enough, once reassured that her virtue was intact, Dot seemed rather relieved.

'I thought I might be getting on the grog,' she said. 'Like my Uncle Ted. He used to pass out all the time.'

'On two glasses of sherry, Dot, not even a moderate sized dog would pass out. You were drugged. Now, would you like breakfast first or remembering first?'

'Breakfast. I feel all right, Miss, really, just a bit slow. A good breakfast and I'll be bonzer.'

'If you say so,' said Phryne. Dot put on her shoes and went out.

Phryne ate a thoughtful croissant. That Dorothy Williams was made of strong stuff. Meanwhile, Phryne needed a few cups of the thought-provoking coffee herself. Who had had the immortal brass-edged nerve to drug Dot? And—she found herself wondering suddenly—what about the coincidence of Magda deciding to sing 'Ten Cents A Dance' so very appositely when Jack Mason was telling her about Jonquil? It was going to be a busy day. And, with any luck, there would be answers. And fjords.

Phryne ate the rest of her croissant and stared out to sea. The wind was cold. She was dressed in a warm woollen suit and soft shoes. Lifeboat drill this morning, she noticed in the ship's newsletter, and then the *Hinemoa* would sail into Milford Sound, South Island which the guidebooks said was magnificent.

Phryne had not half finished thinking when the ship's siren began blowing, bells went off in every corridor, and it was time for her to assume her life jacket and report to Boat Deck Station Three.

The life jacket was not the most becoming of garments, but it was easy enough to put on. Phryne came out into the passageway to find Caroline inserting a returning Dot into hers and shrugging on her own. People were already streaming up to the boat deck. Phryne and Dot joined the multitude.

'Waste of time,' she overheard Mrs. West saying crossly. Mr.

Singer, beside her, turned a pale face to the young woman and snarled, 'Don't say that, you silly woman! You wouldn't say that if the ship was sinking. In the dark, in the middle of the cold sea.'

'Here,' said West angrily. 'I won't have you speaking to my wife like that!'

'He is, however, correct,' observed Professor Applegate, the white calico of her life preserver trussed so high that she could have rested her chin on it. 'Lifeboat drill is essential. Once you know where your station is, and how to get there, you can find it again. Come, don't fuss, Mrs. West. This won't take long.'

And it didn't. Phryne was astounded at how quickly the passengers were mustered, directed to their stations, and ranked by their lifeboats.

'At least there are enough boats,' said Dot. 'Thomas says that's what the sinking of the *Titanic* did for safety.'

'What do you mean?' asked Phryne. 'I rather missed the *Titanic* disaster.'

'How did you miss it?' asked Dot, amazed. 'It was in all the papers. Hundreds of people drowned.'

'In April 1912 I was in the process of being dragged off to England to go to a very tough girls' school. The headmistress did not believe in what are now called current events. I did hear about the ship sinking, but none of the details.'

'They didn't have enough lifeboats,' said Dot. 'They saved most of the women and children in First Class, and everyone else died. It must have been awful. Thomas says that no one will ever forget it.'

'I should think not,' said Phryne, not attending. 'Well, here is our boat, and is everyone here?'

'All present,' said Mr. Aubrey. Roberts, their boat steward, nodded. The wind was cold now, with a nitrogen tang which spoke of ice. It might not be out of question to meet an iceberg in this sea, either. The lifeboat was an agreeably robust looking boat with a stout canvas cover. It was being slung down from its davits. Phryne was pleased. The lines were new, the blocks and pulleys worked with only minimal creaking, and the large boat descended to the boat deck and landed with barely a thud. Four sailors jumped in and urged the passengers to climb aboard and sit down.

This was managed with the usual amount of complaining and a few stepped-on toes. Jack Mason, late and jacketless, joined his boat in a flying leap which tumbled an innocent bystander into the bottom of the boat and earned him a smart clip over the ear from a steward.

'Ouch,' he complained.

'Couldn't you find somewhere else to have the accident?' demanded Phryne.

'Didn't hear the siren,' he said, which was scarcely credible. Anyone not roused by that combination of harsh bells and hooting siren must have been deaf, dead drunk, or just dead.

The boat swung out for a dizzying moment, then was lowered smartly into the sea. It landed with a slap and floated high, like a cork. Other boats were appearing from above; all classes, crew, even the restaurant staff, the stokers and the Melody Makers—all around the large mother duck of the *Hinemoa* they floated.

An officer in a powered boat was gathering the ducklings into a large flotilla. They rowed away until they were perhaps a hundred yards from the ship.

Phryne was impressed. The organisation had been seamless. No one had fallen overboard yet, though Jack Mason would probably contrive it. If this had been a real emergency, the ship would have been emptied of people in less than half an hour.

On the other hand, there was always something missing from a drill. This was the emergency itself, and all the aggravating factors: darkness, panic, people screaming, water pouring in, perhaps smoke or fog or fire. And fear. Fear had a scent which might be hard to detect but infected anyone who smelled it.

Phryne shivered, bobbing up and down in her commodious

lifeboat, and was glad when they were belayed aboard again, and could go into the Palm Court for a little morning tea. Dot, feeling some after-effects, went back to the Imperial Suite, secured all the doors and windows, and lay down on her bed with the teddy for company.

Table three were in the Palm Court in force, both Singers, both Cahills, both Wests, and the usual cast. Phryne ordered strong coffee and petits fours. The conversation inevitably turned to maritime disasters.

'Jolly lifeboats they have on this ship,' said Mr. Aubrey bracingly. 'Cork lined and close to unsinkable.'

'Don't say that,' said Mr. Singer.

'Only "close to", old chap, not "absolutely". *Hinemoa* is a very fine ship, and her lifeboats match her, that's all I meant.'

'And yet *Hinemoa* could be considered to be a jinxed name,' said Jack Mason idly. 'There was another *Hinemoa* in the 1890s. She was ballasted with graveyard rubble, and her captains went, in order, insane, criminal, alcoholic, suicidal and homicidal. Finally she was wrecked off Scotland in 1908, a total loss.'

'Nonsense,' said the professor. 'Kindly do not mention this again, young man! These things have a way of getting about. Do you think that you are the only person aboard who knows about the old *Hinemoa*? The Maoris asked a famous *tohunga* about her, before she was launched, and he said that the other one was cursed not by her Maori connections or any breaking of *tapu*, but by carrying dead men's bones unwillingly from their resting place. That does not apply to us. We are ballasted with good New Zealand gravel. Now hold your tongue,' concluded the professor crisply, and Jack Mason obeyed.

'There was the most famous mystery of them all,' said Mrs. Cahill. 'The *Marie Celeste*, left empty and no explanation.'

'*Mary Celeste*,' said Navigation Officer Green, who had joined them. '"Mary". Not "Marie", sorry. A lot of people make that mistake.'

Mrs. Cahill sniffed. 'Well, what about the *Mary Celeste?*' she asked.

'A real mystery, though not the only ship that's been found empty and still floating. Wooden ships, particularly, were built to, er, as it were, float. The *Mary Celeste* was first sighted by the *Dei Gratia*, Captain Morehouse. She had left New York for Genoa on the fifth of November 1872, if my memory serves me.'

Professor Applegate allowed herself a chuckle. 'Well of course it serves you, my dear Mr. Green. Do go on.'

'*Dei Gratia* sent the mate and two sailors across to *Mary Celeste*. They searched the ship and there was no one aboard: no one at all. Everything was in good order. A flask of oil on the sewing machine unspilt. A bed with the indentations where a woman and a child had lain down upon it. That would have been the captain's wife, Mrs. Briggs, and his two year old daughter, Sophia. Water had washed into the cabins, but there was no damage to the ship. She did not seem, even, to have been in heavy weather. When they pumped her out she was as dry as a tick and rode high.'

'What happened to the log?' asked Phryne, who knew how Navigation Officer Green felt about logs. He smiled gratefully at this intelligent woman who understood the importance of documentary evidence.

'The log was found intact. The last entry was the twenty-fifth of November when the ship was passing Santa Maria island. No more entries had been made and the ship had travelled about five hundred nautical miles since then.'

'What's the difference between a nautical mile and a land mile?' asked Mr. Cahill.

'It's a little longer and much, much wetter,' said Mr. Green with a straight face.

Mr. Cahill thought about this, finally decided it was a joke and laughed.

'Didn't the owners change her name?' asked Mrs. Cahill.

'Yes, the strange fate of the *Mary Celeste* is supposed to be a warning about changing a ship's name. Perhaps as the *Amazon* she might have been luckier. But possibly not. She was run aground, on fire, and wrecked on four occasions before she was sold, repaired and renamed. Not a lucky ship from the beginning, perhaps.'

Much as Phryne enjoyed being told things by Navigation Officer Green, she had an investigation to make. She finished her petit fours and went back to her suite, where she found Caroline at the door.

'She's locked herself in,' Caroline told Phryne.

'And not to be wondered at,' said Phryne. She knocked. 'It's me, Dot dear,' she said.

Gradually, the door opened. Phryne and Caroline went in and Dot resumed her place on her bed. Clearly the small ration of extra alertness conferred on her by unaccustomed coffee had quite worn off. 'I'm that sleepy,' she said.

'I know. Now, remember for me. What happened after you went to dinner with the second class citizens?' Phryne demanded.

'I went along as usual,' said Dot. 'Sat down with the ladies and stewards. Caroline was there. She'll tell you,' she added, yawned cavernously, closed her eyes and fell asleep.

'Caroline?' asked Phryne.

'Yes, Dot came in to dinner,' Caroline replied. 'We all sat down, she was sitting between Maggie and Mr. Thomas. Mrs. West's maid and Mr. Mason's man, you know. We had a really good mulligatawny soup. Is this what you want to know?'

'I won't know until you tell me, so tell me all.' Phryne said, lighting a gasper. Caroline went on slowly, racking her brains for anything suspicious.

'Then a nice cut of beef and vegetables and gravy. The men drank beer, except Mr. Thomas who always has wine. Dot had a glass of sherry with her meal. I had a gin and tonic.'

'What did you talk about?'

'I don't know,' wailed Caroline, distressed. 'Just the usual things, I suppose. Maggie was saying that Mrs. West wanted her to take up the hem of a handkerchief point dress and it was very hard to do without the proper sewing things. Mr. Thomas talked about wine. He always talks about wine.'

'Did Dot offer to help Maggie?'

'Yes, but Maggie said she'd manage it by herself. She doesn't really want help, that Maggie. You see, if someone helped her she wouldn't be able to complain and she likes complaining. We had ice cream for dessert—no, Dot had pudding, a summer pudding with raspberries. I thought Dot seemed a bit tired and she said she wouldn't stay for a few hands of cards or anything but go to her cabin and have an early night. And she knows the way back so I just…let her go.'

Caroline burst into tears. Phryne supplied a handkerchief and a pat on the shoulder.

'All right. So Dot went out by herself and was waylaid by someone or someones who carried her down to the third class deck. Did anyone else leave your dining room at the same time, or just after Dot?'

'No,' said Caroline, wiping her eyes. 'It was early. We always have a game of cards or draughts and a bit of a chat before we turn in. The next watch of stewards was already on deck so there was nothing we needed to do. The girls from the beauty salon were making costumes for the masquerade and I went over to talk to the other Maori stewardesses. We were playing cards for matches.'

'Tell me, why did Tui bring Dot to you?'

'I'm *rangatira*,' said Caroline matter-of-factly. 'An aristocrat. Tui belongs to the same tribe as me.'

'So you're his feudal superior? His princess?'

Caroline did not smile. Neither did Phryne. 'Sort of. More that I'm responsible for him. Tribal chiefs—*ariki*—had to look after their people in the old days. My father is a chief. So if boys like Tui strike something they don't feel they can cope with, they call me.'

'That's how feudal loyalty used to work, too,' Phryne told Caroline. 'Do you think Dot would have accepted anything to eat or drink from a stranger?'

'No,' said Caroline

'Me neither. Therefore she was drugged at dinner. The mulligatawny would have been a good vehicle. That curry soup would hide any odd taste. Easier to do, too. Just drop in a powder and give it a quick stir.'

'Who could have done it?'

'Anyone at the table. And the cooks and stewards. As to why, I suspect that it was to keep Dot away from the Imperial Suite until it had been searched again. Someone may have come in through the French windows while I was asleep.'

'Must be a mountain climber,' said Caroline. 'Or a monkey, p'raps. There's a ten foot gap between each private balcony, and a straight drop into the sea if you fall.'

'Do-able, for a robust young man with a good rope and possibly a helper or two,' said Phryne.

'You mean Mr. Mason,' said Caroline.

'Oh, if it is him, I am going to nail him to a mast. Possibly having to put one up for the purpose, but that can be managed,' vowed Phryne. 'You can get back to your duties, Caroline, thank you. I'll stay here until Dot wakes again.'

'If she's not back with us by lunch time I can bring you some food,' said Caroline, and went out.

Phryne sat down in Dot's chair and considered. No great harm had been done to Dot, who could always do with a bit more rest, but it could have been very bad if she had fallen on something sharp, for instance. And what were they intending to do with her? Why take her down to Third Class and leave her at the head of a companionway? Were they hoping that she might fall and break her neck? If so, the stalwart Dorothy had foiled them. And Phryne was going to feed them to the sharks when she found out who the assailants were.

So that was all right. Phryne gathered up her Chaucer and her glass of gin and tonic and began to construe. As it happens, the 'Pardoner's Tale'. A merry discourse on death, greed, lust and sin. It was just to her taste.

The aged man whom the revellers accosted tapped his stick on the mother earth, the gate of death, and cried 'Loving mother, let me in!' but she would not, and Death would not take him, but he knew where Death was, all right. He directed the revellers to a pot of gold buried under a tree, and thus sealed their grisly but instructive fate.

Phryne read carefully, occasionally resorting to a glossary, while Dot slept peacefully, and the ship *Hinemoa* sailed on.

• • ● ● •

Phryne lunched lightly—a selection of excellent sandwiches. The day was wearing past. Dot woke and lay, attempting to focus. Phryne was pleased to see that her eyes had pupils and she seemed only ordinarily dazed, as one who wakes from a day-sleep tends to be.

'Hello, old thing! How do you feel?'

'I'm all right,' said Dot, rumpling her hair and hauling herself into a sitting position. 'What's the time?'

'Getting on for afternoon tea time. Would you like some?'

'I'd love a cuppa,' said Dot thirstily.

Phryne picked up the phone and ordered tea. Dot got up and washed her face and put her hair into order, firmly suppressing any frivolous intentions as to waving or even curling by a punitive plait. The unnatural drowsiness had gone. Now Dot was beginning to feel angry.

Since she had arrived on the SS *Hinemoa*, she had been subject to a burglar who had ruffled through her intimate garments and an assault on her own person and she didn't like it. This was not what she had signed on for. She said so.

'I know, Dot, but the trouble with travelling on ships is that it is rather compulsory. You go where the ship goes. But when we get to Invercargill I can send you home on another boat, if you like.'

'Not on your life,' said Dot. 'I want to catch up with the bloke who did this. Then I want to have a word with him.'

'Me too. And I can always ask Caroline to lend me her friend Tui. He's about the size of Sampson from the circus. Watch what you eat and drink, keep close to Caroline and the Maori, and we should be all right. Now, I am going to a bal masqué on Tuesday night. What shall I wear?'

Miss Ann Wright
London

I do hope you can come down to Southampton on twelfth of April to see us off, Ann. Though, of course, we are all very glad that you have your own school now, the children will miss their Miss Wright very much. And so will I, of course.

Valeria, Lady Scott

Chapter Nine

Oh me! What eyes hath love put in my head
Which have no correspondance with true sight?

W Shakespeare
'Blind Love'

Phryne loved masquerades. Since, with any luck, the persistent burglar had retired for the moment, muttering 'foiled!' in his teeth, which Phryne fervently hoped were all aching, she might as well plan a new dress.

'What would you like to be?' asked Dot.

'You're having a costume, too,' Phryne insisted. 'What would you like to be?'

Dot thought about this. She had never been to a costume ball. But so many surprising experiences had come her way since she entered Miss Fisher's employ that she was almost getting used to them.

'I don't know for the moment,' she temporised. 'Let's think about you first. You could do a Chinese lady. We've got the silk garments. Or a Japanese one. What will other people be wearing?'

'If I know cruises there will be three distinct classes. Those who are impeccably dressed because they just happen to have brought a Marie Antoinette costume, underpinnings and powdered wig with them. There will be people who contrive costumes out of what they have or can scrounge, like my Chinese lady—that is a good idea, Dot. Then there will be those, mostly male, who decline to wear a costume at all and turn up in ordinary gentleman's evening dress with a domino.'

'They ought at least to try to get a costume,' commented Dot. 'What's a domino?'

'A black eye mask.'

'Oh. Not very interesting.'

'Or enterprising, but there are always some. Now, the pyjama trousers and the long gown, with a few modifications, will make my costume. How about you? Glamorous? Gorgeous? Highly painted? Film star? Lady Godiva?'

'Oh, Miss,' protested Dot. 'I don't reckon I could carry that off. I mean glamorous, not Lady Godiva.'

'Well, what about a saint? Or an angel?'

'I'm not sure…' said Dot. Clearly she was thinking. Phryne stopped teasing her.

'Plenty of time. You said that the girls from the beauty salon were making costumes. What were they going to be?'

'Nymphs, Miss. Dryads. And naiads.'

'Would this have been Mr. Forrester's idea?' guessed Phryne.

'Yes, Miss, how clever of you. He wants to photograph them and they say that if it's all five of them together he can't…I mean, it would be quite safe. I mean respectable.'

'So what are the naiads and dryads wearing?'

'Short loose shifts, and over them long gowns of mosquito net, dyed green and brown for the tree nymphs and green and blue for the river nymphs. And long ribbons in their hair. They're going to look lovely. They're very good with their hands, those girls. They were making papier-mâché for masks. Jack Mason wants a mask.'

'And in what character is the jovial Mr. Mason coming to the revel?' asked Phryne idly, buffing a fingernail.

'Don't know, Miss. They're making a young lady mask for Mr. Charles, who's a bit, you know, and they asked me if I wanted an animal mask. They can do cats or dogs or anything.'

'Would you like to be a bird, Dot? I can see you as a bird.'

'That's a thought, Miss.'

'What's your favourite bird?'

'I've always liked cockies. They're wise. And cheeky.'

'Well, there's a couple of days to think about it. I'll just need some white make-up and some flowers for my hair. Now, I was thinking of going down to the shop and having a little look at the merchandise. Want to come?'

'Yes, Miss. I have to take the teddy down to Third Class. I reckon he's battered enough now.'

'Good. Off we go, then.'

Phryne put on her hat and found her Pierrot bag. Dot tucked the teddy under her arm.

'All right, old thing?'

'All right,' agreed Dot.

Third Class was four decks down, and although it did not have the splendours of First Class, it was very comfortable. Phryne examined the spacious dining room and the games room where a number of men were playing billiards. Dot's family was in the first cabin past the stairs. Dot knocked on a door marked 'Ryan'.

A haggard woman opened the door, finger to her lips. 'I've just got her to sleep,' she said. 'Doctor says if she doesn't sleep he'll dose her tonight. Oh, it's you, Miss Williams.' The woman's tired face lit up as she recognised Dot. 'Have you got him?'

'Here he is,' said Dot, producing the toy. 'Right eye re-sewn, wobbly left ear, well hugged.'

'Teddy!' came a full throated demand from the cot set between the two single beds.

'Here's Teddy, Primmy,' said Primrose's mother. Primrose, a robust child with excellent lungs, had screamed almost incessantly since *Hinemoa* left the dock without Teddy. Her mother handed over the toy and three people watched with bated breath for her reaction. Primrose, a stocky child with pale hair and blue eyes, examined the teddy closely. A spurious teddy had already been foisted on her once. She wasn't going to let that happen again.

She found the wobbly ear. She noticed the re-sewn eye. She gave him an experimental hug and felt the furry body mould itself to her chest, unlike that horrible stiff new one which they had tried to fool her with. This one smelt faintly of a sweet perfume but that was all right. In fact, it was nice. Very nice. She lay down in her cot, Teddy firmly wound in her arms, and shut her eyes. Getting Teddy back against such furious opposition had really taken it out of her. She fell asleep.

Primrose's mother let out a sigh of sheer relief. 'Thank you so much, Miss,' she said to Dot. 'I was going out of my mind. Now I can tell my husband that he can come back. He's been playing billiards for hours to get out of the cabin, and he hates billiards.'

'My pleasure,' said Dot.

'It's not that she's a bad little girl,' said Mrs. Ryan suddenly. 'It's just that when she loves things, she really loves them. And when she wants things, she…'

'Really wants them,' completed Dot.

They climbed the steps towards luxury again and met no one they knew. But the shop was well patronised by First Class. Mrs. West was examining stockings. Mr. West was standing behind her, looming. Professor Applegate was scanning the bookshelves. Dot went to look at the sewing materials. Mr. Forrester was looking at postcards, Mrs. Cahill was looking at dolls, and Mrs. Singer was opening every boxed scarf, shaking it out, disapproving, and dropping it. Each one was then taken up by the clerk, refolded in its original folds, re-boxed and laid aside. They had apparently been doing this for some time, and Phryne detected fraying patience in the clerk.

'Hello, Mrs. Singer,' said Phryne. 'Can't find one that you like?'

'I wanted a blue,' she said fretfully. 'Jos likes me in blue. But even the ones with blue at the edges have some other colour in the middle.'

'They will all be multicoloured,' said Phryne. 'And you don't have to unpack them. That's why they have that little picture on the lid.' Phryne sorted rapidly through the remaining boxes. 'No, not a single one that is just blue. You might be able to get one in Dunedin, or Auckland. But they do have some nice blue beads over here,' she said cunningly. 'Let's have a look at them.'

The clerk drew a breath of relief and gave Phryne a grateful glance as she guided Mrs. Singer away. Phryne grinned back.

'They are rather nice,' said Mrs. Singer. Her voice had an edge of perpetual discontent which was very irritating and Phryne strove not to be annoyed by it. The woman could not help her voice. Or her marriage to a man with dyspepsia. Phryne ran long strings of glass beads through her fingers. They tinkled.

'Those amber ones are very pretty,' she decided. 'I think I'll buy a strand. What about you? There's three sorts of blue here. Aquamarine, sky blue and sapphire blue.'

'I like that dark blue,' said Mrs. Singer. Phryne looked at her as she held the string of beads up to her bosom, looking into the round customer's mirror. She was an 'ish' woman—plumpish, palish, fortyish. Her hair had been kept long, against the fashion, and was originally brown, now heading towards pepper-and-salt. It was wound into an uninteresting bun. Her complexion was good, though she needed to wear less powder and more colour. The hands holding the beads were stubby and the nails chewed. She was wearing an unexciting skirt and jacket of blue serge and a grey shirt.

'The blue looks very good on the grey background,' opined Phryne.

'I think I'll have these,' said Mrs. Singer. 'Or, no, perhaps the paler blue would be better. Have you ever been married, Miss Fisher?'

This was an unexpected and very personal question but Phryne answered anyway, despite Mrs. Singer's defiance of all social convention. 'No, never,' she said firmly.

'It's not all it's cracked up to be,' warned Mrs. Singer with astounding candour for a conversation in a shop with a virtual stranger. 'Take my case. I was a teacher. Never expected to marry.

Then along came Jos. He'd been married before, had a wife and two little kiddies. All dead in some tragedy. I never liked to ask him about it. He decided he wanted me.'

'And you decided you wanted him,' encouraged Phryne, seeing that everyone in the shop was listening. Professor Applegate had frozen at the bookshelf. Mrs. West was standing with a stocking in each hand. Mr. Forrester seemed transfixed by a view of Milford Sound. Mrs. Cahill was trying not to stare, Dot was frankly horrified, and Phryne herself had a string of amber beads dangling unnoticed from her fingers.

'Not really. He just…well, he's a masterful man. And now we're always travelling, and what I wanted was a nice little house and a garden. And perhaps a cat. Of course, we don't…and I wouldn't expect to have children at my age, anyway. But it would be nice to settle down. I do my best to please him,' said Mrs. Singer sadly.

'I know,' soothed Phryne.

'But it doesn't seem to make him like me any better,' Mrs. Singer said pathetically, groping for a handkerchief. Phryne supplied one of her own.

'Come along,' said Phryne. 'Buy the beads, and let's go and have a cup of tea. You're tired, Mrs. Singer.'

'No,' said Mrs. Singer, pushing Phryne's hand away with feeble violence. 'No, I can't. He doesn't like me to talk to people. But thank you for telling me about the beads,' she said, with a sad little gesture. 'I'll have these,' she said to the sales clerk. 'Put them on the Singer account, please.'

Phryne put the amber beads back. She had gone off beads. She looked around. Mrs. Cahill was examining a doll dressed in a crinoline as though she suspected it of concealing cocaine in its skirts. Professor Applegate had taken down a thick book and was scowling over it. Mr. Forrester had selected a view of the SS *Hinemoa* and came forward to purchase it. Dot was still staring, and Mrs. West rolled two pairs of stockings together and put them down. Mr. West was smiling an unpleasant little smile.

'Found anything, Dot?' asked Phryne.

'I never heard anyone talk like that in a shop, never,' said Dot.

'Poor woman doesn't have a chance to talk anywhere else,' said Phryne. 'You heard what she told me. "He doesn't like me to talk to people". Poor woman!'

'She made her bed,' said Dot disapprovingly, 'and she must lie on it.'

Phryne chuckled. 'Don't be censorious, Dot dear, it gives you wrinkles. Let's have a look at the books.'

'I don't need any, Miss, I've brought all those mysteries to read. You can borrow some if you like.'

'Very kind. Hello, Professor.'

'Miss Fisher.' Professor Applegate moved aside a little to allow Phryne full view of the bookcase. 'A nice selection of classics here, and a reasonable number of sensational novels. Which attracts you?'

'Oddly enough, classics,' said Phryne. 'I know the author of those three.' She pointed to *Night of the Sheik, Poisoned Passion* and *Flowers of Sin.* 'A very pleasant woman who kept her elderly mother in Irish linen and lavender water by writing them. But that does not mean I have to read them. Ah, Dickens. My favourite. *Bleak House.*'

'A very charming author,' conceded the professor, 'if you are in the mood to be charmed.'

'I almost always am,' rejoined Phryne. 'But I am also reading Chaucer.'

'Poor Mrs. Singer ought to read the Wife of Bath's prologue,' said the professor.

Phryne thought about it and located the quote. 'Ah, yes. "To speak of the woes that are in marriage", indeed. I am not intending to try matrimony.'

'Wise woman. I never did and I have been very happy.'

'Are you going to buy that?' asked Phryne. The professor examined the thick book. 'I picked it up to cover my confusion,' she said. 'It's a gazeteer of New Zealand and I think it can go back into its place.'

Professor Applegate took her leave and presently Phryne collected Dot, went to the library, and they both spent the rest of the time until dinner reading: Dot was almost finished *The Case of the Blonde in the Library*, and Phryne was researching New Zealand wildlife. It seemed even stranger than Australian wildlife, and that was saying something. Though there was nothing as strange in New Zealand as the platypus, a beast composed of leftover bits of duck, snake, beaver, mole and seal. Then again, there was quite possibly nothing as strange as a platypus anywhere in the world.

● ● ● ● ●

Dinner was an occasion for Phryne to exhibit another of her blue gowns. Her wardrobe was extensive, and it had not been hard to find fourteen dresses which matched the Maharani. This one was very pale blue, almost ice-blue. Mrs. West remarked on it immediately.

'Don't you find that shade very trying to the complexion?' she shrilled.

'No,' said Phryne.

Mr. Aubrey hurried into speech. 'Miss Fisher could wear any colour,' he said. 'What have you ladies been doing all day?'

'A little shopping,' Phryne replied. 'And some reading, and lots of watching the ocean.'

'Really? What are you reading? I've got a box of Agatha Christie and the Detection Club,' offered Mrs. Cahill generously.

'Thank you,' said Phryne. 'Who do you like best, Miss Christie or Miss Sayers?'

The merits of the two crime-writing ladies lasted through the celery soup and the cream of chicken vol-au-vent.

'The only trouble with Sayers is that I have to stop and go back and check that all those timetables and so on work,' said Mr. Aubrey. 'But she writes a dashed fine yarn. I, however, prefer Rudyard Kipling and John Buchan.'

'I like them, too,' said Mrs. Cahill.

Mr. and Mrs. West were having a sotto voce argument, conducted in hisses. Mr. Singer was staring at his omelette with an expression of settled despair. Jack Mason decided to cheer the company.

'I say, I saw dolphins today. And a huge big bird. I wonder that the sailors don't have a few pot shots at some of them. Must have been feet across the wings.'

Phryne spared a moment to send up a fervent prayer to whoever it was responsible for hunters that Jack Mason not be allowed to get his hands on a gun.

'Big bird, you say?' asked Professor Applegate. 'White or brown? Pink beak and feet?'

'Yes, white, black edges to its tail, sort of clown face with a big pink hooter.'

'Ah,' said Professor Applegate with a certain edge to her voice. 'That, my boy, is a wandering albatross. Diomedea exulans, to be precise, and God forbid that you should ever shoot one.'

'Why not? I bet the fishermen would thank me. That thing could empty an ocean in one gulp,' protested Mr. Mason.

'Haven't you read "The Rime of the Ancient Mariner"?' asked Mrs. Cahill. 'I learned it at school. It's by Coleridge.' She stood up and declaimed, '"God save thee, Ancient Mariner, from the fiends that plague thee thus! Why look'st thou so?" "With my cross bow I shot the albatross". It's a famous poem. Awful things happen to the ship.'

'Sit down, Mum, do,' said Mr. Cahill. 'You're showing off.'

'And you have every right to do so,' approved Mr. Aubrey. 'A good memory is a wonderful thing. I've been on a lot of shikars in my time, young man,' he added to Jack Mason. 'And at the end of my hunting days I found myself thinking that the whole thing was a massacre and I had rather had the tiger skin I brought home with such pride back where it belonged, with the tiger still inside.'

'But the tigers were man-eaters,' protested the young hunter, feeling that the table was ganging up on him.

'One, maybe. The rest were just doing what tigers did before the small holders cut down their forest.'

'I've been reading about New Zealands birds,' interjected Phryne smoothly. 'They seem very singular.'

'Islands,' said Professor Applegate. 'Cut off a population for long enough and it evolves out of all knowledge and resemblance. Look at the rock hyrax, whose nearest relative is—'

'The elephant,' said Phryne, who had been told this important piece of information by her adoptive daughter Jane. Jane liked knowing things, and shared her knowledge freely. The professor nodded, as though Phryne was an intelligent pupil.

'And the nearest relatives of the weka, which is about the size of a hen, are the emu and the cassowary. On the other hand they have the largest flightless cricket, a weta, which is the size of my hand and eats anything,' she added.

Mrs. West gave a faint scream. 'Oh, I shouldn't like to see any of them.'

'That is highly unlikely,' Professor Applegate assured her.

'New Zealand never really developed mammals,' the professor went on. 'Instead of the wolf there is the kea. Instead of the badger there is the kiwi.'

'I thought keas were parrots,' said Phryne, dissecting a delicious slice off her veal and chicken galantine and spearing it on a piece of cucumber.

'They are,' said the professor. 'Big strong parrots with beaks of iron who could, I believe, bring down a sheep. The farmers have almost shot them out because they have seen them feeding on dead lambs, though I suspect that they are just opportunistic carrion eaters.'

'Not during dinner,' said Mrs. Singer, patting her husband's hand.

'Let's talk about unknown animals,' said Mr. Aubrey. 'Sea serpents, eh?'

'Have you ever seen one?' asked Jack Mason.

'I regret to say that I have not. Lot of reputable people have, though.'

'Nonsense,' said Mr. Singer, taking another swig of beer and grimacing.

'I reckon there's a deal of unknown beasts out there,' said Mr. Cahill, unexpectedly. He had a strong outback drawl. 'The blacks tell stories about the bunyip and the nargun. They ought to know. Been there thousands of years. Talk about a rainbow snake, too. Australia's a big country, she's a big country all right. Plenty of room for a rainbow snake or two. Wouldn't write it off right away.'

'Especially since animals like the platypus really do exist,' Phryne put in. She had always found platypuses irresistible proof that God likes a joke as much as anyone else. 'A platypus is intrinsically much less likely than a unicorn or a sea serpent.'

'Plenty of sea out there,' agreed Jack Mason. 'But I've never seen one.'

'Have you ever seen a devil fish?' asked Mr. Aubrey. 'Wings yards across, horns like a devil, tears up anchor chains and demolishes boats?'

'No,' said Jack Mason.

'Do you believe that they exist?'

'Yes,' said Jack Mason.

'Why?' asked Mr. Aubrey, plunging a fork into a pile of volcanic curry. It smelt so spicy that Phryne wondered if it would dissolve the cutlery.

'What are we all wearing to the masquerade?' asked Mrs. West. 'I've been trying to think of something new, and I can't. Have you managed a costume, Miss Fisher?'

'Yes, from odds and ends of my own wardrobe,' said Phryne. 'I understand that Mr. Forrester is dressing a lot of the beauty shop girls as naiads and dryads.'

'And very decorative they will look,' he said, smoothing his curly hair.

'And the girls are making masks. Perhaps you might like a

mask, Mrs. West?' asked Phryne. 'I'm sure that they will make one for you. If you ask them nicely.'

'What sort of masks are they making?' asked Jonquil West, interested.

'Well, animal masks,' answered Phryne. 'One lady mask. They offered to make animals. You could be a bird, perhaps?' offered Phryne, though personally she felt that Mrs. West would be admirably represented as a female canine.

'Or a cat,' said Jack Mason. 'You'd look very pretty as a cat.'

Mrs. West fluttered her eyelashes at Jack Mason. Then she jumped as though someone had nudged her.

'What about you, Mr. Aubrey?' asked Mrs. West. 'What are you wearing to the masquerade?'

'Oh, I've got my rajah garb. Always one of these dress-ups on every voyage. What about you, Professor?'

'The usual Maori clothes. Hope it won't be too cold. Those feather cloaks are very decorative but they aren't very warm. The same goes for flax. What about you, Mrs. Cahill?'

'Oh, I haven't thought of anything at all. I was wondering, Miss Fisher, if I might borrow your companion for a little? I'm told she's a fabulous dressmaker.'

'I'll ask,' said Phryne. 'What were you thinking of?'

'I have always wanted to be a princess,' confessed Mr. Cahill, and suddenly Phryne liked her. This was a woman who had worked hard all her life and probably deserved to be a princess, at least for one night.

'We'll have a costume making session on Monday,' she agreed. 'And you will look lovely. Are you wearing a costume, Mr. Forrester? Do you need any help with it?'

'Oh no, Miss Fisher, thank you for asking, but the dear girl insisted that I match them, so they are going as nymphs and am going as—'

'Let me guess,' said the professor. 'Amyntas the shepherd?'

'Wrong,' grinned Mr. Forrester.

'A river god?'

'Wrong.'

'Silenus,' said Phryne and the professor together, and Mr. Forrester clapped his hands.

'Got it,' he said.

'Who's Silenus?' asked Jack Mason.

'The Roman form of Pan,' Phryne told him. 'And very suitable too. Mr. West?'

'I don't do this sort of nonsense,' Mr. West pointed out sulkily. 'I will just wear a domino, as a gentleman should.'

Phryne ignored this.

'And you, Mr. Mason?'

'I'm going as Death,' said Jack Mason, and took another serve of sorbet.

Miss Alexandra Williams
Utah

Dearest Miss Williams, I am so glad to be able to tell you that my financial endeavours at the London office have met with considerable success. I am sailing home soon and I hope—dear Miss Williams—if your heart remains unaltered towards me—to be able to speak to your father when I return.

You have always been my lodestone, so guide me home to your arms.

Your devoted lover
Leonard

Chapter Ten

At first sight the crew were not pleased with the view
Which consisted of chasms and crags

L Carroll
'The Hunting of the Snark'

The Melody Makers were getting into the swing of their music, knowing, perhaps, that tomorrow a pianist would take their place and they would all have the day off to recover. Phryne wondered how musicians ought to spend the day of rest. Attending various forms of divine service, perhaps (Catholic in the second class chapel, sung Eucharist in the first class chapel, Buddhists and pagans presumably to make their own arrangements)? Mend their stockings? Swot up on new music? Instead they played cards and drank beer. Admirable.

Magda, doing a commendable imitation of Bessie Smith, was singing about her kitchen man in a throaty contralto which fortunately blurred the highly coloured words. Phryne was dancing with Theodore Green and almost listening to his information about Milford Sound, which they would reach on the morrow.

'Thirteen miles long, Miss Fisher,' he said solemnly. At least he wasn't standing on her feet. 'Walls of stone and ice rising straight out of the water. And we cruise along very slowly, because of what happened to the *Waikare* in Dusky Sound in 1910.'

'Another shipwreck?' she said, trying to conceal the fact that she had heard enough about shipwrecks to last the remainder of her natural life.

'Well, yes, but it had no tragic consequences. Until 1910 the cruise ships used to go along Dusky Sound quite happily, until *Waikare* found Pinnacle Rock and ran aground, high and dry. The passengers and crew all went ashore and stayed ashore all night. The navy came to rescue them, I believe, but they suffered nothing worse than cold and sandfly bites.'

'Sandflies,' murmured Phryne. The place sounded less and less attractive.

'Oh, yes. Famous for it. When the sandflies go to sleep, the mosquitoes wake up. Won't bother us out on the water, of course.'

'And we aren't going to land?'

'Indeed, if you wish, Miss Fisher, you can go ashore on the tender and have a little walk along a track into the rainforest. The Milford Hotel used to have pet birds which you might like to see. But buy some citronella.'

'Right. Tell me, are you coming to the masquerade?'

'Yes, Miss Fisher,' said Theodore Green.

'What are you wearing?'

'My uniform,' he told her stiffly. 'That's always been costume enough for me.'

'Look for a Chinese lady,' said Phryne. 'And save her a dance.'

Phryne, before sleeping, secured her suite. She locked all the doors. She put chairs under all the doorhandles. She tied the handles of the French windows together.

'That ought to do it, Dot dear.'

'Unless they bring their own battering ram,' agreed Dot. 'I gave your message to Mr. Cec's niece Lizbet, Miss. She says come along after lunch and bring beer.'

'No difficulty there,' said Phryne, and put herself to bed. Dot, after her long drugged sleep, did not expect to sleep, but hearing Phryne's quiet breathing, she drifted off eventually.

Sunday

When Phryne woke it was cold. The French windows disclosed nothing but drifting mist. Not thick enough to be called a pea-souper or a London particular but enough to explain the melancholy sea-serpent cry of the foghorn.

'Fog everywhere,' thought Phryne with Mr. Dickens. Dot was already awake, plaiting her hair with swift fingers.

'Ooh, it's all misty,' she commented. 'How can we see where we're going in all this mist?'

'I have no doubt that we can,' said Phryne bracingly. 'If you really want to know, I'm sure that Navigation Officer Green will tell you all about it. Until your ears bleed. If he wasn't such a darling, I'd have to drop him overboard. Even then he would be telling me valuable and useful things all the way down. I'm for a hot shower and some warm clothes. Break out a wool suit, will you, Dot? Then unlock the door and let Caroline in.'

Phryne dressed in a modish dark grey suit with a flaming red shirt and secured the sapphire to her belt in a petticoat pocket. The fog was breaking up in patches and suddenly a huge wall of green slid past.

'Gosh,' said Phryne, standing transfixed at the window.

'It's the Sound,' said Caroline, bringing in her breakfast. 'Milford Sound. Glaciers and that. Rough country. But amazing.'

'You've got that right,' commented Dot. 'I've never seen anything like it. The hill just drops straight down to the sea, like a curtain. I'm going to breakfast, Miss,' said Dot. 'Then to church.'

'I'll be on deck,' said Phryne. 'Meet you there.'

As she ate her croissants and drank her coffee, Phryne stared out and the cliffs slipped past. *Hinemoa* was moving very slowly, feeling perhaps for a hidden hazard like Pinnacle Rock, and there seemed no end to the backdrop. The cliffs rose sheer, straight up into the grey cloud, with no shelving beach or visible end; just the water, the cliffs, and the sky. It was surreal, alien, astound-ingly beautiful.

And, Phryne realised, very cold. She finished her breakfast, put on her shoes, and donned a fur-trimmed coat.

On the sun deck she found the professor, Jack Mason, Margery Lemmon and both Cahills.

'It's so strange,' said Phryne. 'It almost doesn't look like land-scape. It looks like a sculpture.'

'I've been to Norway,' said Jack Mason unexpectedly. 'Their fjords are all ice. They're beautiful, too, but this is different. Closer to the real world. There are birds and animals in that vertical forest. Men could live there, though I don't suppose anyone does.'

'There were tribes here,' said the professor. 'But never many and never in the rainforest. The insects alone would drive humans away. Those cliffs are impassable. Behind them there are a lot of valleys, also close to impassable.'

'I always wondered what those sandflies ate before people came,' commented Margery. 'I went for a walk last time we were here, and did I get bitten! I couldn't see out of my eyes for two days. If you go ashore, Miss Fisher, bathe in citronella.'

'I will,' said Phryne, gaze fixed on the eerie, moving, ghostly mountains. Here before humans came down from the trees. Will be here when we all evolve ourselves into something which can fly, and will fly away to the stars. Sole occupiers of an empty earth.

She shivered despite her fur coat, and went inside. The Palm Court was setting up for morning tea and gladly supplied her with a cup of hot chocolate and a copy of the ship's newsletter.

Divine service, a talk on spiritualism, a lecture on Maori cre-ation myths from the professor, a simultaneous chess match with Mr. Valdeleur, chess master. Ten boards, already fully booked. Phryne noticed that the chess board was where the navigation officer spent his spare time, which could explain his dancing. He was playing board four. The doctor was playing board five.

Pity I never could master the tedium of actually learning

chess, Pryne thought, sipping the rich, sweet drink. Interesting people play it. But for me a nice respectable Church of England sung Eucharist and then ho for the musicians and the gossip after lunch.

She spent the rest of the morning wrapped in her fur collared coat, watching the endlessly strange landscape, tasselled with white cataracts, slide past her own windows. The *Hinemoa* slid down the sound noiselessly, big engines hardly turning over, until she slowed and came to a halt near a large, tin roofed building which proclaimed itself to be the Milford Hotel.

Just before lunch she was persuaded to go aboard the tender and have at least a little toddle into the wilderness. Doctor Shilletoe offered a distillation of his own invention which he assured her would give any sandfly an acute aversion to her person. Professor Applegate offered to show her keas. Jack Mason threatened to take her swimming otherwise.

Smiling, she consented to go ashore. She slicked all visible flesh with the doctor's potion, which smelt like roses drowned in carbolic. She stepped down into the tender, the MV *Adventure*, and was conveyed to the hotel. It was an ordinary building, until one considered how far each nail, plank, saucepan and sheet of galvanised iron had had to come before it got there. Phryne knew that a good lunch awaited her on the ship so did not tarry to taste the cuisine but followed the professor's sturdy walking shoes up a muddy path and into a forest. The actual rain had stopped. Professor Applegate was carrying a heavy canvas bag.

It was the first rainforest of Phryne's acquaintance and the first thing she thought was that it was certainly rainy. Water gushed off every bush, was funnelled off Miss Fisher's matchless person by the sou'wester she had borrowed from Mr. Green and splashed to the ground. The second was how very dense and dark it was. The trees soared up out of sight, yards in diameter and hung with lianas and vines. The next storey flowed up from the floor to meet the hanging canopy. It was intensely green and grey, and smelt beautiful: an earthy, leafy, almost grapey scent. She was gratified to find that her odour of carbolic and flowers repelled the sandflies. They came flocking towards her in a black cloud, intent on blood. Then they smelled the distillate, braked abruptly, and flew off on other business. A few hopefuls hung at a distance, waiting for the repellent to wear off.

'Just through here,' said the professor, 'there's a bit of a clearing. There was a fire here.'

'How could there be a fire?' asked Phryne. 'You'd think it would take a good soaking in metho to make this lot burn.'

'Close. It was a spilled petrol tank. This is where an old hermit feeds the keas. You mustn't tell anyone. Farmers hate keas. They think that they kill sheep. "Feathered wolves" they call them. But old Rainbird Jim loves them, and so do I.'

They had emerged into a bottle-shaped clearing. The trunks of several of the great trees, in falling, had brought down the lesser vegetation and Phryne could see open sky above and thousands of seedlings underfoot, striving to get to the light.

'Should I be quiet, or sit down?' asked Phryne, remembering a few mind numbing hours she had spent bird watching, forbidden to speak, smoke or breathe loudly. The young man had been very toothsome, but not that toothsome. Phryne had not tried bird watching again.

The old woman laughed. 'You'll be soaked to the bones if you sit down. No need to worry. Keas aren't shy.'

The professor scattered her heavy bagful of lumps of raw fat, chop bones, old bits of cake, bread and butter half nibbled and discarded from breakfast, and mutton bones across the open space. Then she lifted her head and made a rasping screech which sounded a bit like 'Kea! Kea!'

The surrounding trees shook under the impact. Ten keas hit the branches and roosted there, eying the ground suspiciously. They were dark green, but when they flew their underwings were flame orange and scarlet, so that they looked like a flying bonfire.

They inspected the largesse for a few minutes, some hanging upside down, clucking to each other. Eventually a consensus was reached and they dived down on the food, shouting 'Kea! Kea!'

They were clownish, charming, gluttonous birds, and Phryne was delighted. They grabbed with beak and both feet and then tried to eat a chop and a ball of bread and a piece of cake simultaneously. They yelled 'Kea!' with their beaks full. If one spotted another kea with a better mutton bone they'd grab the end and pull, flapping madly, until the winner got the bone and the loser rolled over backwards, tail in the air, screaming 'Kea!' in frustration and loss. They pounced on each other and flapped and shouted like boisterous children playing.

Then they examined Phryne. They flew around her, grabbed her sou'wester, pulled it off, and tore it to pieces in mid-air, clicked a beak close to her face to see whether she'd flinch, dived on the professor and beaked her oilskin hood and then retreated, chuckling, diving, forgetting to fly as they told the next kea exactly what they thought of her, hoisted back into the trees, and were gone in a flame of scarlet and orange. The forest rang with them announcing 'kea!' as they flew.

'Oh, wonderful,' said Phryne. 'They are wonderful. Thank you for showing them to me!'

'Natural clowns,' said the professor, pushing back her holed oilskin hood. 'I should have told you to tie the hat down. If it's tied down they just put holes in it. I remember Rainbird Jim telling me that he forgot to put his boots away one night, and what he heard in the morning was this odd pinging noise. It was the keas. They were eating his boots, and spitting out the eyelets against an iron bucket.'

'Amazing.'

'This way,' said the professor. 'You'll be taking cold in a forest without a hat. Time to get back to the ship and have a nice warm-up and some lunch.'

'Yes,' said Phryne. 'But I wouldn't have missed seeing the keas. Will you call on Rainbird Jim?'

'No use,' said the professor. 'He won't come out while there are so many people around. I always leave some chocolates for him at the hotel, where he buys his supplies. Came back from the war with shell shock, you know. He can't stand noise.'

'I've met men like him before,' said Phryne, and led the way back down the muddy path.

At the hotel the passengers were buying picture postcards of Milford Sound and what looked horribly like stuffed penguins. Phryne left them to it, returned to the ship, had a hot shower and went to break the bad news about his sou'wester to Navigation Officer Green at lunch.

'I should have told you to tie it down,' he worried. He had forgotten to tell Miss Fisher a fact, an important fact! 'They just tear things that are tied down. No matter, Miss Fisher. I'm sure that the *Hinemoa* can afford to lend me another sou'wester. Have some of this chicken Véronique, it's very good.'

'Thank you,' said Phryne. Exercise and cold air always sharpened her appetite. She noticed that the Wests were not at lunch, though the rest of the cast was complete.

'And my niece Margery is going to try a Madrassi curry, which I asked the cook to make,' beamed Mr. Aubrey. 'Did you enjoy the keas, Miss Fisher?'

'Very much,' said Phryne.

'But this is such a strange place,' said Mrs. Cahill. 'Don't you feel those high cliffs closing in on you?'

'No,' said Mr. Mason. 'But I'd like to try climbing them. Must be possible. I mean, trees grow on those slopes.'

'So do supplejack and bush lawyer vines,' the professor told him. 'But you're welcome to try. You'll need spikes if you want to attempt the glacier.'

'No gear,' confessed Jack Mason. 'I left all that stuff behind in Melbourne. Pity. Not country you could just take a nice healthy walk in.'

'Not without a machete and a compass,' said the professor.

'And a gallon of the doctor's insect repellent,' added Phryne. 'Great stuff. I haven't got a single bite.'

'Well, I'm going to try for a walk,' said Mason, getting up. 'Shake some of the fidgets out of my legs. We don't sail till morning, right? I'll be back by then.'

'Take care,' said Miss Lemmon.

'Take care?' said Jack Mason, grinning. 'I don't care.' He strode out of the Palm Court.

'What a trying young man he is,' commented Mrs. Cahill. 'I'm glad my sons weren't like him.'

'Yes they were,' said Mr. Cahill, grinning at his wife. 'You remember when Jim rode the wild brumby? When Andy got thrown and had to bush bash for ten miles to get home? Wasn't it Jim, when he was a nipper, who climbed the water tower and couldn't get down and wouldn't call for help and stayed there all night?'

'Oh,' said Mrs. Cahill, faintly. 'Yes.'

'They were good boys, but,' said Mr. Cahill comfortably. 'No life for a boy, ship like this. Needs to be down with the stokers, living like a man.'

'You're probably right,' Phryne told Mr. Cahill. 'His father wants him to be a lawyer.'

'He ain't got the makings of a lawyer. Give him to me for a year and I'd make him a good cattle man,' grunted Mr. Cahill. 'He's gonna break his neck doing something thickheaded. Boy's bored.'

'If he takes a nice long walk in the rainforest he won't be bored,' predicted the professor.

• ● ● ● •

Phryne met Dot in the corridor outside their suite.

'Nice service from Father Kelly,' she reported. 'I'm going to sit in the library and read my book.' Dot showed Phryne a book about saints' lives, suitable for a Sunday. 'You're going to talk to the Melody Makers?'

'Yes, and I've ordered the beer. You're going to have to do the sanctity for both of us. See you later,' breezed Phryne, and descended the Grand Staircase.

She found the musicians in a large panelled room which had been set up for rehearsal, with music stands and a litter of instrument cases. These had been stacked against the walls and the room now held a long table at which the Melody Makers were sitting, diverting themselves in various ways.

Lizbet rose from the floor, where she was assisting in the hemming of what looked like curtains.

'Hello,' she said. Phryne observed that she was chewing her cud like a cow. Lumberjack gum, she assumed. What a curious pastime. 'This is Miss Phryne,' said Lizbet to the Melody Makers. 'Friend of my Uncle Cec. She's trying to find out who's nicking the jewels.'

'Wasn't us,' said Mavis instantly.

'Everyone says that,' Phryne replied. 'But someone is stealing them. What I want to know is, who? And you ought to be able to tell me. You face the crowd and apart from making your excellent music, you have nothing else to do but watch the dancers. Two of these gems were stolen while the ladies in question were dancing. First Miss Van Sluys and her diamonds, and second the pink pearls of Mrs. West. And when I was dancing on Friday night, I felt a sharp tug at my neck, from behind.'

'Why didn't they get your sapphire, then?' asked Jo, the tenor, previously seen in evening dress, clad today in a nice quiet grey pullover and flannel bags.

'It was secured,' said Phryne. 'Now, I want to provoke your thoughts, so I have ordered a case or two of thought provoker.'

At her signal, Roberts the steward wheeled in a drinks cart. Underneath it was a case of beer bottles.

'Well, that's different,' said Violet, the flute player. There was a chorus of agreement. The vague residual resentment that a foreigner had invaded their sacred Sunday's rest evaporated.

Caps were uncapped. Amber liquid flowed. Sewing was laid aside, as were books, a game of draughts, three letters home, a crossword puzzle and a fiendishly complex jigsaw puzzle, still at the 'looking for a piece with a flat edge' stage. Cigarettes and, in Jo's case, a pipe were lit and the Melody Makers sat down to a good, solid gossip.

'First we must tell you that we like this ship,' exclaimed Magda in her throaty accent. 'My sister and I like the Melody Makers and the *Hinemoa*. The variety of music, it is extending our repertoire. Nowhere else do we get a chance to play Bach at lunch and jazz at dinner.'

'Yair,' drawled Joan, the cello player. 'Good company, good food, pretty good pay. Mind you, that's 'cos Mavis, when she sees a booking agent, comes over all feral and grows these long teeth.'

'With which she skins him alive,' agreed Lizbet.

'And then she sells him back his skin,' added Annie, with the bitterness to which all viola players are prone, while there are violins in the world.

Mavis blushed modestly at these heartfelt tributes. She was a middle aged, middle sized woman with cropped hair which was silvering and bright brown eyes.

'My girls work hard,' she said. 'They should be paid accordingly. If P&O wants us that badly, then they can be expected to pay well. Someone pour me a gin. Shall we introduce ourselves, ladies?'

'I reckon she knows most of us by sight,' said Lizbet. 'She's been looking at us while she was dancing. I seen you, Miss Phryne. Every night.'

'Well, yes,' Phryne admitted. 'You are more interesting than anyone I have been dancing with.'

'Let's see,' said Jo, puffing on her pipe and putting her feet on the table. 'You've had Teddy Green, who is a darling, but scarcely love's young dream. Jack Mason, which must be like dancing with a thunderstorm. Hasn't grown into his legs yet, that boy. Might be quite passable as a bear wrangler or an elephant handler, but ladies, no. That snake West must have been a nasty experience and I note you haven't repeated it. You've got taste. And old Mr. Aubrey, a certified sweetheart. Hmm. I see what you mean.'

Jo gave Phryne what she had only previously received from a man, viz, a slow, lecherous wink. Aha, thought Phryne, back suddenly with the Sapphics in Paris. No real revelation there, what with the male clothing and so on.

'Sorry,' said Phryne in answer to the wink. 'Blatantly hetero-sexual.'

'Can't blame a girl for trying,' said Jo amiably. 'More gin, Miss Phryne?'

'Thanks,' said Phryne, and mixed hers with a lot of tonic. 'You've seen them all,' said Phryne. 'Rack your brains for me, ladies. Do you recall Miss Van Sluys losing her diamonds?'

'Such a hullaballoo,' said Katrina, fanning herself. Screaming and carrying on. She was dancing with Jack Mason when it hap-pened.'

'Was she indeed?' asked Phryne. 'Does anyone else remember that?'

'But yes,' said Magda. 'We were doing a slow foxtrot to "Bye, Bye, Blackbird", everyone was dancing around, it was getting late, Mavis had just told us, two more songs and then "Now Is the Hour", and then—she started to shriek.'

'And she was dancing with Jack Mason?'

'She was,' confirmed Annie. 'I play percussion for the dance band. I'd just had to fight the oaf off when he wanted to play my drums—there is always some idiot who wants to play the drums—so I sent him off to dance with the pretty girl. She was a pretty girl, too. Spoilt as a hothouse flower. But pretty.'

'And pretty rich,' agreed Mavis. 'Her father offered a hundred quid's reward for the return of that necklace so we discussed it carefully. But none of us saw anything. It's hard to see details when the lights are low, because the available light comes through the Tiffany garlands and it's all colours.'

'Yes, of course,' said Phryne, sipping.

'Then when the West pearls went west—sorry—she was dancing with Jack Mason. Don't think we didn't think it was him, but we really couldn't see how he'd done it, and anyway, where did they go? Everyone was searched. He couldn't have swallowed them,' Jo pointed out. 'Besides, I don't reckon he's clever enough to do something as ingenious as this. Not a bad boy, but not that bright.'

'I think he might be cleverer than he looks,' said Magda darkly.

'Just because he's proof against your charms...' began her sister.

'And has he fallen into your arms?' retorted Magda.

'Ladies, ladies,' interrupted Phryne. 'Have another drink. Do you mean that neither of you has managed to...er...engage Mr. Mason's attention? Really?'

Magda glared at Katrina. Katrina glared at Magda. For a moment the room was quiet. Then Katrina laughed and Magda embraced her.

'Neither of us,' they admitted, together.

'He must be ill,' said Phryne, finding this hard to believe. The Czech sisters had 'it' in volcanic proportions, whether one favoured the cool, flaxen, blonde Magda or the dark, smouldering passionate Katrina. 'I may have to look at Jack Mason again,' she concluded. 'All right. Anything that you can tell me which might help?'

'You've probably worked out the cast of people by yourself,' Mavis told her. 'Your table three have been there in all the robberies. Let's see. Old Mr. Aubrey, he's a sweetheart. Everyone loves him. Just don't let him start showing you pictures of his grandchildren. He can go on about them for hours. Oh, and never try one of his curries. Phong, the Malay cook, makes them for him special. Has to use an enamel pot because they eat into the stainless steel. Professor Applegate? Very fair old lady. The Maoris think she's something special. We had some trouble with one of the Maori boys fancying Annie and just a word from the professor put him right back in his box.'

'I don't know what she said to him,' commented Annie, giggling at the memory. 'But he just folded up and slunk away. And she barely clears five feet high and he must have been close on seven feet tall and half a hundredweight. And when the crew tried to blame us for the thefts she told the officer that we couldn't possibly have done them because everyone was on stage, playing. No, nice lady.'

'Jack Mason, he's just a boy. He's here with Thomas, his man, snooty devil. Don't mix with such as us. Only drinks the best of wine. Lah di dah,' said Joan, coarsely.

'Mrs. West, silly bitch, always flirting.'

'Any suggestion that she does more than flirt?'

'Never heard,' said Jo. 'Don't care,' she added. 'Women like her give women a bad name.'

'Mr. West?'

'A snake,' said Jo. 'Never tips. Oily to his superiors and nasty to his inferiors. We don't like Mr. West.'

'How about the Cahills?'

'Nice old bloke, real bushie,' said Violet. 'She's nice too. Come into money late, I reckon, bit out of their depth. That's why they look after the pennies. But he asked us to play "Paddlin' Madeline Home" for her, it being her favourite song or something, and we did, and he gave us a shilling. No harm in them,' opined Violet.

'And how about the Singers?'

'They're not nice,' said Magda. 'He is in pain and cruel to her, she is desperately trying to please him, and the more she tries, the less she pleases. It is sad,' she concluded, looking Slavic.

Her sister nudged her. 'What about Mr. Singer asking you all those questions?' she prompted.

'Ah yes, it was strange. He wanted to know everything about the crew,' she said. 'I told him it was no use asking me, the crew do not like us and I do not know any of them.'

'What was he asking?' Phryne was beginning to feel the effects of too much gin in the afternoon.

'Names, he had a list of names he was looking for. All men. I told him to ask someone else. He swore at me. I cursed him. That was all.'

'Mr. Forrester?' prompted Phryne.

'A lecher,' said Mavis. 'But a polite one. Knows what "no" means.'

'How about Miss Lemmon?' Phryne persisted.

'She's enjoying it. Takes after her uncle. That's about all we can tell you, Miss Fisher.'

'Yes, I'm afraid it is,' said Phryne, getting up carefully. 'Drink the rest of the drinks, girls. When you've finished call Roberts to take the cart away. Thanks for a very nice talk,' said Phryne, and went out.

She leaned briefly against the wall, then tacked her way up the Grand Staircase to her own suite. When she got there she fell into the embrace of her bed and fell instantly asleep.

Mr. Arthur Emery
London

Dear Pa
Mommy says you will be sailing soon on a new big ship. We miss you. Sal says can you bring her some of that Oxford marmalade? And I would like some fudge. That English kind with nuts in. Well that's about enough from me.

Your loving daughter
Marnie

PS and maybe a cute little white doggie? That kind called West Highland? With a plaid collar? Papa darling? Please?

Chapter Eleven

Let the day be time enough to mourn
The shipwreck of my ill-adventured youth

S Daniel
'Sonnet'

Phryne woke, conscious of a headache which drinking gin during the day, as she had often been told, always produced. She sniffed. Odd. She could smell a gamy, male smell, reminiscent of unwashed fox and damp fur. She opened her eyes—carefully, in case any important bits of her head fell off. Two green eyes looked into hers. The eyes were surrounded with nibbled grey fur and topped with two deckle edged ears.

'Hullo, Scragger, old chap,' murmured Phryne, getting creakily to her elbows. 'P&O aren't going to like you napping on their silk coverlet. I, on the other hand, must have coffee, and aspirins, and a lot of cold lemonade, rather quickly. What will you have? Bracing saucer of milk?'

Scragger considered her offer and put his head back on his paws. Phryne reached for the phone and gave the answering voice an order. Then she shut her eyes against the light.

When she opened them again, a tray was being carried in by Nick, the night steward, and Scragger was nowhere to be seen.

'You shouldn't drink with them musos,' reproved Nick, dropping a tablespoon of fruit salts into a glass of cold water and handing it to Phryne to drink. She drank. It was most refreshing.

'You might be right,' she murmured.

'Here's your coffee, extra strong from old Leo. Here's a nice jug of iced lemonade. Got your aspirin?'

'Thanks,' said Phryne, medicating herself and taking a long draught of the lemonade to sweeten the bitterness. 'What time is it?'

'Just on five, Miss. Caroline's helping the poi girls rehearse so I said I'd answer your bell myself.'

'Thank you very much,' said Phryne, pressing a coin into his hand. 'What's poi?'

'Prettiest dance you ever saw,' Nick assured her. He went out, shutting the door. Scragger must have seen his chance of escape and taken it, but his flavour, so to speak, lingered in the air. Phryne opened the French windows. The fog was lifting. The westering sun was silvering the mist and touching the peaks with gold light. Phryne sat down to drink the rest of the lemonade and make a firm resolution about quantities of gin during the day.

But there was something she had forgotten to ask those girls, and she would have to go and ask it. That meant getting up, which she was not keen to do. Perhaps it was in her notes. She found the Pierrot bag and scrabbled in it.

There it was. Both of the ladies whose gems had been pinched from their person had been dancing with Jack Mason in the Grand Salon. That meant that it must have been Saturday, when the dancing was transferred from the Palm Court to that beautiful bejewelled room.

The other two thefts had taken place, respectively, on a Sunday and a Tuesday. From the cabins of the ladies in question. Phryne felt that this might be significant, but could not precisely see how. The masquerade was going to be in the Grand Salon. She must keep her eyes peeled.

But just now she needed more lemonade and a little more rest. She gulped down a couple of glasses and waited to see if they were staying. They were. Leaving the windows open, she lay down and drew the satin comforter over her legs.

When she woke again Dot had arrived and Phryne's headache had left. Both of these events improved her outlook. She stretched.

'Hello, Dot, nice read?'

'Yes, Miss. Maggie and Mr. Thomas wanted me to go for a walk with them but I said I didn't feel like it.'

'A wise decision. Besides, you can only go about a hundred yards along the track and then—forêt sauvage. Straight out of Chaucer with wild boars in. You'd need a bulldozer to get through it.'

'That Mr. Mason, he's gone for a walk,' said Dot, getting out a suitable evening gown for Phryne.

'No doubt. He was threatening to do so at lunch. Well, he'll either catch the ship in the morning or he won't. It's a pity that so young a man is bending such a lot of effort towards breaking his neck, but there we are. What do you know about Maggie and Mr. Thomas?'

'Maggie's Mrs. West's maid. She's been with her for years. She's a bit silly, Miss.'

'Maggie or Mrs. West?'

'Maggie. Well, both, really, but I meant Maggie. She thinks Mrs. West is ever so beautiful and fashionable and lovely. She's generous with clothes that she doesn't want anymore and she gives Maggie a lot of make-up and so on. She says Mr. West is mean to Mrs. West and jealous of her, and in private he begs and pleads, and Maggie thinks he's not very manly.'

'God preserve us from being judged by Maggie!' said Phryne piously. 'In view of the dance she leads him, one might expect Mr. West to beat his wife. Would that be more manly?'

'I s'pose,' said Dot, who had firm views on beating women.

She was against it. 'I told you Maggie was silly. Anyway, she gets herself up like Mrs. West, all shiny and scented and not a lot of clothes. But she's a bit short and stubby and the dresses don't really fit her.'

'Poor Maggie,' said Phryne. Dot, who had not thought of the situation like that, thought about it and nodded.

'Yes, I s'pose. But all the men chase her.'

'Does she favour anyone in particular?'

'Yes, Mr. Thomas. She really dotes on him.'

'And what's he like?'

'I don't see it,' said Dot, puzzled. 'I really don't. There's some nice young blokes amongst the crew. She could have her pick. Well, not for marriage or anything respectable, but for…you know.'

'Dalliance,' supplied Phryne, brushing her perfectly black, perfectly straight hair. Dot blushed and deposited *The Lives of the Saints* face down on her lap, in case it should be shocked. 'She might not be after a full-blown affair, Dot dear, just someone to flirt with. Which is harmless enough.'

'Maybe,' said Dot. 'I don't know enough about such things, God be praised. I never flirted with my fiancé Hugh.'

'You didn't need to. The essential goodness and charm of your character was enough for that excellent young policeman.'

'I wonder how he's going?' Dot said, drifting off the topic.

'I'm sure he is fine,' said Phryne gently. 'Now, by contrast, Mr. Thomas?'

'He's tall and slim,' said Dot, wishing to give the man his due. 'And very well dressed. Mr. Mason is also generous with his clothes and they're the same size, Mr. Thomas says, so useful if one runs out of socks—that's how he talks. He's got dark hair and dark eyes and he's—I don't know, Miss, I just don't like him. He's jokey about Mr. Mason, calls him The Kid, and seems happy to tell everyone about his life—how he hates his father and his father hates him, how he was going to betray his class and play football for a living, how he does Swedish exercises in the nude every morning. He's not what I expected a valet to be.'

'So he's not there because he likes Mr. Mason,' concluded Phryne, putting down the hairbrush. 'I wonder if he owes his allegiance to Mr. Mason senior? Is he, in fact, a spy for Jack Mason's father?'

'I wouldn't put it past him,' said Dot darkly. 'Now Maggie, though she talks about Mrs. West all the time, doesn't say anything about her private life. I was wondering if there was a lover, Miss, because of, well, the clothes and the manner and all, but I couldn't find out from Maggie. She just prims up her lips and says it's none of her business to gossip about her lovely Mrs. West.'

'Very proper,' approved Phryne. 'Do we know what either of these people did before they were servants?'

'This is Maggie's first job,' said Dot. 'Mrs. West picked her from a group of girls straight out of school who wanted jobs as personal attendants. Mr. Thomas is older. I think he said he was thirty-nine. I don't know what he did before. He never said.'

'Any guesses, Dot?'

'Never done hard work,' said Dot. 'He's got no little scars on his hands that brickies and carpenters and mechanics get. Writes very pretty. Could have been someone's secretary, perhaps. Might have worked in a restaurant. He carries a tray like a waiter, flat on one hand. He's a bitter sort of person. Might have been educated for something better and lost all his money. Maybe that's why he doesn't respond to Maggie. She's working class. He might think she was too common for the likes of him.'

'Dot, you amaze me,' said Phryne.

'How did you get on with the musicians?' asked Dot, laying out underwear and stockings and changing the subject. She had never really known how to cope with compliments. Phryne poured herself another glass of lemonade.

'You were right about the way they drink. Like fish. But a nice group of women, no worse than the rest of us. They know the crew don't like them and they return the favour. They work hard. They know a lot of things, but nothing germane to the issue. However, I have worked out that two jewel robberies took place on the dance floor in the Grand Salon, and I think we should take a very careful look at Jack Mason, who was dancing with the ladies at the time they were bereft of their bijoux.'

'He's got reasons,' said Dot. 'No money of his own and no profession that he likes. If he had some capital he could strike out on his own.'

'True. But I wouldn't have said that he had any ambition or any idea of what he would like to do. Not much point in taking that kind of risk if you haven't got an end in view, eh?'

'But he likes risks,' responded Dot. 'You said he was going walking in that wilderness for fun. He used to climb mountains. That's a mad thing to do. If you ask a mountain climber why they are doing it they always say—'

'Because it is there,' quoted Phryne. 'A point, Dot, a palpable point. It is noticeable that the people who lost their jewels were not nice people. A quixotic young man might take the view that they had it coming. Hmm. I'll have to think about this. Any gossip about him and Mrs. West?'

'Lots, Miss, but no one has any proof. No one's seen him go to her cabin, for instance, or seen her come to his. If they are carrying on, it's somewhere secret, and a ship hasn't got a lot of secrets.'

'You've got that right,' agreed Phryne. 'Lord, it's seven already. Off you go to dinner, Dot, I can climb into this dress on my own. And be cautious with the gathering of gossip. You've already been assaulted once.'

'I'll be careful,' said Dot, and went out.

Phryne dressed herself in her fourth dark blue dress, a long brocade garment slashed with green silk like a doublet, and put on the sapphire. It really was a beautiful thing, she thought, watching the light catch the star at its centre. Beautiful and deadly, even though the story had been a complete fabrication, with apologies to Conan Doyle and the Sign of Four. And the stone was, of course, glass. Most of the great stones had curses on them, if not visible blood. It was a solemn thing to hold in the palm of one hand something that (if real) was worth so much. What could one buy with the value of one sapphire? Freedom from a wife or husband no longer loved? A new life in a distant colony? A house, a wife, a different fate?

She shook herself and went out.

• ● ● ● •

Sunday dinner was accompanied by skilled tinklings from the piano. Table three was all present and accounted for as Phryne came in, save and except for the errant Mr. Mason, presumably still walking on the Milford Sound shore.

'Boy's probably knee deep in a morass by now,' said Mr. Aubrey.

'Or lost on a mountain in the snow,' said Miss Lemmon, who had a soft heart.

'Or perfectly safe in the hotel and suffering splendid hardships,' capped Professor Applegate dryly. 'Good evening, Miss Fisher. That is a very pretty gown.'

'Thank you,' said Phryne. 'Hello, Doctor.'

Doctor Shilletoe jumped when addressed, knocked over a glass, and said, 'Oh, hello, Miss Fisher.'

'Done any more long distance medicine?' asked Phryne politely.

Doctor Shilletoe jumped again, spilled the salt he was holding, and knocked his fork to the floor, whence it was retrieved and replaced by an attendant.

'No, it's all been really quiet,' he said. He reached for his glass and Phryne managed to stop him from knocking it over as well. She folded his fingers around the stem and watched him raise it to his mouth. It was indeed fortunate that he had not had to do any surgery lately, what with his hands shaking like that. What was wrong with the man?

Even Mr. Singer had noticed and, being Mr. Singer, commented. 'You been at the surgical spirit?' he asked. 'Ouch,' he added angrily.

'I'm so sorry,' said Margery Lemmon sweetly. 'I seem to have inadvertently kicked you in the ankle. How clumsy of me. Steward, can we get Mr. Singer some more beer? And a gin fizz for me. Miss Fisher?'

'I'm rather off alcohol at the moment,' said Phryne. 'Just lemon squash, please.'

'More beer,' said Mr. Singer.

'A glass of wine,' said Mrs. Singer. The table looked at her. Mrs. Singer had previously confined herself to nothing more intoxicating than ginger beer.

'What sort of wine?' asked the steward. 'Red or white, madam?'

'Oh, I don't know…' Mrs. Singer's courage was ebbing away.

'A nice glass of gewurztraminer,' said Phryne. 'In all probability, you'll like that, Mrs. Singer. And what are we eating tonight?' she asked the steward.

'A little onion soup, Miss Fisher, tournedos of beef, asparagus and creamed potato, trifle for dessert,' said the steward.

'Wonderful. Very French. Make my tournedos rare, please.'

The doctor was sitting between Miss Lemmon and Mrs. West, crumbling bread between his fingers. Mr. Aubrey started a charming but lengthy story about his time in the India Office. Phryne listened abstractedly. Mr. West drank straight whisky and glared indiscriminately at everyone. He was clearly in the sort of temper where no amount of piano accompaniment would soothe his savage breast. Miss Lemmon was adding a few comments about Indian customs and Mrs. Cahill was putting in some remarks about how the local Australian Aborigines had not appreciated attempts to convert them to Christianity. Mr. Singer ate his omelette moodily. Possibly his ankle was still aching. Miss Lemmon was a sturdy woman who could probably give him a reasonably memorable kick. Mrs. West was smiling at Doctor Shilletoe.

Dinner was as good as ever. Conversation drifted from Indian politics to Indian gods.

'Can't offend native sensibilities,' said Mr. Aubrey. 'That's why the missionaries mostly got a less-than-enthusiastic welcome, as you know, Margery. Nothing against them personally, you understand. Just that India is very old and very well balanced, on the whole. Introducing a new religion into the middle of that collection of gods and demons might upset the whole applecart.'

'But they'd say that there are millions of people in India to be brought to the light, Nunc,' protested Miss Lemmon.

'Yes, yes, m'dear, but not unless they want to be,' said Mr. Aubrey. 'I know that it's hard to believe that some of the heathen are happy in their darkness, but they seem to be. Happy and principled and law abiding, which is rather to my point. Anyway, you must have noticed what happened. The Hindu just decided that Christ was an incarnation of Krishna—note how close the names are—and went on as before.'

'I suppose so,' said Miss Lemmon. 'Actually, the missionaries I know spent much more time on the natives' bodies than their souls. Persuading families to take care of girl babies was enough of a feat for them.'

'If they did it, my dear Margery, then they did a heroic thing,' said Mr. Aubrey. 'My goodness yes. But there are ways to use religion to make social changes. Consider the worship of the rat god. That was a real problem in places where the black death is still raging. One good way to foil the advance of the epidemic is to kill the rats, but you can't when the rat is a god.'

Mr. Singer stood up, growled, 'Can't you people talk about anything civilised?' and strode away. Phryne noticed Mrs. Singer automatically rise to follow him, then tell herself something very firmly, sit down again, and sip her wine cautiously. She seemed to like it.

'Odd bloke,' grunted Mr. Cahill. 'Go on, Mr. Aubrey.'

'Oh no, please,' said Mrs. West faintly. 'I mean, rats, they aren't dinner conversation. Or the black death.'

'Tell you later, then,' said Mr. Aubrey gamely.

'And what would you like us to talk about, Mrs. West?' challenged Phryne. 'What do you think civilised conversation ought to be?'

'Oh, I hadn't thought about it,' said Mrs. West. 'People, I suppose, and clothes, and…things.'

'You're a fool,' said Mr. West. This was demonstrably true, but unkind.

'What are you wearing to the masquerade?' Phryne asked Mrs. West directly. 'I saw the musicians hemming what looked like yards of net. Have you thought of a costume yet?'

'Oh, no,' said Mrs. West brokenly. She fumbled for a very small lace edged handkerchief and dabbed at her eyes.

'We're going to make Mrs. Cahill into a princess,' Phryne told her. 'Miss Lemmon?'

'Oh, I shall manage,' said Miss Lemmon smugly. 'But I can come and help you if you like. I can do plain sewing quite well. I used to help my Ayah make our clothes in India.'

'Good. Come along to my cabin at eleven in the morning and we shall see what we can scavenge. All right, Mrs. Cahill?'

'Very kind,' Mrs. Cahill beamed.

'Damn nonsense,' said Mr. Cahill. Mrs. Cahill froze, disappointed and hurt. Then Mr. Cahill grunted, 'Always looked like a princess to me,' and gave her a one armed squeeze which did not interfere with his manipulation of his soup spoon. Mrs. Cahill, Phryne and Margery Lemmon laughed.

'And I am sure that the doctor can let us have some supplies,' Phryne said deliberately, attempting to attract the young man's attention, which seemed to be entirely engrossed in advanced bread pill making.

'Doctor?' prompted Miss Lemmon, giving him a gentle nudge.

'Eh?' he asked, lifting his head but avoiding Phryne's eyes. 'Oh yes, certainly. Anything you want.' He went back to the bread.

Now I wonder, thought Phryne, if this has anything to do with Dot's descent into the unknown? What was the source of the drug that had put her so comprehensively to sleep? Doctor Shilletoe could not have looked more guilty if he had poisoned the entire crew. He was avoiding everyone's eyes. He had eaten little and drunk two glasses of wine. It looked suspicious to Phryne. Of course, there could be other explanations. Her nasty cynical mind was already looking for possible lovers at the table.

And Mrs. West came up as the most likely. Mrs. Cahill and Mrs. Singer were unlikely. Miss Lemmon had a tendre for Jack Mason, though possibly neither of them knew it yet. Had Mrs. West seduced the doctor? If so, why? And was that the source of Mr. West's evil mood? No harm in asking.

'Finish up your trifle,' urged Phryne, 'and take a walk with me.'

The young man shoved his untouched trifle under his spoon and rose with the wholehearted willingness of one being conducted to the close embrace of the Iron Maiden. What on earth was wrong? He had seemed quite straightforward and attractive when she had spoken to him before.

Phryne took his arm and led him up the steps to the lido, where the darkness shimmered on the cataracts leaping down the face of the glacier. The cold was like the breath of an ice-box. Doctor Shilletoe's arm, under her hand, was as tense as steel.

'What on earth is the matter, my dear?' she asked him when they were well out of earshot. There were no other walkers on the sun deck this night.

'I can't tell you,' he gasped.

'You'll feel better if you do,' she advised him, releasing him in order to light a cigarette. 'Let me guess, then. You've made a dreadful medical mistake and poisoned the captain?'

'No,' he said.

'You've found typhoid amongst the crew,' suggested Phryne.

'No,' he said, almost laughing.

'Then it isn't as bad as all that,' she told him.

'Oh yes it is,' he said. 'Sorry, I know you're only being kind. But it's worse than that, a lot worse. You see, I could cope with those things. But I can't cope with this.'

'With what?' asked Phryne.

'Sorry,' said the doctor, and ran away, quite literally, clattering down the stairs like an avalanche.

'Well,' said Phryne to herself. She finished the gasper and went back indoors. She wanted to hear the end of the story about the rat god.

When she returned the table had broken up. Mr. and Mrs. West had gone and Mrs. Singer was on her second glass of wine and was flushed with Dutch courage.

'Tell us about the black death and the rat god,' Phryne encouraged Mr. Aubrey.

'Well, it was quite a problem, you see. Plague on its way. Rat god worshipped in almost every house. Millions of the beggars around, fat as butter. Disaster ready to happen. So my young colleague thought about it and then he sent to England for the Staffordshire potteries to make him a porcelain master copy, which he had manufactured in Benares by the thousand. Thousands and thousands of statues of Ganesha, the god of household happiness.'

'He's a blue elephant,' Miss Lemmon informed them. 'A very lucky idol.'

'And anyone who wanted could apply for a statue of Ganesha, free to each household,' said Mr. Aubrey. 'They were really very beautiful—I believe that now they are very valuable—and most people came to get one. This largesse was explained as the government wishing to honour Ganesha, which was an acceptable explanation.'

'So everyone has a blue elephant,' said Mrs. Cahill. 'How did this affect the rat problem?'

'Oh,' said Phryne, enlightened. 'Elephants are supposed to hate mice. In fact they don't like small things running around their feet, my friend who has elephants tells me. So maybe Ganesha doesn't like rats?'

'A drink for Miss Fisher!' beamed Mr. Aubrey. 'If Ganesha is in the house, the rat god cannot be there. And that goes for his rats as well. A not very subtle gift of packets of rat poison almost cleared the city of rats, and the plague didn't get to my clever colleague's province.'

'Bravo,' said Phryne, and proposed a toast to Ganesha.

Madame Le Roux
Toulouse

Dear wife, I have a good position with a master chef on this maiden voyage to New York. I will look about me when I arrive in America and if there is any chance that we could make a good living there, I will send for you. Kiss little Jeanne for me. And strive to get a good price for the red cow's calf.

Your loving husband
Pierre

Chapter Twelve

Beasts did leap and birds did sing
Trees did grow and plants did spring

R Barnfield
'The Nightingale'

Monday

Sunday night lacked incident, which was nice of it. At dawn Phryne was vaguely aware of the engines starting up and the ship beginning to move again, so gently and slowly that it rocked her back to sleep. She woke knowing that something was wrong with her theory about the doctor. He had cared for Dot in her drug induced sleep without any sign of nerves. Something else must have happened to him since then.

Wondering what, she bathed, breakfasted, and welcomed Miss Lemmon and Mrs. Cahill to her cabin. Mrs. Cahill had an armload of dresses and the ladies spread them out on Phryne's bed to consider them. Dot, who had the quickest eye, selected a loose white satin sacque with a draped back, decorated with crystal beads.

'This one might do for the bodice,' she said. 'If we put it on back to front.'

Mrs. Cahill, in her dressing gown and foundation garments, obliged. Phryne saw that Dot was right. The loose draped back made a very pretty round front and was unshaped enough not to be uncomfortable.

'Then we just need to make a big skirt and stiffen it out, and put on a lot of beads. Or sequins. Or we might be able to paint it,' observed Miss Lemmon.

'We could make the underskirt out of that white petticoat and use another for the overskirt if I can unpick a couple of seams,' said Dot.

'Unpick away,' cried Mrs. Cahill recklessly. 'It can all be stitched up again, I presume. And if not, I can afford a couple of petticoats.'

'I'll go down and see if the laundrymen can find me any unclaimed undergarments,' offered Miss Lemmon. 'Seems a pity to ruin a good petticoat.'

'I'll come too,' offered Dot. 'I'd like to look at the laundry.'

'And we can see what jewels will suit the princess. What do you think, Mrs. Cahill? Would you like your own hair or a powdered wig? What was your favourite picture of a princess?'

'The one in the story book I had as a child,' said Mrs. Cahill, pink with excitement. 'She had a white dress just like the one we are making. Her hair was all loose, and she had a crown.'

'Let's take down your hair,' said Phryne, harvesting pins. Mrs. Cahill had a respectable length of hair. It was not of any particular shade and was dull and lank from being washed with soap, but Phryne knew a cure for that.

'A lovely lot of hair,' she commented. 'The girls at the salon will give you a shampoo and curl it. Not too tightly, just loose ringlets. And perhaps a brightening rinse.'

'Oh, I've never had my hair done,' said Mrs. Cahill.

'Have you a religious objection?' asked Phryne.

'Religious? No, it just seemed like a waste of money in the old days, and we lived so far out of town, and then—well, actually, Miss Fisher, there's no reason at all why I shouldn't go to the salon.'

'I'll call down for an appointment.'

'And you'll come with me?' asked Mrs. Cahill, as though she was being invited to take a frivolous visit to a dentist.

'Why, yes, of course,' said Phryne. 'You'll like it, I promise. Very soothing. Now, let's try out some jewellery.'

Phryne opened her jewel box and exhibited as fine a collection of paste as the art of Holland had ever made.

'Diamonds or pearls?' she asked.

Mrs. Cahill was taken aback at the blaze of facets from the box. 'Gosh,' she said. 'What a lot, and how lovely! The picture in the book had diamonds. Because of the witch, you know.'

'Oh yes, the nice sister who gave her food to the old beggar woman spilled diamonds from her lips whenever she spoke, and the nasty sister who told the beggar to starve somewhere else spat out toads. Just shows you that you have to be careful not to oppress the wrong beggar. This necklace? Or the other?'

'Oh, this one,' said Mrs. Cahill caressingly, opting for the traditional rosette pattern over the filigree deco vines and grapes.

'And you already have a diamond ring, which is good, because I don't have any with me,' said Phryne, who seldom wore rings. When she did they were invariably large and heavy, like the dragon and phoenix she had bought in Shanghai. 'I'm glad you like the rosettes. They belonged to my grandmother and my father was very cross when he found out that he had to give them to me. These earrings go with it, and this tiara.'

She piled jewellery on Mrs. Cahill, who looked in the mirror and saw—her own face, weathered skin, double chin and all. Her whole body sagged with disappointment. For a moment she had almost believed in transfiguration.

'Oh no you don't,' said Phryne, as the older woman's hand went up to tear off the crown. She had seen that reaction before. 'You are always you, no matter what you are wearing. But I promise you will look like a princess tomorrow night. Now, don't worry about the gems, they're paste copies. Keep them on so that you can get used to wearing the tiara. It needs balancing.

Let's order some coffee and then, perhaps, you might give me the benefit of your advice.'

'Of course, Miss Fisher,' murmured Mrs. Cahill, turning her head and feeling the weight of the tiara.

Phryne phoned in her order for coffee, tea and some petit fours, and then posed her question. 'What costume would Dot look good in?'

'She's a good girl, isn't she?' asked Mrs. Cahill, glittering brightly in her gems.

'Definitively.'

'And you're going as a Chinese lady?'

'Yes. In varieties of red. Manchu make-up, for which I'm going to need to buy some really white powder. Little red slippers.'

'Lovely,' said Mrs. Cahill. 'Well, she could go as your amah, you know, your attendant. I've seen them with fine Chinese ladies. In blue tunics and black trousers.'

'Nice, but I want her to look pretty on her own account.'

'I see,' said Mrs. Cahill.

She was artlessly pleased with herself again. Phryne warmed to her.

'How about Mr. Cahill?' she asked.

'He's got his awful old moleskins and his flannel shirt and his terrible old leather hat,' she said, blushing. 'He always brings them in case there's a chance to get on a horse. He'll go as a swaggie. And he'll be quite all right as a swaggie, bless him.'

'Nice,' said Phryne.

The refreshments arrived. Mrs. Cahill told Phryne 'You know, I have never sat around at nearly noon in my dressing gown like this. It feels positively sinful!' She giggled like a schoolgirl and took another petit four.

By the time Dot and Miss Lemmon came back, Mrs. Cahill had assembled a list of things that Dot could be. Dot had been most interested in the laundry, and the laundrymen, recognising Miss Lemmon's unaffected interest, had handed over three unclaimed petticoats, including a vast satin one which could have clothed La Paloma herself.

'This'll do,' said Dot, almost invisible under the waves of cloth. 'I reckon we can glue silver sequins on. I saw packets of them for sale in the shop.'

'Good, and now Mrs. Cahill is sorted out, we need to consider you,' said Phryne relentlessly. 'Here's your list, Dot dear. Pick one. Or make another reasonable offer. You shall go to the ball, Cinderella.'

Dot wondered if Cinderella had ever had moments when she wanted to stay quietly home in her kitchen and talk to the mice. But the list was interesting. Much better than Miss Phryne's suggestion of Lady Godiva.

'I reckon I spent enough time as a schoolgirl,' she said. 'Witches have warts. Indian maid sounds too complicated. But I'd like to sell flowers, or be a nurse, or a clown. As long as the costume is modest.'

'There are very few obscene clowns, flower sellers or nurses,' said Phryne comfortingly. 'I could borrow a nurse's uniform from the doctor, I expect. For a clown you just need to borrow some oversize gentleman's clothes and paint your face. And I've had an idea about the princess, too. What about making an overgown of gauze, like our grandmothers had?'

'It used to be called illusion,' said Miss Lemmon. 'My grandma wore it to meet the regent. Soft sort of transparent stuff, yes, very like gauze. We could loop it up with little knots of sequins.'

'Lovely,' sighed Mrs. Cahill. She settled back on the sofa. Mrs. Cahill was having a lovely day.

By popular agreement, stitching was to take place in Phryne's suite, where there was room to spread out. Caroline came in for the tea tray.

'Meant to say, if you need any seams done, I can do them on the machine,' she offered, and promptly disappeared under a cloud of satin.

Dot decided that she would like to be a nurse. In fact, she

was going as Edith Cavell, for whom she had always had a great admiration. Phryne appointed herself to go to the doctor and obtain a lot of gauze and a nurse's apron and cap.

She was still curious about that doctor. And had Jack Mason managed to get back on board before the ship sailed from Milford Sound?

Both of her questions were answered as she came to the doctor's rooms and heard the young man exclaim, 'But I can't see!'

'Entirely your own doing,' Doctor Shilletoe told him severely as Phryne came in without bothering to knock. 'If you'd used my insect repellent they wouldn't have laid a tooth on you. But no, you have to be a he-man. Not only do you have bruises on your bruises and ingrained thorns, you have about a million sandfly bites and all I can suggest is, if you want to be able to see for dinner, that you keep that wet boracic cloth over your eyes until then.'

'Hello, Mr. Mason, been having fun?' asked Phryne brightly.

The young man on the examination table groaned. 'I got quite a way up the mountain,' he said. 'But the undergrowth kept trying to strangle me and I had to come down. Then, I forgot about the repellent, so everything bit me. Apart from that it was fun.'

'Lucky you've got a mask for the masquerade,' said Phryne heartlessly. 'Shall I walk you back to your cabin?'

'No, curse it, Thomas ought to be outside,' uttered the Voice from the Tomb.

'No one there,' said Phryne.

'I'll sack him without a character,' said Jack.

'But you can't, can you? Daddy pays his wages so he gets to be as insolent as he wants. Which is pretty insolent.'

'Dammit, Miss Fisher—'

'Smeaton, can you get him back to his cabin?' asked the doctor. A smiling assistant in a white coat said, 'Yes, of course, Doctor.'

'Take this bottle of solution, lie him down, and wet the cloth again. And when you find his man, tell him two aspirin every four hours and calamine lotion for all the rest of his body. He's come out of this better than he deserves.'

Jack Mason, horribly swollen and limping, was led out by the assistant.

'And what can I do for you, Miss Fisher?' asked Doctor Shilletoe.

'I want about ten yards of gauze and a loan of a nurse's uniform,' said Phryne. 'And an explanation would be nice, but I don't insist on it.'

'Gauze and nurse's uniform, absolutely. Explanation, I really can't. I wish I could. There's no one I would rather confide in than you.'

He looked so bereft that Phryne came closer, gave him a small kiss on the nose and the benefit of a gust of Nuit D'Amour, and said, 'Never mind.'

A shell-shocked doctor doled out gauze with distracted generosity and Phryne left him to his patients.

The seamstresses went to lunch with a pleasant feeling of a morning well spent. The overgown was cut out and the main seams sewn by the obliging Caroline. Miss Lemmon had contributed just the right sort of sash to cover the gap between bodice and skirt and Dot had glued on several packets of sequins. Phryne had stayed out of the sewing, as her ability to tangle thread was legendary, but had amused the patient while she was being fitted. Lunch was excellent as always.

'We're out in the open sea again,' said Phryne to Navigation Officer Green. She had felt the ship lift and rock 'Where are we now?'

'Going round the bottom of the South Island,' he replied. 'On the way to Dunedin. Site of the first university in New Zealand. A boom town during the Gold Rush, but it has fallen into a bit of a decline. Nice architecture, Miss Fisher. It has an excellent museum and there we shall see one of the *taianui.*'

'What is a *taianui*?' asked Phryne, as she was required to do.

'The Maori people came to New Zealand from Polynesia,' he said. 'In these huge big canoes, the *taianui*. They must have been great navigators. It's not as though you can just fling yourself out on the bosom of the ocean and get washed ashore in New Zealand, Miss Fisher.'

'Yes, where would you end up if you didn't row?'

'America,' he said grimly. 'Eventually. Once you passed all those South Pacific islands.'

'I have a feeling that I have heard of some of Dot's saints doing just that, though,' she said, spooning up a quite excellent green pea soup. 'Irish saints. They just took a few essentials, like a bible or two, and writing implements, and...'

'Navigatio,' said Mrs. Singer very unexpectedly. She had a glass of gewurztraminer to hand and was eating a hearty lunch. Her husband was staring into his omelette with an expression of bitter astonishment. 'We learned about them in Sunday School. Saint Brendan in his coracle. And there was another one who made the voyage on a millstone. They just went out on the sea and trusted God to take them somewhere where they were needed. One of them ended up in Greenland, I think.'

'Not a navigational method which could be used in the present day,' said Theodore Green diplomatically. 'Did the Maoris have compasses, Professor?'

'They're a bit tight lipped about their methods,' said the professor, beginning on her poulet à la reine. 'They say that they were guided by the stars and the flight of birds and dolphins, and also by magic. People who live so close to the sea can tell a lot by how the water tastes and looks, you know. They say that they made a return journey, too, but I rather doubt it.'

'Why?' asked Mr. Aubrey.

'Because they didn't bring back any pigs,' said the professor. 'I can perfectly understand why the original settlers didn't bring pigs, what with the number of women and sacred items and so on that they had to fit into the canoes. But the idea that a return journey didn't pick up a few breeding sows is unlikely.'

'A good point. Nothing like a good roast pork with a lot of crackling,' agreed Miss Lemmon.

Mr. Singer groaned and left them. Mrs. Singer asked for another helping of poulet à la reine and a refill for her glass.

Mrs. West said to Phryne, 'I've decided on my costume, Miss Fisher.'

'Oh, good. Are you going to tell us what it is?'

'Circe,' she said. 'She was a sorceress in the old days, that's what Jack said.'

'She turned men into swine,' said Phryne. 'Not a long journey in some instances. That should be an intriguing sight. Mrs. Cahill is going to be absolutely beautiful, my companion is going as Edith Cavell, and Miss Lemmon is very mysterious about her costume.'

'I want it to be a surprise,' said Miss Lemmon.

Lunch concluded with the usual wishy-washy coffee and Phryne decided that this was a good chance to go for another swim, now Jack Mason was confined to his cabin with multiple sandfly bites. She reposed for an hour to allow her lunch to digest, put on her bathing dress and her cherry red rubber cap, and went out. Dot was still sewing.

When Phryne got to the lido she found that the wind was straight off the ice and it really was too cold. She called herself a piker and, dropping her robe and bag on the chair, dived in.

After that brief moment when the bather's heart stops and they are convinced that their end is nigh, it was brisk and exhilarating, and she swam up and down, occasionally diving, keeping as much of her skin under the water as she could. A cold rain began to bucket down, striking the surface of the pool like lead shot. It was much warmer in the water than it was in the air and she was arguing with herself about getting out. She was halfway up the ladder when a figure appeared from behind a wall and threw something soft over her head. She was pummelled and rolled in the covering, her assailant feeling all over her body, then letting her go with a misdirected blow which was meant to strike her head.

She was supposed to be unconscious, Phryne imagined, so she lay as still as she could, floating on the surface of the water, until she heard footsteps scurry away.

Then she had to unroll herself from the clinging material, which stuck closer than a brother. She recalled the Taoist story about the old man who fell into the rapids and emerged unscathed at the other end. Don't fight the water, let it carry you. Cloth wrapped her limbs like bands of kelp, dragging her down.

She began to feel real terror, tasting brass in her mouth, running out of air. Her lungs were demanding 'Breathe!' and her mind was saying 'Don't breathe!' and it was a toss-up if she was going to suffocate or drown before she broke through the folds and took a welcome breath which hurt all the way down.

She was entangled in her own gown. She gathered it in, got out of the pool, and sat for a moment on the sun lounge on which she had deposited her bag. She pulled off the cap. This was now personal. Someone had tried to kill her, or at least not cared whether she died, and all in pursuit of that wretched stone. Someone had rummaged through her property and ransacked her person. Now they were going to be very sorry, thought Phryne coldly, wringing out the gown and dragging it on. She wrapped the bath towel around herself, over the wet gown, took the bag, and went back to her cabin.

Fortunately Dot and Miss Lemmon were too busy to notice much and she got to her own bathroom without comment. She stood in the shower and allowed the hot water to fall on her freezing shoulders and counted her injuries: none, except for a minor bruise on the shoulder. There would not otherwise have been a mark on her corpse as it was dragged from the pool. Just an unwise young woman bathing too soon after lunch.

And, of course, they had not found the stone. It was in Dot's sewing bag, beside Dot on the floor of the suite, half buried in a thousand yards of white satin and net. Phryne wondered if other jewel thefts had not been noticed because the possessor had died unexpectedly on board *Hinemoa*. She needed to find out about that. Who to ask? Why, of course, Navigation Officer Theodore Green. Man of Facts.

Phryne dried herself vigorously, rubbing her feet and hands with a coarse towel. She put on her brightest red jumper with the grey suit. Being alive was nice. There were silk stockings if you were alive, and nice clothes, and perfumes. And meals. Come to think of it, she was ravenous.

She invited Theodore Green to afternoon tea in the Palm Court and he came in rubbing his hands. He observed that Miss Fisher had ordered a full Devonshire tea, with scones and jam and cream, and wondered where on earth, in that small frame, she put all that food.

'Hello,' she said, waving a hospitable scone. 'Someone just tried to kill me and that makes me very hungry.'

Theodore Green did not exclaim 'What?' or tell her not to worry her pretty little head. He was used to emergencies and alarms, and he just took a scone and said, 'Tell me.'

'I went for a swim, and just as I was getting out someone muffled me in my own robe and searched me, then threw me into the pool all wrapped up, with what should have been a stunning blow on the head. Fortunately I wriggled and he hit my shoulder instead. You may inspect the bruise if you wish. Now, I need to know—have there been any suspicious deaths on the *Hinemoa*? Unexpected drownings, for instance? Any people loaded with expensive jewellery who have taken an accidental overdose of their sleeping mixture?'

'This is awful,' said Theodore Green. 'Let me think.'

He thought about it. He ate another scone and poured himself a cup of tea. Phryne loaded her scone with jam and cream and reflected that the other nice thing about being alive was food. Great stuff. The creaminess of cream, the slightly acid sweetness of raspberry jam. The lightness of the scone. Theodore Green came out of his brown study.

'Perhaps,' he said. Two voyages ago, a Mrs. Reed was found comatose. The doctor had to pump her stomach. It was called an accident, she had been used to taking sleeping tablets and the bottle was left by her bed. The doctor said that she probably fell into a half-sleep and took some more, forgetting that she had taken any. Apparently that happens quite commonly. But at the time I thought there was something odd about it. She had been a cheerful sort of lady and she never seemed to recover her spirits. And there was another, a near drowning—rather similar to yours. That was a young gentleman. I don't recall him being able to explain what happened. Somehow his towel blew off the sun lounge, landed on him, and he became entangled in it and sank. He was a bit like Jack Mason—hanging after Mrs. West. I did wonder at the time if it was as much of an accident as it seemed.'

'Events have taken a nasty turn,' said Phryne enthusiastically. 'Good.'

'Good, Miss Fisher?'

'Yes, it means they are getting desperate, whoever they are. And desperate people make mistakes.'

● ● ● ● ●

Miss Unity Gordon
Somerset

Dear Unity, how sickening for you to catch measles and miss this trip. That's what comes of all that tiresome district visiting you insist on doing. It doesn't make you liked, you know, my dear. Those villagers of yours are just after what they can get. They just take your scarlet flannel vests and chicken soup and give you loathsome diseases. And I expect you have spots. I would hate my Albert to see me with spots. Anyway, pip pip my dear, cheer up and see you on the other side of the pond when you are spotless again.

Your friend, Christine

Chapter Thirteen

For sweetest things turn sourest by their deeds:
Lilies that fester smell far worse than weeds.

W Shakespeare
'Sonnet'

Having left Theodore Green with expressions of mutual concern, Phryne did not rejoin the sewing club but went to the library and read women's magazines. There are days when a good women's magazine, with a few tips on smart dressing on a budget, gardening advice on growing primroses, recipes for appalling canapés and a display of the most unlikely hats, is soothing to the spirit. Phryne leafed through *Women's World*, scanned *Australasian Vogue*, and settled down to read an article on recent developments in TB research in *Women's Choice*, always a good bet for a sensible person.

She was still wound up to a high pitch of nervous tension. What would have been very good for her nerves would have been a few hours in a suitable bed with a suitable lover, but she could not see her way to seducing an officer, in view of the risk they took, and none of her fellow guests were available or advisable, which were frequently not the same thing…

She finished the article, went to her suite and made certain preparations, and then went in search of Mr. Forrester. She found him in his cabin, contemplating an array of photographs spread out across his bed.

'Miss Fisher?' he asked in benevolent inquiry, rumpling his absurdly curly hair.

'I wonder if you would be so kind as to oblige me?' she asked.

'Why, certainly,' he began. 'What can I…'

Miss Fisher was unbuttoning her coat. Miss Fisher was pulling her jumper over her head. Miss Fisher was stepping out of her skirt. He was left in no doubt as to the manner in which Miss Fisher wished to be obliged.

'Delighted,' he said, moving to the door and bolting it. He swept the photographs into a pile and deposited them on the chair. He turned back the covers on his bed.

And there was Phryne. He might have been expected to have become accustomed to female flesh, he told himself as he stripped off his clothes with trembling hands. But he never had, never. She was smooth and beautiful and exceptionally willing and Mr. Forrester had to restrain himself from diving into bed with her, probably beating his chest.

Phryne wrapped herself around him like an amorous cat, and he was lost.

Mr. Forrester was never afterwards able to entirely describe making love to Phryne Fisher. It was, he finally concluded, rather like being hit by a thunderbolt which twined and twisted around the body, electrifying where it touched. A thunderbolt which knew what it wanted and meant to get it. A thunderbolt which, assuaged, turned into a very pretty young woman who was peacefully putting on her clothes while he lay ship-wrecked in his disordered couch.

'Thank you so much,' she said, finding and putting on her shoes. 'I think you can call me Phryne now,' she added, and went out.

Mr. Forrester had a short nap to recover his nerves. Phryne felt much more centred. She went back to the library and read the rest of *Women's Choice*. Then she read *Home*. All of it. Even the advertisement for marcel waves. Even the recipes for canapé Anglais using smoked tongue. Even the cocktail made of pickled onion juice. She contemplated it for a moment. One portion French vermouth, two portions gin, two dashes orange bitters, four dashes pickled onion juice; shake and serve with a pickled onion instead of a cherry. Amazing. And people said that the world was civilised.

Thereafter she watched the water going past and the dolphins dancing on the waves, racing the ship's shadow. It was a nice world, even if it did contain the pickled onion cocktail.

Four o'clock and time for Mrs. Cahill's appointment at the hairdresser's. Phryne sat in a pink plush chair and talked soothingly to the victim as the attendants clucked over the state of her hair, shampooed it with coconut oil shampoo, rinsed it with two changes of water and applied 'Sun Dew'. Mrs. Cahill was as frightened as a woman at an inexperienced tooth-drawer's to begin with, but gradually relaxed under the gentle fingers. The attendants took advantage of her immobility to apply a fine moisturising mask to her face and cucumber slices to her eyes, extinguishing any protests.

When she was rinsed again and allowed to sit up, Phryne judged that the brightening rinse had done its work; not so gold as to seem metallic, but enough to highlight the baby-fine hair. Mrs. Cahill seemed nervous.

'What will my hubby say?' she asked. 'I've never gone in for this sort of thing, even though it is very pleasant, girls, really nothing could be nicer,' she added, anxious not to offend her attendants.

'He'll say you look perfectly sweet,' said Phryne. 'Now, you need to sit under this HG Wells contraption and get that hair dry. Otherwise you will, my mother always said, catch your death.'

'Oh yes, my mother used to say that too. Tell me, Miss Fisher, my stewardess says you are titled! Is that true?'

'Merely the unimportant daughter of an unimportant baron,' said Phryne dismissively. 'Tell me, what is the attraction of all this travelling? You've been on lots of cruises, I understand.'

'I like the people,' said Mrs. Cahill, a little apprehensively, as the metal hood came down over her head. 'I like to travel, but I can't walk like I did once. Walter likes the places we go to. He's lined up a horse ride tomorrow when we go to the Maori village in Otago. Oh, how curious,' she observed, as hot air began to cascade down her neck. 'He hasn't ever got the hang of cars, so we can't go on motoring tours. And, you see, he promised the boys he'd stay out of their way for two years. He loves the station so much, but he has to retire, and they all three of them knew that if he stayed, it wouldn't answer; he'd never be able to let them run the place their way.'

'A very wise decision,' said Phryne. 'But it must have been a wrench to leave.'

'That's why the ship is good,' said Mrs. Cahill. 'It gives him new things to see every day.'

Phryne contemplated a father brave enough to endow his hard-won place on his sons and sensible enough to see that he had to leave it indeed if they were to have any chance of success. She was impressed.

Presently, her hair in loose curls, Mrs. Cahill went back to her cabin to impress her husband and Phryne found that sewing had concluded in her suite.

'All finished, Miss,' reported Dot, putting away the good scissors in their leather pouch. 'Margery and me were just going to order some tea.'

'A good idea. But, Miss Lemmon, I've had a thought. Would you be very kind and go and see that silly Mason boy? He's come back from his ill-advised adventure chewed and bruised, and I don't like that Thomas man of his, I don't believe he is likely to look after the boy. Would you look in on him and make sure he's all right?'

'Of course,' said Margery Lemmon. 'I don't like that Thomas either, Miss Fisher. We'll have tea another time, Dot. See you at dinner, Miss Fisher,' she said and, gathering up her sewing materials, left in something of a rush.

'Miss?' asked Dot suspiciously. 'You matchmaking?'

'She really does like him, Dot,' Phryne excused her meddling. 'She just hasn't noticed it yet. Now, let's have that tea, Dot, and a council of war. We're going to have to catch this jewel thief soon, because he's turned violent.'

'Did you hurt him?' asked Dot.

'I didn't even see him, if it was a him.' Phryne related the occurrence at the swimming pool.

Dot packed her sewing basket with its little reels of thread as she spoke. 'This is bad,' she concluded.

'It isn't good, but it must mean that they are desperate. Now, let's run through the suspects. I am leaving out Mrs. Cahill and her husband—I simply can't see it, and neither of them is spry enough to go bouncing round slippery surfaces. Same for Mr. Aubrey. Jack Mason is out because he was in the doctor's surgery being treated for multiple injuries.'

'Margery was here with me all the time,' said Dot.

'So that leaves Mr. and Mrs. West, Mr. and Mrs. Singer, the professor and Mr. Forrester. I am trying not to assume it is the Wests because I don't like them.'

'We really don't know where the Singers or the Wests were just after lunch,' said Dot. 'But Caroline said that the professor was in the crew's quarters, talking to the men about a haka.'

'What's a haka?' asked Phryne.

Caroline knocked and came in with tea. Phryne asked her the question. 'It's a dance,' she said. 'A war dance. The professor knows some very good ones. She's been with the boys for hours, running through some of them. I reckon they'll give the Moanapipi lot a run for their money.'

'You know, I understood every word in that sentence but I haven't the faintest idea what you mean,' said Phryne.

'You'll see tomorrow,' said Caroline, and left.

'All right, scratch the professor. One of the crew or the officers, or a West or a Singer. I know who I'd favour.'

'Yes, but...' Dot gnawed her lip. 'She's not strong enough.'

'She might be stronger than she looks. She can dance all night. A weakling couldn't do two solid hours of the quickstep, the bunny-hug and the turkey-trot, as I happen to know she can. And it wasn't a very hard blow, Dot. That might have been intentional, so no one would notice a bump on the corpse's head, or it might just have been as hard as she could hit.'

'We have to find out where they were this afternoon,' said Dot. 'I'll ask around at dinner, and you do the same.'

'Oh, and by the way, Dot, something not too nice has happened to the doctor. He's a bundle of nerves, poor man. See if anyone knows what it was. And if I was seen entering Mr. Forrester's cabin this afternoon—it's none of their business.'

'Everyone knows you're interested in his photographs,' said Dot. 'His steward says he's printing some for you special. He was saying that maybe they aren't all that bad. There's one of a lady and a baby that he says looks like the Blessed Virgin.'

'So it does,' said Phryne, and smiled. Gossip, it appeared, could work both ways. 'Now I am going to have a little nap, and then dress for dinner. We're dining at the captain's table tonight, so break out the blue satin and the sapphire panache.'

'Right you are,' said Dot. She opened the wardrobe, where Mrs. Cahill's princess dress glittered in all its sequinned finery. A nice lady, that Mrs. Cahill. Dot hoped that the person who had tried to drown Miss Phryne was caught soon. Otherwise Miss Phryne might have to get rough. And these New Zealanders might not understand.

· ● **●** ● ·

Phryne glimmered on the sight as she waited at the door of the Grand Salon to be announced. She was draped in satin of a peculiar night-sky blue, which showed off her arms and back and her pert profile remarkably like fine china. The Maharani sapphire glowed on her breast. Mr. Forrester, catching up with her, offered his arm.

'If I might have the honour, Phryne?'

'Certainly, Albert.' She smiled on him.

Professor Applegate, wearing her other Molyneux evening gown, a slightly frayed poem in black cherry brocade, smiled. She stopped smiling when Mr. West offered his arm. It was not done to refuse an escort, but she contrived to express, as she walked to the captain's table, that though she might be standing next to this man he was far, far beneath her.

Mrs. West giggled on Jack Mason's arm. The boracic lotion had worked. The inflammation had gone down, though he still looked like someone who had gone eleven bare-fisted rounds with the landscape and lost by a knock out.

Several other people had been in the wars, it seemed. Mr. West had a scratch on one cheek, a matching one appeared, patched with powder, on Mrs. West's face, and Mrs. Singer was walking stiffly, almost limping.

'It's nothing,' she said dully. 'I tripped. On a step.'

Phryne would have bet good money that she had tripped on a husband's temper. Wife-beaters never made the mistake of hitting their wives where it showed. Several bruised ribs, a kidney punch, a kicking of shins, a wringing of the upper arms—all effective, very painful, and invisible in ordinary clothes. Phryne's fingers itched for Mr. Singer's jaw. It was a prominent jaw, easy to hit, hard to miss with a reasonably competent punch. Or possibly a kick. A kick might be more satisfactory.

Phryne came back to herself as the captain took her hand. She surveyed him. A large, strong, healthy man, with white teeth, apple cheeks and those bright blue eyes with crow's feet caused by staring over long distances. His hand was strong but he did not squeeze too hard. Phryne liked him instantly. He said, 'Ah, Miss Fisher, you look lovely tonight!' and she did not doubt his sincerity.

The party from table three sat down. Captain Bishop's eyes had widened a little over the exposure of Mrs. West's flesh, but only a little. Phryne was pleased to see that Mrs. Cahill's newly curled hair, caught back in a clip, looked very becoming. Professor Applegate was affable, Mr. Aubrey charming as always and Mr. Forrester a little elevated, as though by wine. Only the Singers cast a gloom on the festivities. Phryne decided to take the initiative. Captains of cruise ships must have a hard life, she thought, dining with new people every night. Also, she did not want to figure in his memoirs as one of a table from hell. Compliments were required and they needed to be bold and simple to be effective.

'Captain, this is the most beautiful ship in the world,' she said. 'I have never seen anything like her.'

The captain beamed. The dinner was off to a good start. Soup was served, wine glasses were filled, and the evening commenced in good order.

Mrs. Singer took several glasses of sweet wine and said very little. Professor Applegate, who had a deal of worldly experience, gave her one glance, as intimate as a doctor's examination—she could have been mapping bruises—and engaged her in conversation about Maori myths. Mr. Singer scowled at his eggs Benedict and drank beer. Mr. Aubrey and the captain reminisced about the East, and Margery Lemmon and Phryne joined in.

'And what have my guests been doing all day?' asked the captain, smiling in a fatherly way as the roast beef was cleared away and the ice cream and fresh fruit were distributed.

'A little reading,' said the professor.

'A little walking,' said Mrs. Cahill.

'A little swimming,' said Phryne, watching faces.

'Nothing much,' muttered Mr. Singer. Mrs. Singer did not answer.

'We went to keep poor Mason company,' said Mr. West jocularly. 'Eh, Jack? Laid up on a bed of pain with all those bruises and his fellow gone who knows where. Went and played a few hands of cards with him.'

Margery Lemmon raised an eyebrow. 'That must have been after I left,' she said.

'That was kind of you,' said Phryne, abandoning her theory that West must have tried to drown her, but thinking it uncharacteristic. Mrs. West giggled.

'I spent the day on deck,' said Mr. Aubrey. 'Bracing part of the world, this. Wind straight off the ice. When do we dock in Dunedin, Captain?'

'Tomorrow morning. Then there's a visit to a Maori village and, tomorrow night, the masquerade. I hope you all have costumes,' said the captain. 'There are prizes, you know.'

'And I'm intending to win one,' said Mrs. West.

Phryne thought that she had already seen as much of Mrs. West's bosom as was healthy for an adult. She hoped that the Circe costume would be more dramatic and less revealing, but expected that she would be disappointed.

'Are there rules for visiting a Maori village?' asked Margery Lemmon. 'Do you have to take off your shoes as you do in a Muslim temple?'

'Yes, my dear, you approach in a body and wait until you are called to enter. Then you take off your shoes, because the floor is padded with a fabric called tukutuku. Then you sit in a circle on the floor while speeches of welcome are made, there is a meal, and you are expected to put money in the tray which will be passed around to pay for your entertainment. There will also be dancers. The ship's crew have challenged the Otago marae to a dance contest, which ought to be fascinating.'

'Do men and women dance together?' asked Mrs. West.

'Not in these dances. The women dance a poi dance, where they flick and turn a delicate ball of woven flax. It's very graceful. And the men dance a haka.'

'And a haka is…?' trailed Phryne.

'A war dance,' said the professor. 'A very good war dance. You will like it,' she said. It was more of a command than an expression of opinion. 'Every place has their own haka, and new ones are made up every day.'

'But your basic war dance remains "Come out, skulking

enemy, and we will convert you into cat food with these incredibly heavy clubs," ' said Jack Mason.

'Just as your Saxon ancestors must have danced it in the good old days,' responded the professor waspishly.

'Banging sword on shield and yelling insults,' said Mr. Aubrey. 'Nothing stirs the heart and thickens the blood like a good war dance. The Scots still have the sword dance and the kilt and the bagpipes.

'The Aborigines still do it,' said Mr. Cahill. 'Come to a border and yell and wave spears. Mostly don't end up hurting anyone. Makes all the young bucks feel like real heroes. Never saw any harm in it, myself.'

'Boys will be boys?' asked Margery Lemmon.

Mr. Cahill grinned at her. 'Well, Miss, they will,' he said. 'Be boys, you know. Look at Jack Mason there. No need to climb a mountain. Nice comfy ship with food for the taking. Needs to go and spifflicate himself on some cold rock. That's boys for yer,' concluded Mr. Cahill, and Mrs. Cahill sighed and nodded.

Dinner concluded in harmony, and Phryne went to her suite replete but puzzled. She had been sure that the author of her assault was one of the Wests, and now it seemed that it was not.

Jocelyn Chant
Birmingham

Dear Jocelyn, I know about Maisie. I know about the others, too. I can't stand the shame and humiliation any more. I'm taking the children to my sister Joanie in America. I shan't come back. Not again. You can write to me in Ohio but I shan't come back.

Goodbye.
One who was once your loving wife
Lucy

Chapter Fourteen

Rough satyrs danced, and Fauns with cloven heel
From the glad sound would not be absent long:

John Milton
Lycidas

Tuesday

The sun rose. Dot saw it. Phryne didn't. When she emerged on deck, the ship was navigating its way into Dunedin harbour, and there was the city spread out before her.

It looked like North Fitzroy. The buildings were predominantly late nineteenth century, decorated in the respectable colours of beige, brown and dark brown. Like Rome, it was built on seven hills. Unlike Rome, the heights of the Southern Alps made a backdrop for it, high and white and glittering in the early sun. The *Hinemoa* had come in through a fjord, and Dunedin was at the end of it. The mountains closed Dunedin as in a cupped hand. In the depths of winter, it was probably more like a clenched fist.

'That's the Otago peninsula,' said Navigation Officer Theodore Green. 'Home of seals and penguins and such like. Also home of our local Maoris, who mostly live in the North Island, due to it being warmer. I say, Miss Fisher, can you give me any good news about the...er...matter?'

'Last night I thought I had it all sorted out,' said Phryne frankly. 'Today I am not so sure. I am going to set a trap for the thief, and I shall let you know who falls into it. At least with me flaunting my bijou no one else has had anything stolen. Keep up your spirits, Mr. Green. Are you coming on this junket to the Maori village?'

'Marae, Miss Fisher, it's called a marae. Yes, of course. There is going to be a dance contest, and I have reasonable money on our girls. They're very serious about this.'

'And the haka?'

'Ah yes, well, they do have the advantage,' said Theodore Green. 'We have to dance it in sailor's clothes. They get to display their tattoos. But the professor is saying something about a secret weapon. She's a formidable old lady in Maori society, you know.'

'Indeed. Well, I'll go get my coat. Does this outing include lunch?'

'Certainly. I hope you like sweet potato,' he called after her as she went in.

'I shall be interested to try it,' replied Phryne.

An hour later twenty visitors—the maximum the village could accept—and all of the *Hinemoa*'s Maori crew came down the gangplank and boarded a little boat, which putted out into the harbour. It was another MV like *Adventure*, this one called *Wayfarer*. A self-important craft with views of its own on big ships.

Dot was with Phryne. She was still out of breath. She had almost been late, which, for Dot, was unforgivable.

'I'm so sorry, Miss, it was Primrose,' she said.

'The child with the teddy bear? What's wrong with her?'

'Mrs. Ryan said she was in hysterics, but she didn't seem hysterical to me, just furious. She says that someone tried to steal her bear. Came to her cabin and tried to drag him out of her arms.'

'How very singular. Was it true?'

'Her mother was in the recreation room and heard her scream blue murder, but she didn't see anyone by the time she got there.'

'Did the kidnapper get the teddy?'

'No, Miss, but something put a big gash in his belly. I've just been sewing him up again. What sort of devil would cut open a child's toy? They love their toys more than their mum at that age. It was cruel.'

'Yes,' said Phryne. 'Cruel. Did Primrose say anything about the kidnapper? Male, female, tall, short?'

'Said he had a black cloak and no face. Poor little thing must have had a nightmare,' said Dot.

'Nightmares do not cut open toys,' Phryne reminded her.

'Oh. So it was a mask, perhaps?'

'Or a stocking pulled over the face. I bet the child put up a fight!'

'She would have,' said Dot, chuckling. 'But she's all right now.'

'And I fancy that Teddy may now rest secure from further evisceration.'

'You know what this was about?' asked Dot as the little boat chugged across the water.

'The sapphire, Dot. He, she or they thought I might have put it in the teddy. This thief,' said Phryne meditatively, 'is building up really quite a record of bad deeds. He, she or they are going to come to a bad end, Dot.'

'I should think so!' said Dot indignantly. 'When?' she added.

'Oh, quite soon,' said Phryne. 'Quite soon now.' Phryne was angry. The only way that an informed observer could tell was that her lips were a little tighter and her winged nostrils flared as though she was smelling out her prey. Phryne in that mood made Dot uncomfortable. Her employer was about to happen to someone. And when she did, they would be sorry. Well, they deserved it.

'Where are we going?' asked Dot, not wanting to continue the subject.

'Moanapipi,' said Caroline, who stood nearby. 'It means "water of shellfish". I reckon they'll lay on a good feed of pipis. Haven't tasted a pipi for months. And maybe puaua, some crayfish, a few muttonbirds—no, not the season for muttonbirds. Lots of fish and kumara, anyway. It'll be good "kai", whoever wins.'

'I thought that the Maori preferred high places for villages.'

'That's forts,' said Caroline. 'You always put the "pa" on a high place. But this village, it was built for the cruise trade. The tribes in these parts nearly wiped each other out in wars. The survivors made peace and decided they'd better find a way of earning a living and this is it. The chiefs said the old ways were being forgotten, the old words were being lost, the wisdom, crafts, stories. So they put their heads together and came up with Moanapipi. Young blokes go there to learn the ways of men. They might go back to Dunedin to the university, but when they're here they're *iwi*.'

'*Iwi?*' asked Phryne.

'The tribe,' said Caroline. 'The *whares* are corker. All built in the old way. Carved doorposts and all. You'll like it,' she promised, and went back to her group of dancers. Several of them were nervously bouncing little balls of woven material from hand to hand.

The day was, surprisingly, fine and warm. Presently the MV *Wayfarer* put into a little inlet and its passengers disembarked onto a boardwalk over a sandy beach. Inland, this gave way to scrub. From the tangle came odd noises: a squealing, clucking sound like a mob of demented hens, mixed with the braying of a very small donkey, possibly caught in a mousetrap.

'And the noise is…?' she asked Professor Applegate.

'Penguins,' she replied. 'Yellow-eyed penguins. They've obviously got up late this morning. Here they come.'

Hopping, sliding, hurrying so fast that they tripped over their own flat feet, came yellow-faced penguins. Phryne had always liked the blue fairy penguins of her home beach. These were bigger, noisier and looked so brightly painted that they could have just come from the toymaker's hands with their paint still wet. The feathers on the head and around the eyes were bright sulphur yellow and the rest of the penguin was a pacific, decent bluish-grey shade which would match rocks, scrub and dark sand rather well. They paid no attention to the travellers, but rushed down to the water with cries and brays of delight and plunged in, swimming strongly like small bottle-shaped torpedoes.

'Charming,' said Phryne.

Presently the visitors came to a wire fence with a large wire gate in it. A sign in English said 'Moanapipi. Please wait here.'

A tall Maori man, naked to the waist and illustrated with blue designs, came to the gate and unlatched it. He allowed the party in, closed the gate again, and led them perhaps twenty paces through low scrub before he signalled to them to halt.

Caroline came forward, dragging the professor after her. Professor Applegate was actually blushing and pulling against Caroline's hand. 'No, no,' she was saying. 'I don't know these people. It's too great an honour. It ought to be you,' she told Caroline.

'But it's going to be you,' grunted Caroline. 'Hello,' she said to the tattooed man. 'All shipshape. You can start.'

He nodded and waved to someone out of sight behind the scrub. Professor Applegate settled her garments, cleared her throat and called, pitching her voice to carry: 'Hae–ere mai!'

'Hae–ere mai!' came a woman's voice, calling from the depths of history. Phryne shivered slightly. She had been at some strange ceremonies in her time, but this one seemed alien; stranger than the fire walkers in Fiji, older than the Bedouin sheep feast in Egypt. Call and challenge had to be answered by women, perhaps because no war band would have women in it—to have women with you was a guarantee of peaceful intentions.

Professor Applegate led them forward. Rough grass grew underfoot. Before them were a cluster of low houses, each with the crossed doorposts familiar from postcards. They stopped at a flat dancing floor in front of an imposing building.

There, waiting to greet them, stood a huge old man. He was

scribbled all over with warrior designs. He wore a feather cape of special magnificence, studded with red feathers. He was flanked by young men in native dress and behind him were a flock of women and children.

The old man gestured to his warriors and they lined up in front of him. They had spears and clubs. They were very formidable.

'No wonder they had to have a treaty with Britain,' said Mrs. Cahill. 'They look like good fighters!'

Stamp, stamp, came the dancers, their voices deep as the fjords. Stamp, crash, flourish of spears. Professor Applegate was translating.

'It is death, it is death,' said the professor. 'It is life, it is life.' Thump of bare feet on the grass, a horrible gesture reminiscent of neck-breaking. 'Ranks together! Stay abreast! Children of Tane, it is light! It is light!'

The warriors retreated a little as the line from the *Hinemoa* stamped and swayed towards them. Dot, who was hiding behind Mr. Cahill, felt a small warm hand inserted into hers. She looked down. It was an enchanting Maori child of some seven summers, in a little flax dress with a headband and feather. 'Don't be frightened,' said the child. 'It's all show.'

'Thanks,' said Dot. 'I won't be frightened now.'

Professor Applegate was translating again. 'It is fate, it is fate,' she said. 'From the sea, from the sea. Comes death in the morning. To our enemies! They flee! They flee!'

There was a gasp even from the old impassive chief. Professor Applegate had dyed the tongues of all of her haka dancers with blackcurrant juice. When they stuck them out all at once they looked frightful.

Then the chief laughed, lifting a hand. Weapons were put away. Women and children came forward. Caroline led Phryne to the chief. He bent toward her and, nose to nose, they pressed their faces together lightly. 'Hongi', the exchange of breath. Phryne had been briefed. The chief smelt of fish oil, with which his white hair and probably his body had been dressed. A sensible precaution for an Otago climate. He also smelt of pepper, or something like pepper.

'Now you take off your shoes,' the small girl instructed Dot. 'You put them there, in the porch. Can't wear shoes inside the meeting house.'

Everyone obeyed. Phryne was pleased that Mr. Singer and the Wests had not made the trip. They would have complained and it was too much to hope that they would have been speared.

'Sit, sit,' said the chief, conducting them into the building. 'Welcome. This is the *whare whakairo*. Later we go to the *whare kai*. Then we eat, now we talk. And the girls dance.'

● ● ● ● ●

Professor Applegate began her speech in Maori, then changed to English for the benefit of her audience. It was a graceful speech, thanking the chief for his welcome and congratulating him on the fierceness of his young men.

Phryne's attention wandered, as it always did during speeches. She considered the building. It was constructed of wood—where had they got such huge logs in this sandy place?—all of which had been carved to within an inch of its life. The walls were covered with fine fabric dyed and woven in brown and cream. The floor was wood and padded with the same cloth, which explained why they had been asked to remove their shoes.

The chief did not make a speech, but gestured to the tallest of his warriors. He spoke perfect educated New Zealand English, which sat oddly with his savage appearance. His speech, also, followed the same pattern; he thanked them for coming in the name of the chief and the tribe, made many complimentary speeches about the dangerous appearance of the *Hinemoa's* warriors, and then sat down as the young women came on to dance.

They were wearing Maori dress, a shift and bodice of flax and their hair was dressed high with many feathers and pins. They had a small ball of woven material in each hand, which was attached to the wrist by a thin flax thread. And they danced with a gentle undulation which reminded Phryne of a rippling stream.

'So graceful,' said Mrs. Singer. Dot's small girl was sitting beside her, delighted, singing along under her breath.

'Every tribe has their own dances,' said the professor. 'Every action song and dance means something in the life of the tribe, a bit of its history. The Maori didn't have writing until the *pakeha*—Europeans—came, so they remembered by means of songs.'

'What are all those carvings about?' asked Phryne.

'Too many to tell,' said the professor. 'History, myth, legends. *Tiparu*, the ancestors. Unfortunately this part of the world rather went in for civil wars. We're lucky that there are any Maori tribes left in Otago.'

The dance ended, the dancers were applauded and sat down, breathless. Then the *Hinemoa's* women rose, led by Caroline. They were all wearing their uniforms, which looked odd, but once they started to dance, Phryne forgot that they were cooks and cleaners and stewardesses, and watched the clever hands as they flowed, twisted, moved, and the little poi balls danced and spun on the warm air.

It was strangely soporific and very beautiful, and Phryne really only came back to herself when she was led, by Dot and a small girl, from the meeting house into a long house, where places had been laid on the floor, each one marked with a woven mat. Each place also had a small, tightly woven basket containing coarse salt.

The eating house was open, like a verandah, and the seated guests could see older women digging with hoes, dragging aside the sandy soil, until there was a gush of scented steam. Saliva spurted into Phryne's mouth. Suddenly she was starving.

'Hangi,' said Mr. Aubrey. 'Earth oven. Not as highly seasoned as I would like, I admit, but perfectly tasty. And they do have some bush pepper which is quite hot,' he said, a little wistfully.

The lounging men, Phryne observed, did nothing to help the

burrowers as they lifted out packages of steaming food. Dot's little girl vanished along with all the children, to return bearing trays on which reposed sweet potato, pumpkin, potato, something odd which looked like sticks but tasted of asparagus, fish, and the shellfish for which Caroline had been hoping: huge clams, small shells, mussels, crayfish boiled bright red, and sea urchins.

Dot stuck to fish and potato. Phryne tried everything, later admitting that sea urchin was an acquired taste which she hadn't acquired, tasting, as it did, of spoiled, salty egg yolk. There was a subdued 'whoof!' as the *Hinemoa*'s crew fell on the food. Everyone was eating. Dot shared her plate with her little friend, who was called Miri. Miri informed Dot that her daddy was the biggest of the warriors, the strongest, and they lived in Dunedin most of the time where her father worked for the railways. Mr. Cahill revealed an unexpected enthusiasm for sweet potato.

To drink there were gallons of sweet, milky tea. It was a feast. Phryne hadn't fully appreciated the meaning of the term before.

'So,' she heard Margery Lemmon say to the warrior next to her, 'are you the indigenous inhabitants of these islands?'

'Madam,' he said, grinning with a flash of white teeth, 'my ancestors ate the indigenous inhabitants of these islands!'

Margery Lemmon laughed, and so did the rest of the *whare*. Professor Applegate, talking with the old women, obtained some bush pepper which met Mr. Aubrey's requirements for savour. They watched him in astonishment as he poured it all onto the food and merrily ate it. One old woman made a comment which set the rest of them laughing and rocking.

'Let me guess. She said "no sense, no feeling", right?' he asked.

'Well,' said the professor. 'Yes.'

The feast could not have been considered to have ended. It was just that even the stalwart young men couldn't eat any more. The party sat, talking idly, digesting and eating little tastes of their favourite food.

The old women collected Phryne and the other women and

showed them into another part of the *whare*. There there were looms, stretched flat on the floor, and young women pounding flax.

'Hard work,' said Phryne.

'Woolworths better,' said one fabulously aged crone with blue tattoos on her lips and chin. 'But mustn't forget. What if Woolworths gone tomorrow? Freeze in the cold,' she said, wrapping her arms around herself and shivering.

'We just make this for ceremonies,' said the young woman. 'I work in an office. We aren't savages, you know. But this craft was disappearing. We need to keep our history.'

'Very commendable,' said Phryne. 'My ancestors wore less than this. They just wore paint.'

'You English?' asked the young woman. 'That was the Picts. The painted people. We're painted too. But it doesn't wash off,' she added.

The visit concluded with the Solomonic judgment that the *Hinemoa* haka had been superior in terror-inducing quality to the Moanapipi, but the Moanapipi girls had danced a fractionally better poi dance. This was greeted with applause and bets were settled.

Then the women laid out a sale of various handicrafts. Phryne bought a coiled bone carving to hang around her neck on a flax string and a length of the *tukutuku* material patterned in brown and ochre. Dot bought a small basket from Miri, and paid her double for her kindness. Then a plate was passed around and everyone contributed for the feast.

Professor Applegate led them back to the *Wayfarer*.

Phryne drew a deep breath. 'Hello, twentieth century,' she said.

'Back to the ship, ladies?' said the master of the *Wayfarer*. 'Just in time for tea.'

Phryne was not going to be hungry again any time soon. She wanted a gin and tonic and a nap.

She obtained both of these in record time. It was four o'clock before she woke. Dot was in the room, contemplating her Edith Cavell costume.

'Hello, Miss Phryne,' said Dot. 'Feeling better?'

'I'm fine, Dot, it was just that all of my bodily energies were diverted to digestion. How about you?'

'That was a good feast,' said Dot. 'The girls are a bit upset about not winning, but the blokes are so happy about the haka that no one has the heart to be sad.'

'Feeding the dancers blackcurrant syrup was a masterstroke,' agreed Phryne. 'I never saw so many blue tongues. Reminded me of going blackberrying when I was a child.'

'One for me, one for the basket,' chuckled Dot. 'Then it got to be two for me, one for the basket, and somehow there were never many blackberries on all them canes.'

'And by some magic my mother always knew I had been eating them. Are you going to try on that costume?'

'Yes,' said Dot. It fitted. The wrapper was adaptable to any figure and fell to the ankles in the proper fashion, abolishing any dangerous intimation that the wearer might be female. In comparison with, as it might be, Mrs. West, it was refreshing. Dot looked very professional in the uniform, with the starched veil hiding her hair and framing her scrubbed clean face.

'Those Wests…' Phryne began.

'Horrible people,' said Dot. 'And that Mr. Singer, I reckon you're right about him beating his wife. Stewardess heard her crying and him yelling at her.'

'Yes. But doesn't it strike you as odd, Dot, that at the precise time that someone was dropping me into the drink, the Wests should be playing cards with Jack Mason? They never showed any conspicuous signs of compassion before.'

'Yes, odd,' agreed Dot. 'Unless they were skinning him alive.'

'I don't think he's got a lot of money. Not the sort of money to play cards with someone like the Wests. No, there is something strange about it, Dot. I need to speak to Margery Lemmon. She was tending to the poor boy. He couldn't see out of his eyes, you know. Oh,' said Phryne blankly.

'Miss?'

'Just an idea. I'll tell you about it later. I'm going to have something really impressive in the way of baths and take my time dressing. One advantage of a cruise,' said Phryne, stretching luxuriously, 'is that there really isn't a lot to do but be self-indulgent.'

'You've always been good at that,' said Dot affectionately.

Mr. Mauno Vanimoinen
Turku Finland

Dear Mauno
I have heard wonderful things about this place called Minnesota from our cousin. It is well watered and fertile and much warmer in the summer than our country. Though there is not much forest. I am taking a passage on the next ship to New York where I can catch a train to a place called Saint Paul, where our cousin will meet me and Ilmari. They need metalworkers there so we will soon get a job. I will write as soon as I am settled, dear Mauno. Please convey my respects to your wife and daughter.

Lemminki

Chapter Fifteen

Look homeward, Angel, now, and melt with ruth:
And, O ye dolphins, waft the hapless youth!

John Milton
Lycidas

'On with the dance,' sighed Phryne Fisher, slipping into her dark green Manchu trousers, which otherwise did duty as pyjamas. 'Let joy be unconfined.'

Dot had already slathered her employer's face with cold cream and plastered her with Oriental Silk foundation make-up, guaranteed not to rub off on a gentleman's shoulder. Phryne's face was a featureless white oval, on which she had painted the red cheeks and elevated eyebrows of the Manchu beauty. Her hand bore the dragon and phoenix silver ring. The sapphire was secured around her waist in the ever-useful-petticoat pocket.

Dot slipped the green brocade jacket on, careful of the paint, and secured it at shoulder and hip. Then she looped Phryne's fan around her wrist. Phryne sat down at the dressing table to paint her lips into the required cherry shape and blew a kiss to her reflection.

'All right, Miss? You look lovely. I'm going to dress Mrs. Cahill.'

'Do you need my help?'

'No, Miss, I just need the paste jewellery. She's going to look like a princess,' said Dot firmly, 'or me and Margery'll know the reason why.'

'All right. Mr. Singer is calling for me,' said Phryne, who had drawn him in the escort ballot and meant to lose him as soon as she could—preferably overboard. 'We're dining in the Palm Court and going into the Grand Salon for dancing. I hope that Caroline isn't too upset about the girls coming second at the poi dance?'

'No, Miss, she just swears she'll win next year. She told Mr. Green to put some money on our blokes as well so he broke even. Have a lovely time,' said Dot, and went out, Miss Cavell to her fingertips, her white veil fluttering.

Phryne lit a very un-Manchu cigarette and looked out the window. The sun was down, the sea was kicking up a few wavelets. She could hear the usual noises of the working docks; men shouting, wharfies exchanging orders, the whine of derricks, the clump of cargo nets. Hard light flooded her cabin. No matter, she wasn't planning on sleeping much tonight, anyway.

Mr. Singer tapped at her door and she went out into the corridor. He was wearing ordinary evening dress and a domino mask. Phryne put the very tips of her fingers on his arm. The heelless slippers were comfortable on her feet, but she had to shuffle in a very ladylike manner to keep them there. This meant that she and her escort dead-heated the others at the door to the Grand Salon.

It had been strung with Tiffany fairy lights. The band was setting up. Phryne bowed politely to Mavis and the girls and they bowed back. No one ever said the Melody Makers didn't have a sense of occasion. Though the wolf whistle which followed her into the Palm Court was probably just Jo expressing her appreciation of the Manchu costume.

Table three had gone to considerable effort. Jack Mason had pushed back his mask but was otherwise draped in a billowing black cassock. His scythe, hastily improvised from a curtain rod and some silver cardboard, was leaning against the wall. Mr. Aubrey made the perfect rajah, with a ruby in his turban the size of a boiled sweet. Professor Applegate was wearing Maori dress, her feather cloak almost as magnificent as the Moanapipi chief's had been.

Mrs. Singer was wearing a black evening dress borrowed from someone else and a defiant smile. Her newspaper crown declared that she was Miss Print. Mr. Cahill looked like the slightly down at heel sundowner which he might have been. Margery Lemmon was magnificent in Indian dress—a flaming turquoise sari with a gold bodice, which emphasised all of her good points. She had darkened her skin and applied a caste mark.

Mr. Forrester, of course, was with his nymphs and dryads at the party in Second Class. Phryne hoped she might look in on him later in his character as Silenus. She had always felt that Silenus would be fun to frolic with. She remembered a quip she had once made: when pursued by a satyr, always make sure you are caught near the softest available moss.

Mrs. West was partly clad in a Greek tunic which was slipping off one shapely shoulder. It was as green as venom and she had a torc and upper arm ring of green enamel and gold; embossed with adders with tongues of red coral. Circe might have looked something like that, Phryne thought, after all. In which case she applauded Odysseus's courage in making love to her. Those snakes might just bite.

The crowning achievement of the masquerade, however, was Mrs. Cahill. The draped bodice and wide skirts suited her figure. Her golden hair hung in loose ringlets almost to her waist. She dripped with Phryne's paste jewels at waist, shoulder, bosom and ears and she was crowned with diamonds. Dot had made up her face with sympathetic care, not enamelling her with powder, but smoothing the deeper lines, disguising shadows and blotches. She looked, for the moment, as she must have looked as a young girl, when she had married Mr. Cahill and thrown in her lot with one hundred thousand acres of desert and scrub. Mrs. West had already awarded her the evening's accolade: a look of pure, righteous envy. Mr. Cahill kept casting delighted but faintly bewildered glances in her direction. Who would have thought that the old girl would scrub up like that?

Phryne found that eating was not going to be possible unless she repaired her make-up later, and decided to repair it. Those Manchu girls must have eaten their dinners through a straw. Or possibly they were fed a full meal before the make-up was applied, which was more likely. With the soup, she began to talk easily to Jack Mason.

'So glad that you could come,' she said quietly. 'And I hope that your visitors didn't skin you of every last penny.'

'Oh yes, wasn't that nice of them?' he said uncomfortably. 'They only stayed an hour or so, after Margery left.'

'What time was that?' asked Phryne, toying with a cocktail.

'Oh, they must have come about two and left about three,' he said. 'I couldn't see a thing but I could hear my little travelling clock strike.'

Damn, thought Phryne. At about half past two I was being rolled in my own gown and dipped like a candle and it doesn't seem to have been the Wests after all.

'How do you feel now?'

'I doubt I'll be making a late night of it,' said Jack ruefully. 'I caught my head a pretty nasty crack falling down that last bit of crevasse. But Margery said she'd save a dance for me and since I already had my costume…'

'It would be a pity to miss it,' said Phryne.

'She's been really nice to me,' said Jack Mason. 'Telling me stories about India to pass the time. Restful sort of girl. Didn't even mind when I floated off to sleep. Just waited till I came back.'

Phryne smiled and ordered another cocktail. Margery Lemmon, perceiving that Jack was talking about her, gave him a smile across the table. It was a fond, indulgent smile as a sister might give to an erring but well-meaning brother.

'You look spiffing in that gear, Miss Fisher!' said Mr. Aubrey. 'Are you Han or Manchu?'

'Manchu,' Phryne replied. 'The silk clothes are real and so is the ring.'

She took it off and handed it to Mr. Aubrey, who appraised it. 'Dragon and phoenix. Emperor and empress, union of yin and yang principles,' he said. 'Lovely piece.'

'I bought it in Shanghai,' she replied. 'Are you an old China hand as well as an old India hand, Mr. Aubrey?'

'No, no, m'dear, but you pick up things as you go through ports. Busy port, Shanghai. Yellow River meets the sea. Dangerous place, very.'

Mr. Aubrey spoke of piracies past, Mr. Singer glared at his eggnog and then at his wife. Phryne ate a good dinner and the Wests had another of their sotto voce quarrels. Theodore Green strove to distract attention from them.

'You promised me a dance, Miss Fisher,' he reminded her, raising his voice to cover the Wests' hissing undertones.

'And you shall have one, my dear Mr. Green,' Phryne assured him.

'And you'll probably have to dance with the captain,' he went on.

'Does he step on feet?' she asked. 'I'm only wearing slippers.'

'No, no, he's a much better dancer than me,' Mr. Green assured her.

'Will m'lady honour me with the first dance?' asked Mr. Cahill, creaking to his feet. Mrs. Cahill gave him her hand. The band was now playing in the Grand Salon. Dinner could be said to be over.

'I'll just go and repair my face,' said Phryne, and left the Palm Court. The Manchu white had stood the test, she saw as she looked into the mirror in the Ladies' Retiring Room. She took out a lipstick and was aware that the other face, next to hers, belonged to Jonquil West. Phryne surprised a look of such malevolence on that smooth countenance that, had it been rectified spirits, Phryne would have gone up like a torch the next time she tried to light a cigarette.

'You don't carry a bag, Miss Fisher?' asked Mrs. West hungrily.

'No, there's a lot of room in the sleeves,' said Phryne, obligingly turning them out. She was carrying a compact, the key to her suite, a cigarette case and lighter, a clean folded handkerchief, a crumpled handkerchief and a forgotten packet of lemon drops, which must have been there since the last time she wore this jacket. Phryne turned to allow Mrs. West to see that the sleeves flapped empty before loading all the stuff back into them. Phryne repaired her Manchu cherry bud mouth and when she looked up again, Circe had gone.

As Phryne went into the lavatory she reflected that it mustn't be a lot of fun to be as greedy as Mrs. West was. 'These are the four that have never been filled...' Kipling knew about greed.

When she returned to the dancing the Melody Makers were in full swing and the room was thronged with costumed people. 'Who,' demanded Jo in her sweet tenor, 'stole my heart away? Who?' Phryne sat down until the song was over, and before then Theodore Green found her. She was still the only woman he could dance with. All others retired lightly trampled. And Miss Fisher was only wearing slippers! He could really hurt her!

But she glided into his arms and it was all right again. He forgot what his errant feet were doing and he heard no cries of pain from his second waistcoat button, where her neat black head rested. 'We'll make hay while the sun shines,' promised Jo. 'We'll make love when it rains.' Navigation Officer Green danced and was happy.

Phryne liked dancing with the Navigation Officer. He didn't mind her leading. Of course, given his level of terpsichorean skill, he might not have noticed she was leading...

'I wonder why all the songs say that they can only be happy in a nice country cottage with Old Mister Moon shining in through the window?' she asked. 'Most people I know would be bored to tears in a week. The country is really quite crude, you know.'

'I don't know,' he responded. 'I've been at sea since I was thirteen. Before that I lived in an industrial slum. Not a lot of greenery there, unless you count the scum on the river. I might ask Mr. Cahill,' he said, as Mrs. Cahill floated past in the experienced arms of the captain, who knew what he liked and was dancing with her.

'He'd tell you that you needed ten thousand acres before you could even start,' said Phryne. Mr. Cahill was dancing with Mrs. Singer and had even coaxed her into a laugh.

'Miss Lemmon has taken a shine to that Mason boy,' said Theodore Green as the rani and Death circled past. Phryne tried to look at the navigation officer's face, which is hard to do while dancing a foxtrot.

'I fancy she feels sisterly,' she said, in case Miss Lemmon inclined towards a belief in the saying that every nice girl loves a sailor. 'He needs a sister.'

'He needs a straitjacket,' said Mr. Green with uncharacteristic energy. 'And that Thomas, he ought to be the boy's keeper. He doesn't seem to be doing his job. He got drunk with three stokers this morning and I had to confine him to sickbay until he stopped carrying on.'

'What was he saying?' asked Phryne.

'Oh, that he knew things, and people would see what it was to discard him, things like that. Just gibberish,' said Theodore Green kindly. 'It takes some people that way.'

'So it does,' agreed Phryne.

The evening went on. The band played. Phryne collected some champagne—that's not the good champagne, Mam'selle, as Pierre the wine waiter had told her, slipping her a glass of Clicquot—and wandered over to greet the Melody Makers. She observed Lizbet

Yates take her wad of Lumberjack out of her mouth and stick it—horrors!—behind the edge of a Tiffany screen.

'You can tell she was born in Port, can't you?' commented Jo, amused at Phryne's horrified expression, visible even through the Manchu mask. 'It's all right, gorgeous Chinese lady. The stuff won't stick to glass, not bond with it.'

'Useful, though,' said Lizbet sulkily. 'Sets like concrete after a couple of days. We've used it to repair music stands and fix water bottles and mend leaky valves, and you remember that night in Darwin when the bike tyre lost its seal and we thought we'd never get back to the ship in time…'

'All right, all right,' conceded Jo. She stroked her immaculate front complacently. A very male gesture. All Jo's gestures were male. 'It's a tool kit in itself. No home should be without it. But I still say that when you're chewing it you look like a cow.'

'Jo,' Mavis began, as Lizbet picked up her trumpet in a meaningful manner.

'Drinks for the orchestra,' announced Phryne promptly. 'What'll you have, girls? Ask Pierre, he will be delighted to serve you. And can you find another glass of that excellent champagne for me?' she added in rapid French. He grinned conspiratorially, booked orders for the ladies, and sped away on his errand of mercy.

'Sorry,' said Jo. 'I take it back. Face it, Lizbet, I'm just jealous of your boyfriend.'

The Melody Makers laughed with relief. Phryne watched the party begin to wind down. The older dancers had already found chairs and were fanning themselves and wondering about the awful energy of the young. Phryne saw Mrs. Cahill, pink and perspiring, drinking iced champagne cup with Mr. Aubrey and Mr. Cahill. Margery Lemmon was still dancing with Death. The doctor was attending to a guest who had, under the influence of punch, attempted to do the black bottom and landed squarely on her own. Professor Applegate was sitting by the wall, nodding while she listened to some important fact that Theodore Green was imparting to her. The Wests were dancing together to the gramophone which replaced the band during breaks.

The band drank their drinks and limbered up lip, wrist and voice. 'We'll be going up to the sun deck after the captain hands out the prizes,' Lizbet said to Phryne. 'For the last set. Here comes the captain now.'

Captain Bishop had enjoyed his evening. No one had got unpleasantly drunk, immense ingenuity had been shown in the costumes and everyone had been civilised. He liked his ship to be happy. Mind, tomorrow there might be some sore heads, but tonight all was gas and gaiters.

'Ladies, gentlemen,' he began. The drummer gave him a sting to attract attention. But Captain Bishop's powers of projection had been formed as a reefer in a tearing gale going around the Horn, and needed no augmentation. 'It has been a lovely evening,' he said. There was applause. 'And now, before we move up to the lido, I need to present the prizes. For the most beautiful lady,' he said, and paused. 'A dreadful task to choose between so many beautiful ladies, so I left my choice to my officers. And they tell me that the most beautiful lady in the room is...'

Phryne saw Jonquil West start to move toward the captain, confident that her name would be called.

'The Honourable Miss Phryne Fisher,' announced the captain. Table three applauded loudly. Phryne passed Jonquil on her way to the captain, and thought that one of Circe's snakes had uncoiled and hissed at her.

She accepted a silver cigarette box embossed with the ship's name and her own. She bowed in proper Chinese fashion and to her amazement the captain bowed back, to the exact depth required by custom. Captain Bishop had not wasted his time ashore in foreign ports.

'The most ingenious costume,' announced the captain. It went to a young man fetchingly disguised as a billiard table, and

Phryne hoped it made up for the very uncomfortable evening he must have spent inside that green baize box.

'The most popular costume award,' said Captain Bishop, 'is given by acclaim amongst the judges. And that award goes to Mrs. Cahill, a very pearl amongst princesses.'

Mrs. Cahill, with an expression that indicated her night was complete but her feet were starting to hurt, accepted her prize to the accompaniment of good natured cheers.

Then the party began to break up. The professor, Mr. Aubrey, the Cahills and Mr. Singer took their leave and sought their virtuous couches. Phryne, the Wests, Death, Margery Lemmon, Mrs. Singer and the younger persons followed the Melody Makers up the stairs to the lido, where the stars blazed like lanterns. There was no wind, so it was not freezing, but Phryne did spare a moment to hope, piously, that Mrs. West might not catch the pneumonia she was so assiduously courting. Phryne found a corner and a seat and lit a cigarette as the dancing began again. The heelless slippers were not ideal dancing shoes and she was thinking of going below. It had been fun. A really charming evening.

Death swung past her, gown billowing, dancing with a lady in very fluttery garments. Mrs. Singer was dancing with a man disguised as a wizard. Phryne watched for a while, content to sit still. There was something wild and strange about music across the water. The dockyard continued its work, never stopping, as any delay cost someone money. Ships came here from all over the earth and bore away good nourishing New Zealand butter and wool and rock lobsters to a cold and hungry world. Fascinating.

The music went on. Phryne stayed where she was, as serene as a Chinese doll. She was still watching the derrick move, the hook never stopping, the slings lifted and set down with wincing care, when the last dance was announced and she got up to find someone to dance it with.

The party had thinned out to the stalwart, the inebriated and the diehards who never left before someone played 'Now Is the

Hour'. She held out a hand to Jack Mason but Death did not seem to see her. She claimed the doctor and they began the last, slower, nearly-ready-to-go-to-bed circling of the lido.

'Now is the hour, when we must say goodbye,' the song began. Phryne, leaning a little on the doctor's chest, which smelt pleasantly of iodoform, was in the perfect position to see a boathook shoot out of the mass of dancers, hit Death squarely in the middle of the back, and precipitate him into the sea.

One moment the antic figure with flapping black garb was whirling along, holding on to his partner with one arm and his scythe with the other. The next, he was a kicking, screaming stick figure, plunging down into the night-black air until, far below, there was a splash. And thereafter nothing.

Madam Lina Fejes
Kecskemet Hungary

Honoured Lady

I write to inform you that my sister Maurika hereby tenders her resignation from your household. Please inform your brother that she is leaving immediately for America. Any letters will be returned.

Petofi family

Chapter Sixteen

Like a God self-slain on his own altar
Death lies dead.

A Swinburne
'The Forsaken Garden'

As soon as it happened Phryne looked hard at the crowd, trying to imprint the picture on her mind so that it could be examined later, when she was less shocked. The Melody Makers had frozen mid-note. They were all in their places, except Jo. The dancers were milling around, trying to stare down into the water, screaming for help or demanding that someone force brandy down their throat according to preference. The doctor and the other officers had gone to deal with the emergency with well-trained efficiency.

Phryne stared hard. Mr. Singer was holding his wife by the arm; he had decided not to go to bed, then. Margery Lemmon was leaning over the rail, with Jo of the Melody Makers hanging on to her waist and telling her not to be foolish. The Wests stood next to each other. All the rest of her table had gone to bed. Poor Jack Mason. So very young, and now not to get any older or acquire any sense. What a waste.

Phryne backed a little and sat down on her previous bench. Then an officer returned, indistinguishable in white uniform and cap. He raised his hands.

'Ladies and gentlemen, we are doing all we can. Could you go to your cabins now? And stay there while we do what we have to do. If you would be so good,' he added. Phryne knew that he had to be Navigation Officer Green.

Obediently, Phryne turned to the staircase. Guests were now tumbling down it, anxious to be out of the night and the cold and the breath of death. Jo hauled Margery Lemmon back and shoved her towards the stairs. The Melody Makers gathered their instruments and came too. Phryne wanted a drink and some time to contemplate what she had seen. She spoke a few sentences to Pierre in passing and he supplied her with a bottle wrapped in a white napkin in a deep basket. Conversation in the Grand Salon was shrill and hysterical and Phryne did not want to hear it. She made it to her suite, locked herself in, and placed herself and the Manchu make-up for a sinfully long time under a hot shower.

Her face felt dry, so she sat at the dressing table and applied cream. The she opened the basket, unwrapped the bottle, and poured herself a full glass of the Petit Duc cognac. The basket also contained a selection of cocktail canapés. She was thinking so hard that she jumped when something laid a respectful paw on her knee. She looked down. It was Scragger, appearing slightly less disreputable than usual, politely intimating that crabmeat vol-au-vent did not come his way very often.

Phryne was pleased to see him. She spread the napkin on the carpet and supplied the more fishy of the available treats with a liberal hand. The cognac was soothing her nerves. And it was nice to be able to smile without feeling that she was going to crack her face.

Scragger made a good meal. As an old campaigner, he ate with a certain amount of whoofling and spattering, but then he meticulously cleaned up every edible scrap and sat down to give his fur a lick and a promise.

Phryne ate the rest of the canapés while she wrote out her statement describing exactly what she had seen, and appreciated his company.

When Dot came in disgracefully late, Phryne was asleep, and there was no trace of Scragger but the white napkin, decorated with paw prints, still lay on the floor.

•• ● •• •

Detective Inspector Evelyn Minton of the Dunedin constabulary was having a bad night. Awful enough that he should be named Evelyn in a man's profession like the police. Still, he reflected, it could be worse. He could be either of his brothers—Beverley or Cholmondeley. The fact that he still visited his aged mother every Sunday and brought her his children to spoil with homemade scones and blackberry tart was an indication of his compassionate and forgiving nature. His sons, however, were very firmly called James and Michael, and his daughters were Jane and Mary.

But this was going to be a headache, he could tell. First it seemed an ordinary accident. Drunken cruise passenger does header off lido deck while dancing. A not uncommon circumstance. Then several people, including the navigation officer of the ship, had told him that the drowned man had been pushed—with, of all things, a boathook. It would help if they could find the body but the deceased had evidently gone down like a stone. All that enthusiastic dredging had found so far was a black garment and a dissolving papier-mâché skull mask.

No, it wasn't going to be funny at all. In person, the Detective Inspector was a well dressed forty year old with a deceptively diffident manner, brown eyes and fading chestnut hair, which was retreating backwards over his scalp. Years of training by his daughters had made him familiar with the female psyche, though not less puzzled by it. Five o'clock in the morning and a faint presage of dawn found him, his assistant Detective Sergeant Donald Peace, Navigation Officer Green, the purser and the doctor, in the Grand Salon, drinking tea or coffee, according to taste, and worrying.

'What was the deceased's name again?' asked Peace, taking

out his very own fountain pen and opening his notebook. 'I'd better make it all official.'

'Go to it, if it gives you any pleasure,' said his boss gloomily. The newly promoted Peace's youthful enthusiasm occasionally filled him with a sense of how old and cynical he had become. Without noticing. One day he just woke up and there he was, old and cynical and getting short of hair.

'Jack Mason,' said Green. 'His father is a judge in Melbourne.'

'Date of birth?' asked Peace, imperturbably.

'Here's his passenger card,' said the purser. 'You can copy it. Nice enough young bloke,' he added.

'So he was,' agreed Mr. Green. 'But wild.'

Detective Inspector Evelyn Minton pricked up his ears.

'What sort of wild?' he asked. This was a world he knew very well. 'Other men's wives wild?'

'Well, he did seem to have a sort of infatuation with Mrs. West,' admitted Theodore Green. 'But what I meant was he was restless. He tried to climb one of the fells at Milford Sound, for instance. Got quite a long way before he had to come back.'

The navigation officer was feeling unreal. At the same time he was horrified that something like a murder could have happened on his own ship and at the climax of a very good party. Captain Bishop had told him to talk to the police, stay with them, and give them anything they wanted. But he would not allow them to wake his first class passengers in the middle of the night. Tomorrow would do—they weren't going anywhere. *Hinemoa* had moved out from her mooring so that the sea-bed could be searched for the body. There was no way off the ship except the route Jack Mason had taken.

'So he was restless. What was he doing on a cruise? These things are mainly for the rich and old, aren't they?' asked Minton, taking a deep swig of tea.

'Not at all,' the navigation officer bristled. 'We have quite a number of young people aboard. Now, let me tell you all I know about Jack Mason and why he was here.'

He did so. Peace took notes. Roberts the steward supplied more tea. Roberts had met policemen in his time, and knew that all police forces were fuelled and lubricated by tea. Minton rumpled his hair and then stopped in case any more of it fell out.

'All right, I've got a good picture of what the lad was like,' he admitted. Theodore Green had not omitted one fact and had indulged in a reasonable number of hypotheses, much against his usual practice. 'Basically a good boy, at a loose end, quarrelling with his father. Best bet is probably this Mr. West. If he's as jealous as you say, then he might well have decided that Mason wasn't wanted on the voyage. We'll talk to him after breakfast. And all the others. Oh Lord,' he said, reading the passenger list. Then he leaned over and grabbed Green by the forearm.

'This Miss Fisher—she isn't a fashionable little woman with Dutch-doll hair and green eyes? Comes from St Kilda?'

'That's her,' said Green, considerably astonished, trying to get his arm back.

'She's some sort of nob?'

'She's an Hon,' said Mr. Green, a little proudly.

Evelyn Minton passed a hand over his eyes, incidentally releasing the navigation officer's arm. He was rather pleased to get it back in one piece.

'Oh, jeez,' he said.

'What's the matter, Boss?' asked Donald Peace, capping his fountain pen. 'Headache?'

'Biggest one of all,' said Minton. 'My wife's cousin is married to an officer in Melbourne. Nice bloke. Works for Homicide. He came over to stay in the bach for a bit of fishing a few months ago, and he told me all about this Miss Fisher. His boss, Jack Robinson, says she's given him a whole forest of white hair. She's a private investigator,' he said, and Doctor Shilletoe dropped his cup.

It rolled and spilled. The men at the table watched it. No one said anything. Then the doctor got up, scraping his chair clumsily, and almost ran from the room.

'Your doctor always this jumpy?' asked Minton.

'No,' said Theodore Green. 'I don't know what's come over him lately.' Mr. Green was wondering if he ought to tell these policemen that Miss Fisher was indeed on the ship in her professional capacity. He decided that he would subject the idea to a rigorous analysis when he had time, and then decide.

'How did he get on with Jack Mason?'

'Very well. Spent a lot of time attending to him when he came back all stung and bruised. They got on fine.'

Nothing is more depressing than the room in which a very good party has ended in disarray. Streamers hung forlornly from the decorations. The floor had been swabbed and the crockery and glasses cleared away.

Minton was adding pipe smoke to the already close atmosphere of the Grand Salon. Peace did not smoke and Green did not commonly smoke in uniform. But it looked like being a very unusual night. He found his packet of Gauloise. Navigation Officer Green's view was that if you were going to endanger your health and cut your wind smoking, the cigarette ought to have punch. He drew the line, however, at Navy Capstan, reputed to be composed of old rope.

He dragged his wandering mind back to the business at hand. He and the purser, from their several viewpoints, knew a lot about the passengers, and in an hour Donald Peace had a neatly written summary of the major players which he could readily transfer to a typewriter when he got ashore, if he ever did.

Periodically the draggers would come back with news of no progress whatsoever. 'He must have gone down like a stone, Boss,' said one. 'No splashing and bubbling, just straight down.'

'That's strange,' Theodore Green observed. 'He could swim like a fish.'

'The boathook might have hit him in the spine and broken his back,' said Minton. 'Paralysed him instantly.'

They all thought of how it must feel, being unable to move,

sinking rapidly in black water. Choking. Smothering. The knife-like pain as the lungs give up and breathe water. Donald Peace, who had almost drowned in a surprise encounter with a vicious undertow, remembered struggling in utter despair towards the surface, impossibly out of reach, and shivered.

'Or he might have been real drunk,' said Minton. 'Drunks make a hole in the water like that. Just straight down and nothing until the body washes up a week later. Well, nothing to do until we can talk to the passengers, and we already know a lot about them, thanks to Mr. Green. Let's see if P&O can rustle up some breakfast for us, eh, before all the rich people wake up.'

Roberts was already giving orders to the first class kitchen. He also knew that policemen ran on fried bacon, fried bread, fried eggs, fried mushrooms, fried tomatoes and anything else which could be conveniently cooked in fat. The night chef was a Kiwi. He'd know how to make Fried Cuisine.

Wednesday

Phryne Fisher was woken with her usual coffee, and far too much information for a woman whose last drink before sleeping had been Petit Duc cognac. She retreated into the bathroom, bathed and brushed her teeth, while Caroline was telling Dot all about it. Actually, she didn't have a headache. Her calves were sore from a lot of dancing in slippers, but above the neck she was in tiptop form. This was an asset, because from the sound of the news Caroline was even now imparting, it was going to be a trying day.

Bathed and brushed, Phryne sat down to her coffee and attended to Dot's narrative.

'You know that Mr. Mason was wearing Death's costume last night, well, he went over the side,' said Dot. 'And Caroline was saying that he was pushed!'

'I know,' said Phryne. 'I saw him go.'

'Oh, Miss,' wailed Dot. 'Can't we go anywhere without a murder?'

'It does seem unfair, Dot. This, however, was no doing of mine. I did not expect it either. Who is investigating it?'

'A nice policeman from Dunedin, Miss. Called Minton. His second in command is a Maori called Peace. Caroline's brother is married to his second cousin.'

'Then we will talk to him in time,' said Phryne. 'How was your party?'

'Oh, it was lovely. I had such a nice time. Everyone liked my costume. Nice things to eat and that Mr. Forrester did an Ancient Greek dance with his dryads and naiads.'

'I bet he did,' said Phryne, and grinned.

'No, it was all quite proper, they had body stockings on. Caroline's girls danced again. We had lobster. I had a very good time. And now this has to happen.'

'Not your concern, Dot dear. The only people near enough were the first class passengers. It was during the last dance, and most of our friends had gone to bed. Ask Caroline for my usual breakfast, will you, and I will dress. By the way, what happened to our feline companion?'

Dot found underwear for Phryne and then stood, staring into the wardrobe. What did one wear to be interviewed by the police? She decided on a respectable dark green suit and a dark ivory blouse.

'Scragger?' she asked absently. 'Was he in here? I did wonder why there was a napkin on the floor. He must have got out when I came in. I was late, Miss. After two. I've never been up that late before. I mean, for a party. Sat up all night at plenty of sickbeds and so on but I never stayed at a party so long.'

'Then you must have been enjoying it, Dot. A good sign. You will be frivolous yet. Just not very frivolous,' concluded Phryne.

Frowning—she didn't think that frivolous was at all respectable—Dot ordered Phryne's breakfast and went to her own.

Phryne had just eaten the last crumb of croissant and drained the last drop from the coffee pot when a knock announced

Theodore Green and two policemen. Phryne admitted them. They stood, uneasy in this bower of luxury, until she ushered them onto the private balcony and sat down on a steamer chair herself.

The one with the notebook was clearly Mr. Peace, Caroline's relative. He was slim and tall, with light milk coffee coloured skin, and the aristocratic face she had come to associate with the princely class of Maori; high nosed, high cheekboned, almost Ancient Egyptian. A prince of the captivity, thought Phryne.

The other was older, balding, and anxious. He shook her hand and introduced himself.

'Well, Detective Inspector, I have drawn up an account of exactly what I saw last night. Here it is,' she said, and handed over three closely written sheets. Minton scanned it.

'I have to tell you, Miss Fisher, I have heard a lot about you,' he said, eyes widening as he read. 'This is very good,' he added. 'You'd swear to all of this?'

'Yes,' said Phryne. 'From whom?'

'Oh, a bloke who works with Jack Robinson.'

'And you are about to tell me not to interfere,' prompted Phryne.

'Yes,' said Minton, looking into her eyes.

'I have no intention of interfering,' she said. 'I'm on holiday. I have affairs of my own to pursue.'

'Right,' he said. 'What did you think of Jack Mason?'

'A nice boy with not enough to do,' she said. 'If I might make a suggestion, you should talk to Mavis and the Melody Makers. They were in the middle of the dance. They might have seen something. Or heard something.'

'They're on our list,' he told her.

'Take beer,' said Phryne, 'if you want them to loosen up.'

'What a suggestion,' said Mr. Minton. 'They'll cooperate because it is every citizen's duty to cooperate with the police.'

Phryne was about to reply when she caught a gleam of mischief in the policeman's deep brown eyes.

'Of course,' she said demurely, folding her hands in her lap in the manner made popular by Her First Sermon.

'We can take these?' Donald Peace asked, indicating Phryne's notes. Phryne nodded. They took the notes, and their leave, and Phryne decided to stay put for the moment. She tried Chaucer and found that she could not concentrate, so she picked up one of Dot's detective stories and was soon deep in *The Murder of Roger Ackroyd*.

• • ● • •

Detective Inspector Minton read the summary about Professor Applegate before he knocked on her door. 'Tough eminent old lady not to be trifled with' it said, and when she opened the door and met his eyes with her own calm, wise ones, he saw what the navigation officer had meant. The professor was wearing a severe grey serge coat and skirt. The only mark of distinction which separated her from any other old lady of independent means and strong character was a greenstone ornament which made his partner step back a pace.

'Kia ora,' said the professor to Donald Peace.

'Kia ora,' he replied in a subdued tone. 'I'm Donald Peace and this is Detective Inspector Minton and we'd like to ask you some questions.' There was a pause, after which he added, 'If you please.'

'Come in,' said the professor.

Ten minutes later, they left her cabin. The professor had given them a pithy summary of every person about whom they had inquired. She was not constrained by politeness, as Theodore Green had been. Thereafter her crisp assessments occurred to Detective Inspector Minton as he spoke to the other people on his list.

'Inadequate dyspeptic; beats his wife.' That was Professor Applegate on Mr. Singer, which entirely agreed with Mr. Green's 'enjoys poor health and has an uncertain temper' but was somehow a lot more informative.

Mr. Singer was sharp and nervous. Mrs. Singer was polite but terrified. Partly, Peace realised, it was because he was a Maori. That was expected. But it was more than that. The poor woman was trembling, and to get any sense out of her they would have to remove her husband from the equation. Miss Fisher's notes said that Mr. Singer had declared that he was going to bed and had actually left with the professor and the other older people, but he was on the lido when Jack Mason did his boathook-assisted high dive.

'If you would be so kind as to come along with me, sir,' said Peace, communicating with his chief by one glance. 'We'll go up to the lido and you can show me where you were standing. My boss just has a couple of questions for your wife.'

'I ought to be here if she's going to be interrogated,' declared Mr. Singer. 'I'm not going!'

'Come along now,' coaxed Mr. Peace. 'We don't want to make a fuss, do we?' The gentle pressure on Mr. Singer's shoulder increased a little. He shrugged it off.

'Don't you say a thing, you hear?' he snarled at his wife. 'Not a thing! I shall know if you do!'

Then the door was shut. Mr. Minton said to Mrs. Singer, 'He won't know what you say to me.'

She shook her head. 'He'll know,' she said in an utterly defeated voice. 'He always knows. I've crossed him before. The last time he broke five of my ribs. But actually I haven't got much to tell you. I stayed at the party when it moved up to the lido. I haven't been to a party for a very long time. I was having fun. Dancing. I knew he'd make me pay for it but it was such a beautiful night, last night. All those stars and music on the water.'

'Yes,' said Minton gently. 'It was a corker night, all right.'

'And I knew I'd have to come back here, but I was free, just for that moment. I danced with the doctor and Mr. Green, and I even danced with Jack Mason. I saw Miss Fisher sitting out, looking just like one of those Chinese dolls. She's very beautiful, you know. Let me see, the Wests were there, several other people I didn't know. I didn't see the poor boy fall, only heard the screams. Then suddenly my husband grabbed me from behind. He hustled me down here and I haven't even looked out this morning. He wouldn't let me open the window.'

Minton could see, under the loose short sleeves of her blouse, the darkening marks of fingerprints on Mrs. Singer's fragile upper arms.

'What, no breakfast?' he asked cheerfully. 'Can't have that. You cut along and have something to eat, and I'll tell your husband I sent you there. All right?'

'Thank you,' she said, and scuttled out in case Mr. Singer should return.

When he did he was not informative. He had gone up to the lido to search for his errant wife when she didn't come back to the cabin. He had heard a scream and someone had told him that Mason had fallen off the ship. It was no business of his. He had escorted his wife back to their cabin. Neither of them had gone out again that night. That was all.

Mr. Singer worried Minton. There was an air of barely suppressed glee about the man which was foreign to his character, as described by both Green and Professor Applegate. What was the secret that was giving Mr. Singer so much pleasure? He was hugging it close to his chest like a greedy child hugs a stolen pudding. Peace shifted uncomfortably. He had noticed the same thing.

'All right, Mr. Singer, that will do for now. And just a hint, sir, if you'll forgive me. If I see any more bruises on your wife, I'll have you taken up for battery. Is that clear?'

'What has the bitch been telling you? She's mad, always has been, she makes things up!' shouted Singer.

'She didn't say a word. I've got eyes,' said Minton curtly. He collected his sergeant and left, trying not to slam the door.

'Phew,' said Peace.

'You bet,' agreed his inspector. 'I hate these wife-beating

bastards. Got to be something wrong with someone who has to hit women. Who's next?'

'Mr. Aubrey,' said Peace. Both Mr. Green and the professor had agreed that Mr. Aubrey was a charming aged gentleman of impeccable character.

He invited them in and asked if he should order tea.

'I reckon I'm about filled up with tea to pussy's bow,' said Minton. 'But thanks for the offer. What did you think of Jack Mason, Mr. Aubrey?'

'A good boy with time on his hands,' said Mr. Aubrey judiciously.

'That's what everyone says,' sighed Mr. Minton.

Peace was looking at Mr. Aubrey's cabin. It was draped with Indian painted cloths, enriched with brass idols, and stuffed with interesting handicrafts.

'I tend to collect a lot of things on voyages,' Mr. Aubrey explained. 'Then when I haven't room to move, I give them all away and start again. I'm a perpetual traveller, as I am sure they have told you.'

'Very pretty,' approved Mr. Minton. 'You didn't go out again after you left the dance last night?'

'No, I watched the stars for a while and went to bed,' said Mr. Aubrey, and they left him.

Miss Margery Lemmon, described by both informants as a nice girl, probably looking for a husband, fluent in Indian languages, Mr. Aubrey's niece, was not helpful. She was lying down and crying. She had been crying for hours by the state of her eyes.

'I just saw the boathook shoot out from the crowd,' she said. 'Then he was gone. Poor boy. Poor boy!'

'Mr. Forrester wasn't at the first class party at all,' said Peace, consulting his notes as they left Miss Lemmon to the ministrations of her stewardess. 'Next cabin is Mr. and Mrs. West.'

Mr. Theodore Green had said 'An unstable couple, always quarrelling. Mrs. West is flirtatious and Mr. West is jealous.' The professor had said 'Jonquil is a greedy slut and her husband is a perpetually tormented wreck, expecting at any moment to be crowned with horns. Both of them are superficial and tedious.' Professor Applegate did not habitually mince words.

The Wests were, however, polite. Mrs. West was wearing a trussed-tight dressing gown and her husband was still in his silk, monogrammed pyjamas.

'We were dancing the last dance when all of a sudden the poor boy fell,' said Jonquil in her high, child's voice.

'Did you see him fall, Mr. West?'

'No, I had my back to the rail. Jonquil gave a shriek and I asked her what on earth was the matter and she just pointed and screamed. Then a lot of other people were doing the same. Gave me the jumps. As soon as they let us go we came down here and we stayed, like the officer said.'

'And I was having hysterics,' said Jonquil proudly. 'The doctor had to give me brandy and sal volatile.'

Neither West had anything else to offer, except to say that Jack Mason was a nice boy. Mr. West said it through gritted teeth, but he said it.

'Not helpful,' commented Peace as they drew a breath outside. That cabin had been foul with sweat, cigarette smoke and expensive French perfume in about equal measure.

'It's all information,' said his boss. 'Now what?'

The Cahills were next. They hadn't seen a thing, and they had seen it together.

'I suppose we'd better talk to the Melody Makers,' said Mr. Peace as they left the Cahills's cabin. 'What if you do the musicians and I go down and see if I can talk to the Maoris?' Peace seemed uneasy.

'What have they told you about the Melody Makers, Don?'

'Just that they're man-eaters, sir, and I've never been very good with them sort of women.'

'Well, today's your day to learn a new skill. Come along with Papa, boy.'

The Melody Makers took one look at Peace and decided that he would do for breakfast. Then they considered his boss and decided that maybe they would leave the young man, so deliciously terrified, for another time. Detective Inspector Minton was a nice, polite, well spoken policeman who looked like a man who might see how a night in the cells would subdue a cheeky wench who got in his way.

So they were affable and absolutely unhelpful. No, they hadn't seen anything. Yes, they had been playing the last dance, the Maori Farewell. They were tired and inattentive and at least half of them had been on the booze, to the extent that some of them were only playing from conditioned reflex.

'We'd been playing for four hours almost nonstop,' said Mavis. 'And people kept bringing my girls drinks. What can you expect at that time of the night?'

'You grabbed a young woman and stopped her from falling,' said Peace to Jo, greatly daring.

'So would you have,' she retorted. 'I thought she was going to go down after him. And that's your lot,' said Jo. And it seemed that it was.

Hans Blum
Wilhelmshaven, Saxony

Dear Papa

I have left the shipyard and I am going to America. I do not want to build the Kaiser's warships. This can only end in disaster for the Fatherland. When I have a job I will send for you and Mamma.

Your son
Anton Blum

Chapter Seventeen

He hath at will
More quaint and subtle ways to kill;
A smile or kiss as he will use the art
Shall have the cunning skill to break a heart.

J Shirley
'The Last Conqueror'

Lunch was a fairly dismal meal. Margery had kept to her cabin, Phryne was feeling sad, Mr. Aubrey and Theodore Green were shocked, the Wests were subdued and not even bothering to quarrel, the Singers were distant, the Cahills horrified and Mr. Forrester was still demanding details, as he had missed the whole event. Finally the professor, who had long ago outlived her fear of death, explained the happenings of the previous night to him in crisp, measured tones. It was an excellent account. Everyone at the table nodded in agreement.

'He danced with several of you ladies,' said Mr. Forrester. 'Did he say anything about being threatened, feeling in danger?'

'No,' said Phryne. 'But he did smell rather strongly of spirits. Whisky, I believe.'

'Certainly did,' said Mrs. Singer. 'Definitely whisky.'

'When he was dancing with me I didn't smell a thing, except starch from his shirt,' protested Mrs. West.

'That's odd,' said Phryne. 'Not even a masking smell, like peppermint?'

'No,' said Mrs. West. 'And he didn't say a word to me. I thought he was angry. He seemed very tense. You can tell, if you are dancing with someone,' she said. 'Their back muscles are all hard.'

Odd, thought Phryne. Then she spoke aloud: 'I talked with him, but it was just the usual nonsense; lovely night, lovely party. Did he talk to you, Mrs. Singer?'

'Same sort of thing,' replied Mrs. Singer, watching her husband like a hawk. But Mr. Singer was still possessed of that strange glee which Minton had noticed and did not seem to be listening. 'Who'd want to kill that poor boy?'

'We'll let the police do their job,' said Mr. Aubrey firmly. 'And help them as much as we can. I wonder what they are going to do about this cruise? They can't hold a whole ship up for long.'

'No,' said Theodore Green. 'They're letting us go on with the cruise. We are taking that policeman and his assistant with us. Meanwhile the Harbour Trust will keep dredging for…the body. We leave tomorrow. Only one day late. We're one day at sea and then we'll report in at Christchurch. They've been very fair,' he said lamely.

'Good, good.' Mr. Aubrey rubbed his hands together. 'We'll all feel better when we're moving again. Ah, here's my vindaloo, and the chicken fricassée for you people without asbestos tongues. Come along, now, eat up. Mr. Green, could you signal to Pierre? I believe that we would all be comforted by a nice drink. On me,' he added.

'Thank you,' said Phryne, as the fragrant chicken dish was placed in front of her. 'You're quite right. We can't help Jack Mason now.'

Mr. Singer emitted a sound which was almost a giggle and waved away his usual omelette. He tucked into a plate of fricassée. Phryne felt a deep sense of unease. Mrs. Singer was also watching her husband in disbelief. He hadn't kicked her once. He was enthusiastically eating ordinary food as if there was no such thing as dyspepsia in the world. And he didn't even raise an eyebrow when she ordered a glass of that heavenly Rhine wine.

Phryne went to her suite very puzzled. Dot was there, sewing. She had finished her drawn thread work and was embroidering Australian flowers onto her tea cloth. This required less concentration than counting threads so she looked up when Phryne came in and exhibited the design.

'Nice,' said Phryne, shucking her shoes and throwing herself down on her bed. 'I always did like boronia. Dot, something very odd is going on with Mr. Singer.'

'He's a bad man,' said Dot, not surprised. 'What sort of odd?'

'He's got a secret, and he's delighted with it,' said Phryne slowly. 'And being a bad man, it's got to be a bad secret. I wonder what it is? I'd like to seize him by the throat and shake him until he told me. But we women are denied these simple pleasures. How are the crew taking this?'

'They're shocked,' said Dot. 'They liked Jack Mason and they don't think this'll be good for the company. I listened when they were all talking at breakfast and at lunch today, and no one seems to know anything. Except they've not found the boathook.'

'Where did it come from?'

'There's one stowed alongside each lifeboat,' said Dot. 'They're for pushing the boat away from the side of the ship when it's being lowered, as well as a lot of other stuff. Big ugly things with a brass head with a hook on.'

'Not much different from a good old English pike,' murmured Phryne. 'And this one is missing?'

'Yes,' Dot replied. 'And so is Mr. Mason's man. Thomas. The one who was so snooty about wines. They reckon he must have got off the ship while she was moored, and they're looking for him in Dunedin. It's not a big place and he's a stranger, he won't get far.'

'You've been talking to Detective Inspector Minton, haven't you?' accused Phryne, closing her eyes.

'No, Detective Sergeant Peace,' said Dot, not even blushing. 'He was in the crew's recreation rooms with the Maoris. He knows Caroline's father. I think he's some kind of relation. They all sat down and talked about the murder but no one knows anything. It was so sudden and unexpected that I don't think it'll be solved, Miss.'

'Oh, it'll be solved,' said Phryne. 'Ring up, Dot, and make me an appointment with the doctor at, say, three o'clock? Just a headache, that's all. I'm going to read for a little while. I want to think.'

Dot made the appointment and Phryne perused *The Murder of Roger Ackroyd*. If only real life could be that neat.

At three o'clock she was at the doctor's surgery door and was admitted by an affable Maori nurse. She was middle aged, plump and comfortable. Her white uniform shone with cleanliness and starch. Phryne could smell it. Which argued that Mrs. West's nose was also in good working order. And she had been dancing with Jack Mason late in the evening, after the others. And she had not smelt spirits on that spirit sodden young man. Strange.

'Doctor will see you now, Miss Fisher,' she said, and led Phryne into a well-equipped surgery. Doctor Shilletoe was sitting with his head in his hands.

'Nip out and order the doctor a cup of strong coffee, will you, Nurse?' she asked, and the woman gave her a conspiratorial grin and went out.

'Hello,' said Phryne. 'It's not as bad as all that, you know.'

The doctor raised his head. His eyes were bloodshot. His skin was grey. His mouth was loose. Phryne had seen more animation on corpses dug out of shell holes.

'It's worse,' he groaned.

'I think I know most of it,' said Miss Fisher, taking hold of both his hands. They were unnaturally hot. 'And it can be fixed. Both problems can be fixed.'

'How do you know?'

'You are not the first blackmail victim I have met,' said Phryne bluntly. 'Here is your coffee. Lots of sugar,' she instructed, watching him load it into the cup. 'That's right. Now, have you any aspirin? Take two. Have you had anything to eat today? I thought not. Sorry to ask again, Nurse, but can you rustle up some sandwiches for the doctor?'

'Right away,' said the nurse. 'You're doing him good, Miss. I've been that worried about him.'

Doctor Shilletoe, after the first few mouthfuls of coffee, began to resent this conversation.

'If you ladies have quite finished with your consultation about my state of health—'

'No use getting shirty with us,' his nurse told him firmly. 'You're the one who's eating your heart out. I'll go get some grub. Back soon. And you do what she tells you,' she added.

'She's been with me a long time,' apologised Doctor Shilletoe.

'And you're lucky to have her. A very competent person. On an empty stomach that aspirin ought to start doing its stuff pretty soon. But meanwhile, why not wash your face, shave, perhaps a clean shirt? You'll feel better.'

'Very well, Miss Fisher,' he said wearily. He got up and went into his own quarters. When he emerged ten minutes later, much cleaner, the nurse had returned with a tray.

'There,' she said, pouring him another cup of coffee. 'There's no one waiting and if anyone comes, I'll send them to Nicholls. And these are ham and cheese, your favourite.'

He picked up the first one languidly, then quickly demolished the plateful and another cup of coffee.

'There,' said Phryne. 'Human again. Tomorrow night I am setting a trap for your blackmailers, and I shall succeed in apprehending them. I will tell you all about that in a moment.'

The doctor made a broad gesture which swept the sandwich plate onto the floor, where it smashed. Phryne recalled that he did tend to break crockery when stirred.

'Miss Fisher, if that happens, I shall be ruined!'

'No, you shan't, if you do as I say. I've done this—and harder—things before. No one wants a fuss. If I can produce a neat *Murder of Roger Ackroyd* solution, everyone will be happy and no one will inquire further.'

There was a silence while a newly renovated doctor stared at Phryne Fisher in her blue suit, her hands folded in her lap in that Millais pose, her eyes as sharp as emeralds.

'Who are you?' asked the doctor. 'You are not the standard cruise passenger, I can tell you that.'

'Thank you,' said Phryne in a self-possessed manner. 'You are correct. I am a lot of things, some of which do not concern you, but mostly I am Phryne Fisher. Come along, Doctor. You have plunged yourself so deep into the soup that only one nostril is presently above the surface. I can extract you, but only if you trust me.'

'I have to think about it,' he muttered, avoiding her eyes.

Phryne stood up abruptly. 'You have until dinner. If, in the interim, you are intending to go and ask your blackmailers whether you should hand them over to justice, then you are a moron and I wash my hands of you. But your nurse and I think you are cleverer than that.'

'I hope you are both right,' he mumbled. 'All right. How, in fact, could things be worse? What do you want me to do?'

'Talk to me,' said Phryne. 'First, what did you do with the boathook? I want it back.'

He stared at her, utterly aghast. No wonder he had been reducing himself to a nervous wreck over the past few days, Phryne thought. This was a nice young man with a fundamental honesty which was being cruelly outraged by the minute.

'Fingerprints,' she explained. 'You're labouring under the delusion that there is only one criminal conspiracy aboard this ship. So you assumed that the boathook and the jewels are connected. But they aren't. So I want the boathook back, please. And then I want to examine your surgical instruments.'

'It's in the lifeboat,' said the doctor. 'Above the davits. Someone ought to find it soon. But it won't have fingerprints. I wiped it.'

'You are doing everything you can to ensure your own destruction, aren't you?' asked Phryne. 'All right. Now, the second question. Where is Jack Mason?'

His mouth worked. His eyes rolled back in his head. With a sense of timing which really could not have been worse, the doctor fainted. Phryne swore. Some people were very hard to rescue.

Phryne and the nurse managed to get the doctor to his own bed and Phryne left the stalwart woman to care for him while she swore her way to her suite, swore her way into her bathing costume, and snarled her way up the steps to the pool. She dived in and swam vigorously, allowing some of her exasperation to wash away, enjoying the water sluicing over her bare shoulders. She swam two lengths as fast as she could and pulled up puffing.

'Too much dancing and not enough swimming,' she told herself. At least there is no one around so I shall not have to try not drowning again. Curse that Shilletoe! What a time to faint!

Then again, she thought as she clung to the edge, getting her breath, he's clearly got no talent for intrigue. He is a good, straight, healthy, clean-living young man who would be putty in any blackmailer's hands. Poor doctor.

Phryne swam until she was tired and tinged a light but attractive blue. Dunedin weather had turned around and the sky was clouding over. She dried herself quickly, donned her robe, and was about to go downstairs when a huge hand closed on her arm. Another huge hand enveloped her face, cutting off both sight and the chance of screaming. Her attacker was so gigantic that Phryne guessed he was one of the Maoris and did not fight. Early, compulsory bible study had taught her that there was no use in kicking against the pricks. But once she got free and found out where she was, then the pricks would have to look after themselves.

She became aware that someone was murmuring in her ear.

'It's all right, Miss,' said the huge voice. She could feel it in his barrel chest like an organ note. 'Caroline sent me.'

'She could have asked,' said Phryne against the giant hand, but it was no use.

Down and down they went, via some sort of lift. Where on earth was her captor taking her? Phryne hadn't seen any lifts on the ship. Down and down and thump to a stop. A door clanked open.

'Bloody hell, Tui, I just told you to go get her, I didn't mean carry her here like a sack!' exclaimed someone very crossly. 'Put her down right now!'

'Gently!' said Phryne, as the enormous hands relaxed their grip all of a sudden and she started to fall.

Tui caught her and set her on the deck as though she was a lightly boiled egg and he didn't want to crack her shell. Phryne tied her gown closely about her. She was striving not to laugh.

'Caroline, I presume?' she asked.

The stewardess flushed bright red and plaited her apron between strong fingers.

'I'm so sorry, Miss Fisher. I only told him to get you quietly, and he didn't think of just asking you. He didn't mean any harm.'

'And he didn't do any harm. How did I get down here? Where am I? And what do you want of me?'

'This is a cargo deck,' said Caroline. Phryne looked around: crates, boxes, trunks, anonymous bales of stuff. Cargo, self-evidently. 'You came down in the cargo lift.' She indicated a steel door with buttons beside it. 'They put it in so the caterers could get a supper up from the kitchens without having to pass through the salons. You're here because Alice heard what you said to the doctor.'

'Alice being the nurse?'

'Yes.'

'And I'm here because you've got Jack Mason and you are wondering what to do with him?'

'Yes,' said Jack Mason. He seemed unhurt. He was clad in pyjamas and his hair needed brushing but apart from that he was in one piece.

'Why are you here?' asked Phryne.

'Well, you see, I still felt a bit rocky and I had definitely had too much to drink, so I went back to my cabin. Thomas was there and he asked me if he could borrow the costume. He wanted to dance with the pretty ladies. Always had ideas above his station, that man. Apart from him being my father's spy.

'I didn't see why not and I just wanted him to go away, so I said yes. Then my steward Roberts came and woke me early in the morning, saying that as far as anyone knew, I was dead, murdered, and what did I want to do? And I said I wanted to hide, to think about it. Sobering thought, having someone want to kill you. I didn't think anyone hated me that badly.'

'But you will be exposed as soon as the body is found,' said Phryne.

'But we'll be on the way to somewhere else by then,' he said, as though this was an important point.

Phryne felt like clipping his ears. 'My dear fool,' she replied, 'your murderer is on the ship with you. No one else but one of the dancers could have poked Thomas overboard with that boathook. Consider. Use your intelligence.'

There was a long pause while two was slowly and carefully added to two, the sum examined to see if it could be anything other than four, and the attempt abandoned. The young man's eyes widened.

'Oh,' he said, at last. 'What shall I do?'

'We shall contrive,' said Phryne. 'You stay down here for a few more hours and I'll go and talk to that nice cop. Caroline, I don't want to get anyone into trouble. We can manage this. But, tomorrow night, I might need your help. Can I, perhaps, borrow some things?'

'Anything,' said Caroline, vastly relieved that someone was

going to take the Jack Mason problem off her hands. Caroline, like the doctor, preferred to have a clear conscience and hers was sooting up in the manner of a back country stove.

'Thank you,' said Phryne, and named her needs.

Caroline grinned at her. 'Just as you say, Miss Fisher. Too right.'

'Good. Now get me back to the swimming pool, I've got things to arrange.'

Phryne Fisher, reclad in the usual habiliment of the gentlewoman, called in on Detective Inspector Minton and Detective Sergeant Peace as they were gloomily staring over the rail at Dunedin vanishing into heavy cloud.

'Reckon that might carry snow,' observed Peace.

'Reckon you're right. Just what the divers need, snow. Makes the water real comfy,' replied his boss, bitterly. 'What can we do for you, Miss?'

Detective Inspector Minton was not comfortable leaving Dunedin, where anything might happen if he was not there to protect it. He was definitely not in the mood for confident young women.

'Just a bit of news,' said Phryne breezily. 'The body you are looking for is the personal assistant Thomas, not Jack Mason. He borrowed Death's costume in pursuit of some jape or wheeze and therefore Thomas, not Mason, collected the boathook in the back and is now improving his acquaintance with the fishes.'

'How do you know this?' bellowed Minton.

'You told me not to investigate, so I didn't,' she said flatly. 'I have come into some information which is of use to you so, like any good citizen, I am telling you about it. It would be appropriate for you to say "Thank you, Miss Fisher" at this point, instead of shouting at me.'

'Thank you,' mumbled the policeman. 'But, jeez! This means we're looking for the wrong bloke.'

'Yes, you should call off the chase.'

'But, no one knew it was Thomas inside that costume and mask,' put in Mr. Peace. 'They thought they were killing Mason all right.'

'Where is Mason now?'

'I'll take you to him, provided there is no nonsense about either bullying the poor boy or charging him with anything. He was woken in the dark after a crack on the head, and he panicked. Also, I don't want any nasty legal repercussions against anyone who might have been aiding or comforting him.'

'Otherwise?' asked Minton, who did not like threats.

'Otherwise, you can start searching the ship for him,' said Phryne. 'And I don't think you'll find him until he wants to be found.'

'I don't like this,' said Peace slowly. 'If he's that well hidden the crew must be in on it. And if that Caroline knows about it, wild horses won't drag it out of them.'

'It's a ship,' snarled Minton. 'It can't be that big.'

His deputy looked at him significantly.

'It's that big,' said Phryne. 'And there are only two of you. The task is impossible. Come along,' she coaxed. 'It won't be as bad as all that. You go down and talk to Jack Mason and satisfy yourself that he's alive and had nothing to do with the murder. Be a good policeman. Then I'll give you a murderer for supper.'

'You will,' said Minton with heavy irony.

'Oh yes,' said Phryne blithely. 'Well, what'll it be?'

'Can't hurt,' said Detective Sergeant Peace, who had met Caroline's grandmother and didn't like to think of what she would do to him if he insulted her granddaughter.

'All right,' said Minton grudgingly. 'As long as you give me my murderer.'

'On toast,' said Phryne. 'With truffles.'

● ● ● ● ●

Spiridion Theotocopoulos
Corfu

Honoured father

I saw Theo in London as you told me and he got me the tickets for the ship and also showed me many places, like the Tower of London and the British Museum which has some marbles which belong to the Hellenes, and also the zoo which has lions. I never saw lions before. They are very big and fierce. I sail tomorrow, confident in the protection of our island's saint.

God bless you Papa.

Your loving son
Spiro

Chapter Eighteen

Weigh the vessel up
Once dreaded by our foes
And mingle with your cup
The tears that England owes

William Cowper
'Loss of the Royal George'

Dinner on Wednesday evening began rather sadly. Everyone seemed depressed. Table three, however, picked up their spirits as, with captain's compliments, Pierre was ordered to provide them with free drinks. The presence of two policemen at the next table went largely unnoticed. Margery Lemmon had joined the feast, mopped up if not recovered. Mr. Aubrey started a conversation with her in Farsi about love poetry.

Professor Applegate was talking to the Cahills about cattle stations she had visited. The Singers were present. Mrs. Singer was more puzzled than afraid, though she ordered her usual gewurztraminer. The Wests were marginally cheerier. Mrs. West had returned to her former mode of dressing and was partly clad in a purple crepe dress which slid off one shoulder all the time. Detective Sergeant Peace kept telling himself not to look. And looking.

Phryne Fisher wore dark blue and a collar of sapphires, with the great stone depending to her porcelain bosom, which drew Mr. Forrester's eyes. She was a poem in blue and white. He wished, very fervently, that someone would invent colour film, though he thought it very unlikely that science would ever progress that far. Only then could he really capture the white skin, blue gems, green eyes and pink lips of the divine Miss Fisher.

He sighed. Phryne patted his hand. She had put a lot of planning and effort into this dinner. When it was over Mr. Forrester might prove lucky again. He perceived this by some sexual telepathy, and smiled.

Conversation turned, for some reason, to shipwrecks as the waiters brought in the soup, a calm and gentle chicken broth. Phryne spooned it down. She might need her strength and chicken soup, it was well known, fed the wits as well.

'There is a difference between a wreck from natural causes and something like a torpedo,' said Mr. Aubrey. 'Or so it seems to me. One is an act of human malice. One is an act of foolishness, as in the *Titanic* disaster, or perhaps an act of God, like being caught in a typhoon. I was in a typhoon once. I swear, the wind caught us and the ship spun on her axis. The sky was yellow as poison and I commended my soul to God. Luckily, he didn't want it. That day.'

'I was in a typhoon in the Bight of Benin,' responded Margery Lemmon. 'It was awful. So hot, you know, the air like the breath out of an oven, and poor birds whirled like feather dusters through the air, and all the crew screaming…'

'I've been in some hard weather,' said Theodore Green, shocked that a crew should so far forget themselves as to scream. 'I remember one night in fog with every member of the crew that wasn't sailing the ship or tending the engines, even the cooks and the boys, hanging over the side looking for the faintest glint of ice. The sea was as flat as a plate, so we couldn't see the little ruffle of breakers which tells you there's an iceberg ahead. It was like that the night the *Titanic* sank. No moon and no sort of a sea.'

'Is it true that nine-tenths of an iceberg is underwater?' asked Phryne, putting a warning hand on Mr. Forrester's thigh. She hadn't been able to get around to him and the pressure of the hand asked him to play along. Mr. Forrester was quite willing to play along, especially if that hand stayed on his thigh.

'Yes, fully nine-tenths. You just have to look at the ice in your drink,' said Theodore Green earnestly. 'See how it rides?'

Mrs. West held up her glass and looked through it. 'Oh yes, I see,' she said. 'Most of it's under the surface.'

'Quite. They say that the iceberg that *Titanic* hit was as huge as a small island. Someone saw it later, and identified it because it had a streak of White Star red along its side.'

'Horrible,' said Mr. Cahill, whose idea of safety depended on at least a thousand acres between him and any sea water. Mrs. Cahill, who had left her hair in its loose ringlets and now wore a mere brush of powder and a little lipstick, patted his arm.

'You're thinking of John,' she said. 'My husband had a friend who drowned in the *Lusitania*,' she explained to the table at large.

'I was on the *Lusitania* when it was torpedoed,' announced Professor Applegate. Mr. Singer made his strange giggling noise again.

'Lord, you never told me that, m'dear!' said Mr. Aubrey. 'Tell us about it,' he urged.

'Not a nice story,' said the professor. 'But perhaps instructive.'

'I would like to hear it,' said Theodore Green.

'And so would we,' said Mrs. West.

Waiters took away the soup plates and served a very canonical Irish stew, made with local vegetables and strongly flavoured New Zealand mutton. It seemed to Phryne, as she listened, that the taste of the Irish stew infused the terrible story of the wreck of the *Lusitania*.

'It's what you were saying, Vivian, about the difference between being sunk by malice and sunk by inadvertence,' said Professor Applegate, tucking in her napkin. She was wearing her only formal evening dress again and could not afford to get it stained. 'I was travelling from New York, where I had been to a conference, really a very good conference, on Polynesian and Plains Indian creation myths. We left on May the first and six days later we were off the Irish Coast, expecting to dock fairly soon, when suddenly there was an enormous cracking noise, and a torpedo hit the ship. It was two in the afternoon. I was on deck. I could see the beastly thing as it surfaced to see what it had done and I am ashamed to say that at that moment I hated those men in their metal coffin and would have boiled them alive if I could.'

'Hate,' murmured Mr. Singer. Mrs. Singer leaned away from him.

'Then everything was confusion,' said the professor. 'The crew were trying to launch the boats, and there were enough boats for all of us, the *Titanic* disaster had taught the shipping lines about that, but the ship was going down fast, listing to starboard.'

'As her watertight bulkheads filled,' said Theodore Green. 'Makes it hard to launch boats.'

'Impossible,' said the professor. 'I saw them spill and no one in those boats ever came up again. I can't really convey how very horrible it was. I can still hear that screaming, men and women and children, all crying out against an unjust fate. They were being murdered and they knew it. The crew were doing their best, in most cases, and we weren't even very far out from the shore, but it was misty, and we seemed to be all alone, like a—like a fallen buffalo, a crippled horse, and that predator lying smugly in the water, waiting, watching us die. Ever since the *Lusitania* I really can't bear crocodiles.'

'But you were brave enough to sail again,' said Theodore Green, with great respect.

'Well, U-boats don't happen once wars are over,' replied the professor briskly. 'I'm not likely to meet another one of those again. I was lucky, I was with a female friend of mine, and we found ourselves in a lifeboat, one of the first to reach the little boats who had come out to help us. I was there with Elizabeth Duckworth. What a woman. When we passed people in the water, she asked if we could help, and when the crew member said no, Elizabeth said yes, and hauled people out by main strength. We got aboard the *Peel 12*, a fishing boat, and I was so glad to see it, and hear those soft Irish voices. They wrapped us in blankets and gave us cocoa and I've never tasted a drink so delicious. My friend Annie was so overcome she kissed the Irish boy who brought the cocoa and he blushed like a rose.'

The main course plates were cleared away, and waiters brought dessert, which was a selection of ice creams and fresh fruit, and a cheese board. The professor ate her ice cream and peeled a meditative nectarine.

'Yes, she was a wonderful woman, Elizabeth Duckworth. When a boat came in with only three men aboard—it had been capsized—and wanted to go back for other people, the petty officer said he couldn't spare anyone and Elizabeth said, "You can spare me!" and jumped aboard. They kept coming back with more people. I believe they saved forty.'

'Unlike the *Titanic*,' said Mr. Aubrey. 'But the water was so cold then. No one could live long in water with ice in it.'

'About four minutes without special clothing,' Theodore Green informed the table.

'Not such a bad death,' said Phryne, and heard Mr. Singer choke. Now she was sure. It just needed special care in approaching the point. Her table companions were doing splendidly. In a very short time they had bonded, and were now responding as a group.

'But a lot of people died in the *Lusitania*,' she said to the professor.

'Oh yes, dear, most of the children died. I think it was over a thousand bodies washed ashore eventually. The Irish villagers buried them as they came in, as an act of faith.'

'Not many ever washed up from the *Titanic*,' said Phryne.

'No, but it was in the wide ocean,' said Theodore Green. 'In the very deep water. That was a terrible thing, that *Titanic*. Folly, pure folly. I was on the *Carpathia*. Our radio operator was fooling around when he heard the distress call. He should have been in bed like the Marconi op of the *Californian*, who was closer to the sinking ship. I was just a boy at the time, you understand. All I knew was that the Old Man said, "Turn the ship", and suddenly we were racing through that same ice field, every spare man staring at the sea looking for ice, praying to any number of different gods.'

'Under those circumstances, my boy,' said Mr. Aubrey, 'they are all the same God.'

'Probably,' conceded the navigation officer. 'It was black dark and we zigged and zagged. When dawn came up and the captain saw what he had steered through, he said that some other hand than his must have been on the helm.'

'Very proper sentiments,' approved Mrs. Cahill.

'Captain Rostron was a very fine officer,' said Theodore Green. 'We had everything ready by the time we caught up, and we got those lifeboats aboard as though it was a drill. But there weren't many of them, and some of them weren't full...'

'And most of the survivors were from First Class,' said Phryne.

'Yes, Miss Fisher, and they were very shocked. Cold, scared, horrified. They said that the steerage passengers, when they finally gained the decks, ran like ants to the highest part of the wreck, and then...'

'She sank,' said Phryne.

'Yes,' said Professor Applegate. 'Taking thousands of people with her. Criminal. That captain was sensible in deciding to go down with the ship.'

'And they said that some of the stewards and sailors had barred the entrances to the decks so that the first class passengers could get away,' said Mr. Aubrey sternly.

'Murderers,' whispered Mr. Singer.

'Mr. Singer, I know your secret,' said Phryne to the man, who seemed about to cough or laugh.

'Eh? My secret?'

'You knew it wasn't Jack Mason in the Death costume.'

'Yes, yes, knew it was Thomas,' said Mr. Singer, and laughed again. 'What of it? No reason to kill Thomas.'

'Oh yes you had,' said Phryne gently. 'Wife and two children, was it, dead in some tragedy? Mrs. Singer told us that much. What tragedy, Mr. Singer? How did they die?'

'They drowned. She was taking them to her sister and they drowned,' said Mr. Singer.

'On the *Titanic*?' Phryne pressed.

'Yes,' said Mrs. Singer over Mr. Singer's escalating laughter. 'I've seen the certificates. That's where he got the capital to start his business. White Star paid out two hundred pounds for his wife and children. His name was Chant then, Jocelyn Chant. I never thought he cared about his family,' she added, wonderingly.

'She would have brought them back!' screamed Mr. Singer. 'She'd left me before, she'd left me often, but she wrote me a letter and said, you can write to me at my sister's, she would have come back to me, but they killed her.'

'Yes,' said Phryne in that same gentle, hypnotic voice. 'You have been tracking them down, haven't you? All of them that you can find. That's why you always check the crew register. The stewards who barred the way for the steerage passengers. The ones who condemned your wife and children to drown in the dark recesses of the sinking ship. Someone like Thomas, perhaps.'

'Like rats,' mourned Mr. Singer. 'Like ants, they say, never saying, like women, like children. Thomas was there. Told me so. Told Jack Mason so. On the crew manifest for the *Titanic*. I saw Mason go back to his cabin, he was drunk, then I saw Thomas come out. He had his patent leather shoes on. No one else wears them but him. I knew him. And I killed him,' said Mr. Singer. 'Well, I had to, didn't I? Put it to yourself,' he said.

His wife cringed away from him. 'And you know, I felt better,' he told Detective Inspector Minton as he raised him to his feet and applied handcuffs to his wrists. 'I felt much better after he was gone down to drown in the dark like my girls. I felt better every time. And I shall be well, quite well, when they are all dead!'

Minton gave Phryne a nod. She pointed to his table. On it, Pierre had just placed two glasses of cognac and a platter of pâté de campagne, toast and truffles.

The policemen led Mr. Singer away.

'I think you should have another glass all around,' said Phryne to the table at large. 'That was very skilled, friends.'

'Rather a good show,' said Mr. Aubrey. 'But surely he won't hang?'

'No, he's completely insane,' said Phryne. 'I'm sorry I couldn't get you out of this, Mrs. Singer. You shouldn't have had to watch that performance.'

'Yes, I should,' she said. 'Otherwise I might not have believed it. He talked about them sometimes, but I never thought he loved them, any more than he loved me.'

'Since we are being so frank, I believe that love has nothing to do with it,' said Mr. Forrester. 'It is all about power, influence and ownership. You're better off out of it,' he added.

This was so clearly true that table three just nodded and went on with cheese and coffee. The Melody Makers came in and began to set up. Phryne did not feel like dancing at present. She was suddenly very tired. However, she patted Mr. Forrester's thigh companionably. He had done very well for someone who was completely unrehearsed.

'Imagine him following all those stewards,' giggled Mrs. West. 'It's creepy!'

'Mrs. West,' Mrs. Cahill began.

Phryne could tell that the tension was about to be released with a nice quarrel, in which Mrs. Cahill would finally get to give Mrs. West a piece of her mind, and though that would be very instructive for Mrs. West and amusing for the rest of table three, it did not accord with Phryne's plans.

'Let's talk about something else,' said Phryne. 'Does anyone know anything about Christchurch? I need to do some souvenir shopping. Rather a lot, in fact. I believe Mr. Aubrey mentioned dolls?'

'Oh yes, Miss Fisher, there is an excellent doll maker in Christchurch,' he said, picking up the hint very quickly. 'You will love his shop, Mrs. West. Every possible sort of doll you can imagine.'

'And books,' said Phryne. 'Possibly handicrafts? I already have a length of that beaten flax fabric.'

'*Tukutuku*,' said the professor. 'It's very fine. You might wait until we get further north, near Rotarua, for any more Maori things. But you must buy a few hand-knitted shawls in Christchurch,' she said. 'Perfect for anyone who feels the cold. New Zealand wool is very fine,' she said, then, deferring to Mr. Cahill, 'though not as fine as Australian wool, of course.'

He accepted the compliment. 'Nice of you to say so,' he said gruffly. 'I reckon we might turn in. Been a real interesting evening, but,' he said. He collected his wife and went away. Mrs. Cahill left him by the door and came back.

'Mrs. Singer, perhaps you'd like to come to our suite? The police will…er…probably be in yours for some time.'

'Thanks,' said Mrs. Singer. 'Very kind of you. But I'm sure the ship can find me a little place somewhere. I don't want much. But I do want to be alone tonight,' she said fervently.

'I'll make some arrangements,' said Theodore Green, getting to his feet.

'And I'm going to dance with Mr. Forrester,' said Mrs. West, and dragged him away. Mr. West scanned the table for a partner, struck out with Phryne and Margery Lemmon, and went to find suitable company.

The Melody Makers were playing 'Romona' when a familiar figure came in and was immediately enveloped in Margery Lemmon, who hugged him tight and then clipped him over the ear.

'Oh, Jack Mason, I cried for you!' she exclaimed wrathfully.

'Sorry about that, old girl,' he said, rubbing his ear. 'Is it all over?'

'It's all over,' said Mr. Aubrey. 'Come and sit down, boy. Might as well have some of that pâté and toast, maybe some more cheese, some cognac for us too, eh, Pierre? How are you, Jack?'

'Bit confused,' said Jack Mason. 'But once Miss Fisher started sorting out my life, it all came good. You're a miracle worker, Miss Fisher. I'm sorry you cried,' said Jack to Margery Lemmon, who was proving that she had by doing it again. 'Here, take my handkerchief. Never meant to make any lady cry,' he added. Margery took the handkerchief and slapped his hand.

'Mrs. Singer, there's a nice little cabin ready for you.' Theodore Green had come back with a steward. 'Joanie here's ready to take you to get your things and then she can show you where it is and get you all settled in.'

'Do you want some company?' asked Phryne. Mrs. Singer bent suddenly and gave Phryne a fast, throttling hug.

'No. I'm on my own,' she said with a faint exultancy in her voice. 'I'll be fine now. Thank you for…finding him out. He would have kept on doing it. Now he won't be able to hurt anyone anymore. I'll come right now,' she told Joanie, and they went out together.

'Sit yourself down,' said Mr. Aubrey to Theodore Green. 'And drink this glass of cognac, for which you will be forgiven, and tell us what is happening.'

'Just this once, then. It's not every day P&O carries a murderer. Well, the policemen have locked the prisoner in the punishment cell. There's a crewman on guard outside. They're on their way back, I believe. Say they owe Miss Fisher a drink. The radio operator has sent a message on to Christchurch police and they will take custody of him.'

'Imagine that man brooding all his life about the death of his first family, and waiting sixteen years for his revenge!' said Mr. Aubrey.

'He didn't have anything else to think about,' said Jack Mason. 'No other children. Hated his wife, poor woman. Anyone could see that.'

'Yes,' said Phryne. 'Did you know Thomas had been on the *Titanic?*'

'Oh yes, he made no secret of it. Said it was a magnificent ship. Raved about its wines. Never told us how he got off it, though, when so many other crewmen drowned. Probably bashed someone over the head and dragged them out of their lifeboat. He wasn't a nice man,' concluded Jack Mason. 'Just the sort of person my father would hire to keep an eye on me. I'll have to send the old man a telegraph tomorrow. I'm glad the ship hadn't got around to telling him I was dead.'

'Oh but we had,' said Theodore Green, looking stricken.

'Then perhaps he'll be pleased that he doesn't have to go to the expense of a funeral,' said Jack Mason. 'I say, this pâté is rather good.'

'Isn't it?' said Miss Lemmon, and piled her toast high.

When Detective Inspector Minton and Detective Sergeant Peace returned to the diners, the party had become rather hilarious, partly with relief. Jack Mason was dancing with Margery Lemmon, who didn't seem to be able to stop laughing. Mr. Forrester, who had palmed Mrs. West off on an unoccupied officer, was telling stories of Paris and artist's models, and Phryne was retailing how she had once found herself entirely naked and freezing, the only blanket in the atelier being used to cover the artist's pet wolfhound, and decided at that point that being a model was not as glamorous as she had been led to believe.

'Buy you a drink, Miss Fisher?' asked Minton.

'Only if you sit down and eat your pâté, toast and truffles, and drink your cognac,' said Phryne.

'For you,' said the Detective Inspector, 'I'd eat uncooked crow. That was a corker effort, Miss Fisher. You know that he's done it before?'

'I thought he might have,' said Phryne. Detective Sergeant Peace picked up a piece of toast, truffle and pâté, nibbled dubiously, then ate the rest with relish.

'This is real good, Boss,' he urged. 'Come on, Boss! Let down your hair a bit. You made a great pinch tonight.'

'Yes,' said Minton expansively. 'So we did. Ladies, gentlemen, we made a great pinch. I hope the lot of you never take to a life of crime because you'd be bloody good at it. Gimme that glass, Peace, and don't hog the truffles.'

Rachel Rosenbaum
Brooklyn, New York

Dear Sister

By now you will think that we are on the high seas on the way to visit you, but you will be wrong. Why is this? Because Israel went mad, it seems, we were all on the ship, all ready to go, they had blown the going ashore siren, then suddenly, up comes Izzy, red, puffing, grabs my arm, says come with me, bring the girls, you aren't sailing on this ship, well, I didn't know what to say, but people were looking so I went with him, anyway, he was dragging me. I was so ashamed! And all our trunks gone with the ship, the girls were crying, I asked him, Izzy, what are you doing? And all he could say was that he had a dream and—there we were! We're sailing tomorrow on another ship and we've all got new things so I suppose it's all right but he has me worried.

Do you think it could be true what that Maxie told us that Izzy had an uncle who had to be put away somewhere nice and quiet? And I never did get to the bottom of that family fuss about his sister.

Puzzled,
Your sister Minnie

Chapter Nineteen

Fair Cloe blush'd: Euphelia frown'd
I sung, and gazed: I play'd and trembled:
And Venus to the Loves around
Remark'd, how ill we all dissembled.

Matthew Prior
'An Ode'

Phryne danced, after all. There was an air of satisfaction about the ship, as though a large beast had sought attention from a tick bird which had found and removed an irritating parasite. She thought about Mr. Singer in his long revenge, hating until his soul was irremediably putrefied within him, blood flowing with the acid which rotted even his stomach. She shivered slightly and Mr. Forrester held her tightly.

'All right?' he asked.

'Yes,' she said. 'You know, I just don't have the concentration to do what Mr. Singer did. I forget about injuries soon enough.'

'You have other things to think about,' said Mr. Forrester. 'He didn't. He narrowed his focus down to one thing and could not be distracted.'

'A good definition of a murderer,' agreed Phryne.

'And Mrs. Singer will recover,' he said soothingly. 'Some

women immediately go out and find another heavy-handed brute, but I don't think she will.'

'No, not now she has escaped.'

Phryne and Forrester danced away. Mavis and the Melody Makers were really putting their backs into their music tonight, Phryne observed. The tempo was a whisker quicker, the notes more accurately struck or hooted. Lizbet Yates was dragging notes out of her trumpet which perfectly harmonised with the effortless jazz voice, floating above each note before hitting it like an arrow to a target. Bull's eye.

'I went down to Saint James' Infirmary,' sang Magda. 'And I saw my baby there...so cold, so white, so bare...'

Phryne's mind was suddenly presented with the picture of a sea covered in corpses, cold and white and bare.

'I'm worn out,' said Phryne to Forrester. 'I'm going to bed. Thank you for your company,' she said, leaning up and kissing him gently on the mouth.

Mr. Forrester did not press her to join him in his cabin. He escorted her to her door and was rewarded for his forbearance with another kiss.

'Dot, you in?' asked Phryne as she stepped into the room.

'Yes, Miss,' said Dot from her own room. 'So you got him?'

'I got him,' said Phryne.

'I knew you would,' said Dot. 'I told them you'd get him. That policeman was cock-a-hoop. They telegraphed from Christchurch that he'd done it before when he was called Chant. How's poor Mrs. Singer?'

'Relieved,' said Phryne. 'Oh, you've got Scragger.'

Scragger, lying in a pose made fashionable by the sphinx, was near the French windows, staring blandly out at the night.

'He was in here when I came from dinner,' Dot responded. Phryne stooped to caress the nibbled ears and knocked against Dot's sewing box, sending reels of thread rolling all over the floor.

'How clumsy of me,' she exclaimed, dropping to her knees as

Scragger, leaping to his paws, began to chase them. 'Dammmit, Scragger, don't, they'll go everywhere.'

Several of the reels had gone under Phryne's elaborate bed and she dived in after them. Dot heard her say, 'Well, well,' and then Phryne crawled out, put her arms around Scragger, and started to laugh.

'Miss?' asked Dot, plucking the last reel out from between Scragger's iron claws and replacing it in the sewing box. Scragger, who was not used to being embraced, oozed out of the importunate arms and resumed his place by the windows. Phryne kept laughing.

She stopped before Dot could really begin to worry about her.

'Well, that explains everything,' she said at last. 'No need to worry, Dot, I haven't taken leave of my senses. Or, at least, I don't think I have.'

'Diving around the floor in that delicate brocade,' grumbled Dot as Phryne got to her feet and allowed Dot to peel off the misused dress. Her employer was still struck with occasional fits of the giggles as they went through the evening ritual of bathing, the brushing of hair and the donning of pyjamas. Only once did Dot ask why she was amused, and Phryne said, 'Ever since I started explaining my solutions, Dot dear, you've been saying that they are simple. This time I am going to make an effect. Goodnight,' she said, and threw herself into her bed.

Dot went to her own, puzzled. She devoted some moments to praying for the soul of Mr. Singer and his victims, and all who perished in the sea, and then for Mrs. Singer alone in her cabin. Then she went to sleep, leaving her puzzles in the hands of God, who knew the answers. She slept like a log in that confidence.

Thursday

At breakfast Phryne announced that her maid was leaving her for the night to sleep in the crew's quarters. 'They're making a dress,' said Phryne. 'Dot is a very fine needlewoman. Apparently one of the stewardesses is getting married and they are getting her trousseau together.'

'Very nice,' said Mrs. Singer, who was washed and brushed and seemed already more at ease. 'I always think it's more fun to sew in a group. That's how our ancestors used to do it, you know. All get together to make a quilt or any big project.'

'I would have been supplying the refreshments,' said Phryne. 'I can't sew a stitch.'

'No necessity, Miss Fisher, when you have so many other talents,' said Mr. Aubrey. Phryne wondered if she had really caught a mischievous glint in the old man's eyes. 'I am sure that you read aloud very well. That would please the needlewomen. I believe that my grandmother, in her time, read her way through the entire works of Walter Scott, though, now I come to say it, it does rather beggar belief. How are you occupying the day, then?'

'I'm swimming,' said Phryne. 'Then perhaps a little reading. The usual.'

'Come up and watch the deck tennis,' said Jack Mason. 'You don't have to play. Mr. Green will explain the rules, I am sure.'

'Delighted,' said Theodore Green.

'We shall see,' said Phryne. Hell would freeze over, she thought.

'So you'll be quite alone tonight?' asked Mrs. West. 'I wouldn't like that. If my husband isn't with me, I've always got Maggie.'

'Ah yes, your maid,' said Phryne. 'Has she been with you long?'

'Oh, forever,' said Jonquil West airily. 'She's a bit upset at the moment. She was close to Mr. Thomas. I've told her that she has to get over it. He wasn't at all a nice man.'

'But she might have liked him,' said Margery Lemmon. 'Even the most evil characters have someone who likes them, even if it's only their mother.'

'And that's true,' said Phryne, rising to take her leave. 'See you at lunch,' she said, and left.

To Phryne that day passed with geological slowness. As the *Hinemoa* pottered along towards Christchurch, Phryne half expected to see fossils forming on the shores as she watched: fossil trees, fossil horses, fossil men. Hours dragged their feet with the bright alacrity of aeons.

Phryne swam herself to exhaustion and had a short nap before lunch. She went to interview the doctor and secured his puzzled acquiescence to whatever she felt like doing to save him. Then she was driven, after Dot had been exasperated to the point of screaming by her mistress walking around the suite picking things up and putting them down again—in the wrong places!—to the library, where she decided she had better stay.

Phryne found notepaper and pen and began to translate her Chaucer. This was difficult. Even though some words appeared to mean the same as they did in 1928, she could not be sure of that, and attempting to translate and keep the rich rhyme was almost impossible.

'The Pardoner's Tale' was a moral treatise on the dangers of greed. Of course, he didn't like gluttony either: 'Oh womb, oh belly, oh stinking cod! Full filled of dung and corruption!' But then, pardoners made their living out of sin. If everyone heeded their strictures and became moral, they would be out of a job. There did not seem to be much likelihood of that happening, however.

Phryne read on as the young men gathered around the pot of gold and began, instantly, to plot to kill each other off. And did, the last being poisoned by food which he had forced one of his early victims to prepare. The gold remained where it was, a glittering, beautiful, nectar-trap, poised like a sundew, for whoever walked past it.

It was getting dark. Phryne closed her book. At last, the long day was over and it was time to dress for dinner.

• ● ● ● •

Dinner was, as always, excellent. Phryne found herself sitting next to Mrs. West, not her preferred seating. However, Jonquil appeared to be in an affable mood. She talked lightly about the dolls she would buy in Christchurch and the difference in washing survival of various sorts of silk.

'Of course, you can always sponge the dress with vinegar and dry it in the shade, but that doesn't seem entirely clean to me,' said Mrs. West, leaning close to Phryne.

'I suppose not,' said Phryne, who had given up on domestic detail ever since she had been able to afford people to do it for her. They presumably knew all about how to wash things, it was their profession, so who was Phryne to interfere?

'No sense in washing good silk,' said Mr. Aubrey unexpectedly. 'Takes the gloss off it. Needs to be pounded with fuller's earth and shaken. They make a silk in China, I'm told, that only retains its shine in darkness. Moonlight, it's called. It loses colour as soon as it is exposed to the sun. Fabulously expensive,' he added.

'And foolish extravagance,' said the professor. 'I've never seen any point in spending that much money on clothes. Not when books are to be had,' she said.

'No, indeed,' said Margery Lemmon. 'No offence, Miss Fisher, Mrs. West.'

'None taken,' said Phryne, sliding her glass under the table and gently pouring the liquid into a towel which Pierre had placed there on her instructions. It was a pity to waste good wine like that but she was fairly sure that it was not as the vintner had left it.

The meal went on. Phryne ate lamb chops, roast potatoes and green peas, which were excellent. She disposed of three glasses of wine and a dessert soufflé of surpassing delicacy.

Then she yawned, apologised, yawned again a few moments later and told the company that she was suddenly very sleepy, and that she must bid them goodnight.

When she got back to her cabin, Dot was waiting. 'You're sure you don't need me?'

'No, and I don't want you anywhere near when it all happens. Off you go, Dot dear, have fun sewing, and I'll come for you as soon as it's all over.'

'You promise?' demanded Dot, eyeing Phryne narrowly.

'I promise,' said Phryne, wetting her finger and crossing her heart.

'All right, then,' said Dot. She took her sewing basket and went out. Phryne locked the door and did the usual night-time things, in case anyone was watching or listening. She dressed herself in her pyjamas, which were of green silk, and lay down on her bed with a packet of gaspers, an ashtray, a flashlight, her little gun, and a sense that the end justified the means. Her preparations were all complete. Now she had to wait.

She fretted and smoked for half an hour, then fell into the cat's watching trance. Her mousehole was covered. Phryne lay as still as any sleeper. There were no lights in the suite. Dot's room was innocent of occupation. Surely the robber would take this opportunity, which might never come again, to gain the big blue stone which had once been an eye of Krishna.

There was a faint noise—far too faint to wake a sleeper—then four hardened paws hit the bed and Phryne found Scragger had joined her little tête-à-tête. He had clearly been hunting, but luckily had not brought his rat with him, probably having consumed it in situ. Phryne stroked down the knobbly spine and Scragger purred his rusty purr. He lay down, tucking his paws under him, and Phryne readjusted her hearing.

It was very late when Scragger tensed under her hand and Phryne woke from a light doze. There were definite scraping noises coming from under her bed, and at the same time, someone tried the door. She heard the handle make its characteristic creak as it was turned. Scragger stood up, interested.

Then there was a snap and a howl, and Phryne turned on the lights. She took the little gun in hand, went to the door and unlocked it. Two policemen, Tui and Caroline were there. So was Mrs. West, securely held by the stewardess.

'Come in, ladies, gentlemen,' Phryne invited.

Both policemen entered. Tui bent and hauled on a wire, and out from under the sumptuous bed, noosed like a rabbit and kicking like one, came Mr. West. He was wearing black clothes and a black stocking over his head. Tui stood the robber on his feet and pulled off the stocking.

'Hello,' said Phryne. 'Were you looking for this?'

She dangled the sapphire in front of his nose.

This, in retrospect, she considered to have been unwise. West wrenched himself free of Tui and dived for Phryne, grabbing at the stone. She dropped it and kicked him very hard in the place where she felt it would do the most good. All the men in the room winced. Tui reclaimed his captive.

'Now, Mrs. West, what were you doing here outside Miss Fisher's cabin?' asked Detective Inspector Minton.

Jonquil West flew at him, nails forward, and was restrained by Caroline. Neither of the Wests had spoken a word but this action seemed to break their silence.

'But I saw you drink that wine,' said Jonquil artlessly.

'Jonquil, shut up!' yelled Mr. West frantically.

'I didn't drink it,' said Phryne. 'I bet an analysis of it will show how much laudanum you put in it.'

'Just to put you to sleep,' protested Jonquil, as Tui gagged Mr. West with one huge hand. 'Just to get the gem, you see. My husband found that hole under the bed one night while we were staying in this suite. It's an old ventilation shaft. It leads down into the doctor's surgery, so we could always say that's where we had been. Wasn't it clever of him?'

'Very clever,' said Minton, delivering himself of the usual warning. 'Come along with me, Mrs. West. Mr. West. And Miss Fisher,' he added. 'There's still a lot of explaining to do.'

'I'll just go and tell Dot that I'm all right,' said Phryne. 'And when Caroline has handed Mrs. West over to someone else, I'm sure that she can supply a very good meal for Scragger. Fish, Lobster, perhaps. I never would have worked it out without him.'

Scragger had seldom been kissed on the nose by a beautiful lady, but he didn't seem to mind. He sat enthroned on Phryne's silken bed and blinked benevolently as the prisoners were removed. Scragger, like most cats, understood as much English as he needed to. The future, if he understood Miss

Fisher correctly, would contain fish. A lot of fish and perhaps even lobster. That was good enough for Scragger.

It wasn't until they were out in the corridor again that Mrs. West started to scream. Phryne collected her bag, the sapphire, a surgical instrument and her key and went with the party. Her endgame had been staggeringly successful. Perhaps she should take up chess, after all.

Henry Tolhurst
Fitzgerald, Georgia

Dear Hank

She sure is a mighty fine ship, this one. We're moving like a running horse. The rep from the company is on board and I reckon he's making the Cap try the ship's paces. I'm longing to get home and smell the magnolias. They ought to be blooming in every tree by now. Remember me to your Mama and Papa and that fine woman your sister Josie. I'll post this at Cherbourg.

Your friend
Roy

Chapter Twenty

But busy, busy, still art thou,
To bind the loveless joyless vow
The heart from pleasure to delude,
To join the gentle to the rude.

J Thomson
'Fortune'

The meeting was in the captain's ready room, a charming place with navigational instruments and charts, terribly nautical. In it, the pyjama-clad Phryne and the black-clad Mr. West rather stood out. Now provided with handcuffs, the prisoners sat sullenly in their chairs, and Phryne was free to roam, accept drinks, and expound. Pierre had broken out the Veuve Clicquot for the occasion and the captain did not even seem to notice.

'I became suspicious of the Wests because they didn't seem to enjoy cruises,' said Phryne. 'Mr. West is very jealous and Mrs. West spends a lot of time flirting. So why bring her—repeatedly—into a place where she has an endless supply of young men to flirt with? Seemed strange. All of the others are on the ship because they really like it; the professor and her beloved Maoris, Mr. Aubrey and his perpetual travelling, Miss Lemmon who is having a wonderful time. The Cahills are here because she can't walk like she did and he can't drive, and both of them need to stay away from their property to give their sons a chance to run it alone. The Singers, well, we know about the Singers. Mr. Forrester has an endless supply of the female form divine, his passion. But the Wests were uncomfortable and unhappy—so I wondered, why would they spend all this money in order to be uncomfortable and unhappy?'

'Reasonable question,' grunted the captain.

Captain Bishop was profoundly disturbed. Miss Fisher had suggested to his officers that she could extract everyone from out of the soup. He hoped it was true. She looked far too much like a Dutch doll for his complete confidence. Her delivery of her investigational report, however, was as crisp as one of his own officers reporting on navigational conditions. There might be hope for the *Hinemoa* yet.

'I examined all the other thefts carefully, thanks to the excellent briefing notes made by your navigation officer,' said Phryne. Mr. Green bowed politely. 'There were two sorts of theft; the one from the lady's actual cabin, as in the case of La Paloma and her ruby and Berengaria Reynolds and the Attenbury emeralds. They occupied the same suite that I am staying in. Sealed room mysteries are well explained in John Dickson Carr, and one of his solutions to a sealed room mystery is that it is not entirely sealed. That is, there is some sort of trapdoor or secret passage, the roof lifts off, and so on.

'I did wonder how the admirable Scragger was able to wander into my suite whenever his heart desired. But in each case, he might have come in with someone. It wasn't until I found the hole in the wall under my bed that I realised it was a John Dickson Carr solution. The occupant never stirred because either Mrs. West (in my case) or Maggie (in the case of my companion) had stirred a solid dose of laudanum into their supper. I guessed about the mask because a small girl, who nearly had her teddy bear stolen by that man, said that he had no face. No, don't say anything yet, Mr. West. You may hear something to your advantage.'

West's eyes were fixed on Phryne. His gambler's instinct told him that somewhere in this quiet woman's words there was a ghost of a chance of some sort of escape.

'The other gems, Mrs. West's pearls—they were stolen to divert suspicion from this unlovely couple—were stolen by means of a trick. I wondered how it could be done, some sort of magnet, a hook, perhaps? Then I realised that in their perambulations into the doctor's surgery they had picked up one of these.'

The captain examined it. It was a pair of long steel pincers with two blunt-ended blades and some sort of screw arrangement.

'What's this thing?'

'Used to extract bullets and so on,' said Phryne. 'For the Wests' purposes, however, note that it has very sharp blades. Mrs. West just danced close enough, and then inserted a blade under the fastening. Snip, it parted, and the necklace was caught by the hook.'

'But we searched everyone!' cried Theodore Green. 'No one left the salon!'

Phryne held out her glass to be refilled and laughed.

'You were aware, were you not, that Lizbet the trumpet player always parks a huge lump of her revolting chewing gum behind one of the Tiffany panels while she is playing? And what could be simpler than to just stick the glittering prize on the chewing gum? It's quite strong enough, and no one would see the jewels through that multifaceted, gorgeous, semi-opaque border.'

'And then reclaim them once the room is searched. Very clever, Miss Fisher.'

'Thank you. The question remains, however, what are we going to do with the Wests? Do we want a huge scandal, in which both the *Hinemoa* and her officers are plunged into ruin? Or have we an easier solution?'

'Miss Fisher,' said Detective Inspector Minton, 'are you leading me into temptation?'

'Not precisely,' said Phryne, smiling at this dutiful minion of the law. 'Now, consider. We cannot prove the previous thefts.

They are past and gone and insurance has been paid for them. All of the people in question have been compensated for their losses. Right?'

'Yes,' said the captain. Light was beginning to dawn, even though it lacked some hours to sunrise. He felt hope stir in his heart.

'The Wests would doubtless strenuously resist any attempt to charge them with the previous thefts, wouldn't they?' she asked. West was quick on the uptake. He had been waiting for an opportunity and took it.

'Strenuously,' he said. Jonquil West, who seemed entirely stunned, nodded.

'But they would probably accept a plea of guilty on the attempted theft of my sapphire. Ought not to cost you both too many years in the clink, Mr. West. Or perhaps you would like to think about an attempted murder charge? You could have drowned me. And it's no use saying that you had an alibi. All you had to do to fool that poor blindfolded Jack Mason was to alter his clock. He was calculating the time by its chimes. Shall we talk about drugging my companion?'

'No,' said West. 'You've got your guilty plea.'

'And an undertaking of silence, of course, and on the under-standing that if either of you show your noses on a P&O vessel again, the captain has firm instructions to have you keel-hauled.'

'Actually, I don't believe that we keel-haul people anymore…' began Mr. Green. His captain glared at him.

'For these two, we could revive an immemorial custom of the sea,' he growled. 'Well, West? Do you agree?'

'But,' said Mr. West, thinking quickly. This was a very good deal. Such a good deal that he began to wonder what else Miss Fisher was hiding. Phryne caught him calculating and said, very sweetly, 'Yes or no, and you can't change your mind. We are playing, as the children say, for keeps.'

'Yes,' said West. 'Yes, for both of us.'

'Well, that's it,' said the captain. 'Good riddance to bad rubbish. How about it, Detective Inspector? You've got your criminals and my ship won't be compromised.'

'Well…' said Detective Inspector Minton.

Sergeant Peace stared wide eyed. He had never seen his chief at a loss before.

'Come along,' coaxed Phryne, now well flown on expensive champagne, rhetoric and adrenalin. 'I only promised you one solution. Now you've got two for the price of one. You can get off the ship in Christchurch, take them all back to Dunedin, and I bet your chief will be pleased with you.'

'Lay on a tender,' offered Captain Bishop. 'No need to waste time. Get you back to Dunedin by sea much quicker. You can take Singer and the Wests.'

'All right,' said Detective Inspector Minton slowly. He was aware of undercurrents so strong that they were almost over-currents, but it was another good pinch. 'You give me a set of sworn depositions, so I don't need you in court, and I reckon we can do it.'

'I can swear the depositions,' said the captain. 'Now, how about a glass of wine? I see that Pierre has been so good as to open the Roederer. It'll only go to waste now the bottle is open.'

'Done,' said Detective Inspector Minton, and smiled.

Two Days Later

When the *Hinemoa* arrived in Picton, Phryne Fisher, decked out in all of her diamonds and a wisp of gauze, was reclining on Mr. Forrester's bed while he fussed about the position of her feet. Sitting in a good light near the window was Dot, embroidering boronia onto her tea cloth. Dot was coming round to the conclusion that Miss Fisher had been right about being an artist's model. It was not compromising. But it was tedious.

Miss Fisher's visits to Mr. Forrester's cabin were thereafter assumed to be in connection with his photography, and no mention was made of them. Mr. Forrester's afternoons had suddenly become filled with interest and excitement.

● ● ● ● ●

On Charleston Thursday, the prize was won by the unexpected team of Miss Fisher and Navigation Officer Green, who danced to the tune of 'Roll 'em, Girls, Roll 'em' and 'Varsity Rag' with what was judged to be superior enthusiasm and dash. Green thought it worthwhile, even though he had to wear surgical bindings on his mistreated ankles for two days thereafter.

Five slow and languorous days since the arrests, Phryne and table three had returned from a visit to a hot spring, where they had been massaged and soaked and boiled until Phryne began to feel a gentle pity for lobsters. Phryne, Mr. Aubrey, Professor Applegate and Mr. Forrester were seated in the Palm Court, repairing their strength with iced lemonade. Jack Mason and Margery Lemmon had gone to play deck tennis with the doctor, who had quite recovered his nerve.

'But you mustn't try anything like it again,' said Phryne carefully to the table at large. 'I only managed to keep you all out of it by making a shameless deal with the Wests.'

'What do you mean?' asked the professor, sharply.

'The doctor betrayed himself at once,' said Phryne, studying the sprig of mint in her glass. 'Being a nice young man he was naturally pie for such a woman as Mrs. West. She seduced him and blackmailed him into letting her repellent husband get into my suite through Scragger's entrance. He was easy. Poor idiot even wiped the boathook because he thought West had killed Thomas. But, I wondered, why did the Wests keep at this jewel theft caper? It was hugely risky. Surely one of those gems was worth enough to make retirement sound good? And then I thought, yes, they might just be amazingly greedy, but what if they managed to steal the gems, and somehow didn't manage to keep them? What, in fact, if they were still as poor as they had been?'

'An interesting theory,' said Mr. Forrester, alertly.

'I thought so. And then I recalled that each one of the people who lost jewels had left someone in need. La Paloma's child. Miss Reynold's companion. The young man Mr. West ruined. And I wondered if some public-minded people might not feel that keeping the jewel, selling it in a suitable port, and sending the money to the afflicted one might not be rather poetic justice. Minus, of course, ten percent for handling fees.'

'A charming idea,' said Mr. Forrester. 'Very Raffles.'

'I thought so,' said Phryne. 'But now the Wests are gone, to languish for some time in a Dunedin jail—at least Mrs. West won't have anyone to flirt with there—it can't continue, however good the cause.'

'No, under those circumstances, of course it could not continue,' said Mr. Aubrey. 'Speaking hypothetically, you understand.'

'And, speaking hypothetically again,' said the professor, 'how did you come to these conclusions, Miss Fisher?'

'Call me Phryne,' said Phryne. 'You had an auditor. I worked it out from a sequence of coincidences in choice of song. By some freak of acoustics, the Melody Makers could hear every word said at this table.'

Phryne had her answer. Everyone at the table changed colour, jumped, or began a course of advanced fingernail study.

'They gave us away?' asked Mr. Forrester.

'They didn't say a word,' said Phryne. 'I understand that the Wests gave you the jewels just because you could have put them in jail. But they will be punished and I don't think it's an unhappy ending. And was it the Professor who sprang my mousetrap?'

'It was,' said Professor Applegate.

'Now, I get to hand over this hunk of glass to Theodore Green, and enjoy the rest of the cruise.'

'Here he comes now,' said Mr. Aubrey, grinning an expansive grin. 'Oh, Officer? Miss Fisher wants to hand over her piece of worthless paste.'

Phryne was tossing the sapphire from hand to hand, watching the play of light in its centre. It really was a wonderful fake. The way that the star in the middle seemed to glow in sunlight. The depth of the indigo colouring. Really, even Venetian glass wasn't usually this good. A horrible suspicion rose suddenly in her breast and she closed her fingers around it.

'Oh no,' she said.

'Oh yes,' said Theodore Green. 'It wouldn't do to try to palm off a paste replica onto an experienced jewel thief. That sapphire belongs to one of the director's wives,' he said, taking it very carefully from Phryne. 'And if she doesn't get it back, there will be trouble. It's insured for ten thousand pounds.'

'Oh,' said Phryne faintly, conscious of having dropped, flung and tossed this priceless gem.

'I've come to tell you that the board is very grateful to you for your good work,' said the navigation officer. 'They'd like to offer everyone here a reward for trapping Mr. Singer into a confession and for—well, saving us a lot of unpleasantness. Perpetual travel, Mr. Aubrey, Professor Applegate, Mr. Forrester, Miss Fisher. First Class for as long as you like.'

'Thank you,' said Mr. Aubrey. 'I am most gratified. And delighted to be able to assist P&O.'

'Indeed,' murmured the others.

Theodore Green departed with the sapphire. Table three caught each other's eyes and began to laugh.

●　●　●　●　●

'I bought such a nice doll for my little sister,' Dot told Phryne that evening. 'And I'm sure that the girls will like their presents.' Dot looked at the pile of souvenirs. Shawls made of very soft wool, dyed in earth tones, for various female relatives. The bones of a Moa's head and neck for Jane. A huge tin of different sorts of fudge for Ruth. Maori dolls in flax dresses and headbands for little girls. Carved greenstone charms for others. Phryne had found packets of seeds for Jack Robinson. She looked forward to his attempt to grow a pohutukawa tree. Phryne had a necklace made of hundreds of little pieces of paua shell, polished like opal.

'What a fascinating place,' said Phryne. 'Every sort of scenery you could want, all packed into one little island. And the friendliest people in the world.'

'Except for Mr. Singer and the Wests,' said Dot.

'They were imports,' said Phryne.

Phryne came in to dinner with a resolution, and said so. Other resolutions had also been made. The table three jewel thieves had forsworn a life of crime. Mrs. Singer had decided to go home to Melbourne, realise Mr. Singer's estate and buy a small house. Delivered, she had lost most of her more iritating traits.

'I shall have a cat,' she said. 'I always wanted a cat but I knew that my husband would have killed it. He hates cats.'

'I shall learn deck tennis,' said Phryne. 'Tomorrow.'

'And now Margery has turned me down,' said Jack Mason cheerfully. 'And quite right, old thing. We would not have suited. I've found a profession. Not going to waste my life anymore. A nice respectable profession but one which is going to make my father foam at the mouth.'

'And what is that?' asked Mr. Aubrey, accepting his plate of vindaloo.

Jack Mason beamed. 'Those chaps were a real inspiration. I'm going to become a policeman,' he said.

Kevin O'Connor
Sligo, Eire

God and Mary be with you, Kevin my brother. I don't really know how to say this, but that fine ship the 'Titanic' may still be on its way to New York harbour, but I shan't be upon it. I don't know what it is but I couldn't be staying on it after what that great gentleman said who built it. 'Even God Himself couldn't sink this ship' the man said the other day. Father Doyle would have given us the larruping of a lifetime had we said such a thing of the work of our hands. Blasphemy altogether is what he would have called it, and there's myself thinking of my skinned knees praying before the man back home in Sligo with you. Father Doyle was a terrible man for his denunciations as you well remember. So I jumped ship and here I am, walking the roads of old Ireland. Expect me in the summer.

Your loving brother
James

Author's Note and Pre-Emptive Apology

I have always been in love with the sea and ships, my father having been a wharfie working for the Union Steamship Company of New Zealand, but when I came to research the New Zealand–Australia route in 1928, I found that I needed to construct my own ship, due to lack of information on the SS *Aorangi*. I have made the *Hinemoa* as much like a ship of the time as I could from pictures and descriptions, but I will have made mistakes. Forgive me. Though I confess to hours of fun designing the interior and ordering my glass panels from Tiffany.

The same goes for New Zealand, the most civilised country in the world, which I may have unintentionally maligned. There just isn't a lot of published information about New Zealand in 1928 and I have had to use such sources as I could scrounge. If you are reading up on NZ, don't miss Mr. Reed, the last of the great walkers.

Any similarity between real people and the cast of this book is purely coincidental. Feel free to email me on kgreenwood@netspace.net.au if you would like to do so.

Bibliography

Baillie, Captain DGO. *A Sea Affair* Hutchinson, London, 1957

Baty, Scott *Ships that Passed* Reed Books, French's Forest, NSW, 1964

Bisset, Sir James *Commodore: War, Peace and Big Ships* Angus and Robertson, London, 1962

—— *Sail Ho!* Rupert Hart-Davis, London, 1961

—— *Tramps and Ladies: My Early Years in Steamers* Angus and Robertson, Sydney, 1960

Britten, Sir Edgar T *A Million Ocean Miles* Hutchinson and Co, London, 1936

Broadbent, Michael *Vintage Wine* Websters International, New York, 2002

Chambers, John H *A Travellers History of New Zealand* Interlink, New York, 2004

Chaucer, Geoffrey *Complete Works* Oxford University Press, London, 1969

Dovaz, Michel *Fine Wines* Assouline Publishing, New York, 2000

Durrell, Gerald *Two in The Bush* William Collins, London, 1966

Ellis, Richard *Monsters of the Sea* Doubleday, New York, 1994

Farquhar, IJ *Union Fleet* New Zealand Ship and Marine Society, Wellington, 1968

Frazer, JG *The Golden Bough* MacMillan Press, London, 1922

Gardiner, Robin and Dan Van Der Vat *The Riddle of the Titanic* Orion Books, London, 1996

Hoeling, AA and Mary Hoeling *The Last Voyage of the Lusitania* Longmans Green and Co, London, 1957

Kennett, Frances *Fashion* Granada, London, 1983

Kipling, Rudyard *The Second Jungle Book* Pan Books, London, 1967

Lord, Walter *A Night to Remember* Longmans, Green, London, 1956

Main, Jim *Australian Murders* Bas Publishing, Melbourne, 2004

Marsh, Ngaio *Colour Scheme* William Collins, London, 1943

——— *Vintage Murder* William Collins, London, 1937

New Zealand Lonely Planet Publications, Melbourne, 2003

Olney, Richarde *Romanee-Conti* Rizzoli, New York, 1995

Orbell, Margaret *A Concise Encyclopedia of Maori Myth and Legend* Canterbury University Press, Christchurch, 1998

Park, Ruth *Pink Flannel* Pacific Books, Sydney, 1963

——— *The Witch's Thorn* Pacific Books, Sydney, 1962

Reed, AH *The Four Corners of New Zealand* New Holland Publishers, Auckland, 2004

Riley, Murdoch *Maori Love Legends* Viking Sevenseas, Paraparaumu, New Zealand, 2003

Wilson, Damon (ed.) *The World's Greatest Unsolved Mysteries* Magpie Books, London, 2004

Wylie, Elizabeth and Sheldon Cheek *The Art of Stained and Decorative Glass* Todtri Productions, London, 1987

To see more Poisoned Pen Press titles:

Visit our website:
poisonedpenpress.com
Request a digital catalog:
info@poisonedpenpress.com